AF445023

Predator Pit

G.L.Newman

Published by G.L.Newman, 2024.

This is a work of fiction. Similarities to real people, places, or events are entirely coincidental.

PREDATOR PIT

First edition. June 27, 2024.

Copyright © 2024 G.L.Newman.

ISBN: 979-8227175731

Written by G.L.Newman.

Table of Contents

PREDATOR PIT

THE YEAR IS 3023. FIFTY years ago, global warming caused the world's ice caps to melt, leaving just twenty-five percent of the land not covered in water. The coastal towns and cities were the first to be swept away when the water level rose drastically, killing many millions of people. Temperature upon the land became so hot that if you were caught outside for any length of time, your skin would blister and burn.

The whole world descended into chaos, governments fell, and anarchy reigned supreme. To try and bring some order to the broken civilisation, a group called the Commission sought to bring structure into the chaos before the people destroyed what little land and resources they had left. Constructing vast walls to keep out the rising tides and using satellites orbiting the planet to put a barrier around what was left of the world, which had been aptly named the Last Isle. Although this helped to stop the blistering temperatures from killing the last of civilisation, this barrier preventing the blazing hot sun's rays from scorching the land, and keeping the people safe, came at a cost. The leader of this group, the High Commissioner, a man called Hector Forthright, now held what was left of the world in his grasp.

The Commission controlled everything from food to water to the temperature of each sector and even the amount of sleep they received, all dependent on the Sector's hard work. There was, however, a huge disparity between the haves and have-nots. Some walked around in the latest fashions, while others wore rags that haven't been washed for weeks. Some ate like Kings and Queens, while others scavenged for scraps amongst the waste discarded by the higher in society.

Life for some was a lavish affair of privilege and parties; others lived a life full of dread and despair. Everything was a struggle, and life was about as much fun as being torn apart by hungry wolves. Something that was a real possibility if they were unlucky enough to have to face the PREDATOR PIT. A cruel game devised by the High Commissioner to provide entertainment for the more prevalent in society, but also a chance for the Sectors to win their freedom from a life of suffering.

Could an ancient legend help these oppressed people fight back against the tyrannical rule and bring hope to those whose lives are viewed as little more than slaves? Have the people still got the strength to unite together as one? An ancient gift said to give one the ability to communicate with the animals may be the only hope that these people have, but can this unique ability still be nurtured in the desperate and desolate surroundings?

CHAPTER ONE

Two Sides of Life

A LOUD ALARM RESONATING throughout huge speakers sounded off at six o'clock in the morning. It was a punching air-raid siren that wasn't at all pleasant to your ears, or any other part of your body, to be exact. The tremor-like vibrations shook the ground so violently, the poorly constructed huts the unfortunate people in the Sectors inhabited almost collapsed. The vibrations could be so acute that many couldn't hold onto their bodily functions either; if you were lucky, it was just the bladder that was affected.

"Please make it stop," complained Luna, who had her hands over her ears, trying to drown out the awful noise.

"Get up now. You know what happens if we are late to the announcement," said her mother in a flap.

As thousands of people piled out onto the streets, everyone wore the same frightful expression. This was the day that everyone dreaded, one among them would be chosen to face a deadly competition.

The reason for this mind-numbing alarm was to wake up the people living in the Sectors. There were eight Sectors that all stemmed from a raised central hub called the Inner Sanctum. The High Commissioner lived in the very centre of the Inner Sanctum, housed in a vast mansion where only a few select people lived and worked. This impressive building was so big, its total square meterage was almost as large as one of the Sectors itself. Sadly, the Sectors housed many thousands of people, all cramped into wilderness-type spaces. Some had forests, some had mountains, and some had meadows, but all were now surrounded by the sea.

Surrounding this well guarded mansion was a very affluent city that housed around one-hundred-thousand lucky people. They lived an entitled life; they wanted for nothing and had everything they would ever need. Their lives were one of privilege, and parties where slaves plucked from the Sectors tended to their every need. This was a stark cry for the conditions in which the people of the Sectors lived. If they were lucky, they would have enough food and water to keep themselves on the side of the living. They lived in makeshift huts and worked the land to provide food for themselves and those who lived in the Inner Sanctum. It wasn't all bad for the Sectors, once a month they would get to trawl through the Inner Sanctum's rubbish to find any discarded food, clothes, or anything at all that might just make their dire existence bearable.

The people of this new world were promised a life of luxury once the walls had been constructed. It was sold to them as the fairest way to split resources. However, once the work had been completed, they were tricked into a life of servitude. Their hard work had helped to build the massive, one-hundred-foot walls that now separated them from the higher in society. A huge divide that represented the disparity between both areas. Many lost their lives and many others worked until their hands bled and their backs broke, all believing that when the walls had been completed, they would get to share in the fruits of their labour. How wrong they all were!

Each Sector housed roughly the same amount of people, and everyone would get the same amount. However, the frivolous people of the Inner Sanctum gorged on more in a day than the Sectors could hope to have in a month, forcing them to work even harder to provide the highest in society with enough sustenance to continue their privileged way of life.

The Inner Sanctum soon became the upper class, and the Sectors were not even as low as the working class. They were seen as little more than slaves, needed to keep the more affluent of society in the way that they had been accustomed to. However, they could move about freely within their Sector, unlike the actual slaves that had been forced to serve the Inner Sanctum's residents. Made to wear retention collars which stopped them from wandering where they shouldn't be, providing a horrifying electric shock to any who stepped, talked, or dared to do anything outside the strict rules they were expected to adhere to. These people would serve, or they would be severely punished. Kept like dogs in kennels by night, they lived a very persecuted and uncertain life.

The rich and poor divide had never been greater. The High Commissioner controlled everything, and if you wanted to stay alive, you had to live by his rules. He could scorch the land of any given sector if he so pleased. He controlled the amount of water each sector received, deciding if he would let them have the conditions they desperately needed to grow their own food, most of which would be taken by the Inner Sanctum anyway. To give these downtrodden people a little ray of hope in their lives, or at least that's another lie that was sold to them, the High Commissioner created two games in which the people of the Sectors would compete. Participation in the games, however, wasn't optional.

Each month, the wheel of chance would be spun. This wheel looked like your classic game show wheel, which was divided into eight equally sized portions, each relating to a Sector. Huge screens in each Sector displayed this wheel, which was spun once a month by the High Commissioner in a very lavish and entertaining showcase display. There would be music and dancing, and the wheel, which was as tall as a house, was brightly lit with colourful lights, resembling that of a ferris wheel. The big, extravagant show did little to hide the fear that everyone felt when the wheel began spinning.

Sadly, Luna's father and brother had both met their end while competing in these deadly games. "I hate these cruel games. Why should we have to compete for a better life? We already give them everything, now they want our actual lives," Anna frustratingly said.

"Shush, mum, the guards are looking over here," Luna whispered, fearing what might occur.

The High Commissioner saw the people living in the Sectors as nothing more than meat for his most loved entertainment, one of which was called the Predator Pit. Entertainment was the real reason for the Tourneys, giving hope to the poor people who lived in the Sectors was just an unhappy and very unexpected after effect. For the luxury of being protected by the satellite shield, which allowed everyone the mercy of not being cooked alive by the sun's blistering-hot rays, which now stood at a scolding sixty-five degrees. Along with providing them with the means to grow their own food, even if the majority of it was taken to feed the Inner Sanctum, the High Commissioner required payment. This so-called payment was more of a sacrifice, because it was very rare that any of the unfortunate souls who competed in these games would survive.

Each month, eight people selected by the wheel of chance would have the opportunity to face the Rabbit Run. These unlucky participants would be forced to face a deadly gauntlet. There was no saying no, or backing out. If you didn't compete, you would be killed along with the rest of your family.

The High Commissioner was an avid animal buff, having previously owned a Zoo, before the world came crashing down around everyone's ears. He loved animals of all kinds, and he knew how to take care of them. He also loved the fighting arts, himself being a great fighter in his day. The sport of fighting had always interested him, and he loved all types of the fighting arts from Boxing, Karate, Kickboxing, Judo, Sumo wrestling and so many more. He'd studied the fighting arts throughout history and always wondered who the best fighter was from all the different styles. Competitions like the Ultimate Fighter came along, which saw men of any size and weight, versed in many different battle styles, fight it out against each other to see who was best. Unfortunately, like everything else, this was soon regulated, and weight classes brought a regiment order to what was such a pure no-holds-barred fighting contest. This, however, was still not enough, the High Commissioner wanted to pit man against beast in an elaborate show that not only provided hope for those living in the Sectors, but also great entertainment for all. Wanting to see if anyone had what it took to survive against the most powerful predators in the land.

The Predator Pit was essentially a reinforced glass box. Its hexagonal base had five sides that rose up at a steep seventy-five-degree angle to a height of twenty feet. The sleek glass surface made the sides too slippery to climb up, but they could be used to gain a height advantage over their opponent, or as a way to escape an attack. The Pit was located beneath the High Commissioner's mansion, and a glass ballroom floor allowed him to view the contest from above while still perusing with his guests.

Crowds of people came to watch this unusual and horrifying occurrence, and they would bet against either man or beast. It was the highlight of the year. The glass structure of this fighting zone made viewing extremely up close and personal, especially if you were lucky enough to have a seat in the viewing room, where you could literally be face to face with the action. Being so close to a person being torn apart by an angry beast was like nothing the world had ever seen before, and they absolutely loved it. The world had gone feral and violence was the norm for so many years until the Commission brought a regimented order to the slaughter.

Before these unlucky people could get the chance to face the perils of the Predator Pit, however, they would first have to survive the Rabbit Run. If a person was lucky enough to survive a Rabbit

Run contest, they would spin their own wheel of fate. This wheel was divided into many Sectors, sadly, these people wouldn't be spinning to get some sort of prize, there were no cuddly toys or speed boats available in this game. This wheel held the fate of which predatory beast they would be facing inside the Predator Pit. Among the possible choices were Lions, Tigers, Crocodiles, Grizzly Bears, and so many more terrifying beasts that could tear your body into many little pieces.

There were also creatures that had been altered from their original D.N.A. These hybrid beasts added an extra level of fear to proceedings. The fighters weren't left completely unprotected, they wore suits of armour which allowed them some protection from the huge teeth and claws that they would be facing. Weapons could also be gifted by those watching and betting on the outcome, giving them a higher chance of surviving. Extra incentives were on offer for any who managed to slay the beast, but survival was the main aim of this game.

The first competitors in this new bloodsport didn't have the luxury of this protection or weapons, however, the fights would be over far too quickly and they would be torn apart like rag-dolls. Not many would survive long against the deadly predators of the land, and this didn't please the onlooking fans one bit, they wanted to see a contest, not just a slaughter.

High stakes were on offer to those who competed, and not just the luxury of staying alive. If they managed to survive five minutes against their chosen beast, they would be welcomed into the Inner Sanctum, where the richest of society lived. There was no poverty in this place, everyone wore fancy clothes and they had all they could ever hope for. They discarded more food than the people living in the Sectors ate, in fact, it was the leftovers from the Inner Sanctum that would be given out to the Sectors as a gesture of kindness. This was never enough to feed everyone, and with the crops they could grow all dependent upon the High Commissioner's allowance of water in their Sector, many still went hungry. Most Sectors also retained the protein rich food for the warriors, who would be facing the Predator Pit. After surviving the Rabbit Run, they needed as much help as they could get to give them the best possible chance of winning.

The Sectors had no control over who would face these grotesque contests, all were forced to train in some way to prepare for the eventuality they might one day be picked. Every Sector would be forced to provide someone to face this more often than not, death sentence. The wheel of chance would then determine who would be the unlucky person forced to face the Rabbit Run. It was always a tense wait, hoping and praying that your name wouldn't be called out. Those chosen to face the Rabbit Run would do so once a month. If they managed to complete this deadly gauntlet in one piece, they would have the chance to compete inside the Predator Pit. Only the strongest would get a chance to face this terrible contest and the chance to earn a better life for their families.

The Rabbit Run survivors would face the Predator Pit on Christmas day. Christmas had become an extinct tradition. No one had enough for themselves except those who lived in the Inner Sanctum, who wanted for nothing. Out in the Sectors, however, it was all they could do to survive the devastating fate that had befallen them. The giving of gifts was definitely not an option in this cruel new world. The people living in the Sectors didn't usually have enough food and water to survive, let alone enough to be giving any of it away. The only water these people had was what they had collected when the rain fell. Once a month, each Sector would be granted a small amount of rainfall. The collected water had to be used for drinking, bathing, and growing crops. This meagre amount wouldn't usually be enough for one of those activities alone, so very few ever bathed properly and water was rationed to the very last drop. If they wanted to survive, they would have to be extremely conservative in its use.

Whilst thousands of people starved, the animals in the High Commissioner's Zoo were fed like kings. They ate as well, if not better, than those who lived in the Inner Sanctum, however, no one in this prevalent place went hungry. The disparity between the rich and the poor had never been greater. Those who lived in the Inner Sanctum were surrounded by one-hundred-foot-tall walls, which were guarded day and night. High-tech sensors would also detect anyone who was stupid enough to think they could climb this huge perimeter to access a better life for themselves. Anyone who was caught trying to scale the wall would be shot down, that's if they had managed to somehow bypass the powerful electric charge that would fry you on contact and/or negate the wall's circular saw defences that would turn a person into chop-suey. Many had tried to scale this wall to a better life, but all who had tried, quickly died.

The High Commissioner lived in a vast building, surrounded by the latest technological defence systems. This place was an impenetrable castle, and not even the highest in society had access to this place. Only the High Commissioner's family and an array of countless servants were permitted in this building. Beyond another high security fence, and out past the vast walls were the Sectors. Each one was roughly the same size and it was walled in on three sides. Outside this, the people were still at the mercy of the rising sea levels, which fluctuated greatly with the tides. Whole years' harvests had been ruined by seawater, not only contaminating the crop itself, but also the land on which it was grown. No one could predict these tidal waves that almost destroyed the very few things these people held dear to their hearts. With each Sector's own prosperity relying on a good harvest, it was totally soul-destroying when the seas washed away their bounty. This was the only food they had, along with the few scraps that were tossed aside once a month by the highest in society.

The satellite shield placed around the territory was controlled by the High Commissioner. He could choose to open up any part of this protective dome, allowing the harmful, blistering-hot sun's ray to scorch the land. This not only made it totally unbearable to live in, but the scorched land would be ruined and the growing of crops going forward would be significantly reduced. Sector's could win extra rainfall, sea flooding defences, and even hampers of food, however, the price they had to pay was extremely high. They had little to bargain with other than their lives and the High Commissioner loved to see people mutilate themselves for a chance to gain extra resources. What good is it having all of your fingers if you were going to die?

Every month, eight people, one from each of the Sectors would get the chance to compete in the Rabbit Run. This was an assault course designed to be extremely gruelling. It had high climbs, harrowing transverses, tunnels, and many other difficult apparatus to navigate. However, if this course wasn't tough enough to begin with, there was something else that made it almost impossible. The competitors would also be chased down by one of the fiercest, fastest, angriest and most agile of beasts. A hybrid of the High Commissioner's own making, which saw the savage strength of a Lion fused with the acrobatic agility of a Leopard and the lightning speed of a Cheetah to make a creature that's roar alone would have you shaking in your boots.

The competitors would naturally get a head start, but many would fall foul of this creature's snapping jaws, which were chock-full of razor-sharp teeth. Men, women, and children were all expected to compete in both of these deadly events. Only those younger than sixteen would be given a pass from competing, along with anyone over the age of seventy. The High Commissioner did have some compassion, or was it the fact he knew these people wouldn't be strong enough to put on a good enough show for the baying crowd?

Winning the Rabbit Run was highly important, it meant that the winning Sector would have enough food to not only feed everyone, but they would also be provided with some protein rich food to give to their Predator Pit participant. A strong competitor gave that Sector the best chance of surviving either contest. Those who survived the Rabbit Run would get the chance to face the Predator Pit, and if said competitor survived five minutes inside the Pit, against their deadly animal foe, their whole family would be moved into the Inner Sanctum. Not only would the survivor's family get to move up in society, the whole Sector would be rewarded for their efforts. They would receive more food and water than ever before, along with many more resources. They could stop the growl from their stomachs, nourish their bodies, and hopefully have enough energy and resources to make it through the winter.

Winters were extremely hard for those living in the Sectors. People lived in self-made huts with little or no insulation. These poorly constructed sheds did little to keep out the cold. Most Sectors had one big fire in the centre of their dwellings, so all could benefit from the heat, but this did little to stop the pain brought with the sharp decline in temperature, which sometimes reached as low as minus forty degrees. This bone-chilling snap of frosty weather saw many who weren't strong enough lose their lives to hypothermia. The High Commissioner could have shielded them from the worst of the cold snap without using hardly any of his precious resources, but while some sat in front of roaring fires that heated their lavish homes, stocked with enough food to feed an army, the Sector's inhabitants lost fingers and toes to frostbite.

Everything was a battle if you lived in one of the Sectors. It was an almighty battle just to stay alive, let alone anything else. Still, in these unforgiving conditions, they not only had to survive, but they had to become strong enough to compete in the High Commissioner's sick games. Many tried to rise up and take the fight to the cruel Commission and their unfair treatment, but while they had sticks and stones, the Commission had the latest in high-tech weaponry, as well as an army of brainwashed soldiers and genetically engineered beasts that would tear you limb from limb.

Sadly, after the resolve and conviction had been starved and beaten from most, they had little fight left. The only way out of this nightmare was to compete in the High Commissioner's sick games. They would literally have to fight for their lives to pull themselves out of poverty and despair, but when all the cards are stacked in the Commission's favour, could anyone find the strength to fight back against this cruel and callous organisation?

CHAPTER TWO

Choosing Day

THE DREADFUL ALARM sounded once again, gathering everyone to the big screens. As always, music started playing and the over the top performance began. It was quite a spectacle to behold, but this extravaganza was only enjoyed by those who lived in the Inner Sanctum. For those living in the Sectors, it meant that at least one among them would be chosen to compete in the High Commissioner's deadly games, where the odds of survival were extremely slim. Mothers, fathers, sons, and daughters were all plucked from their families to face an uncertain fate. The percentage of those who survived either deadly game stood at about ten percent, however, ten percent was still a chance. A chance to live a better quality of life, a chance to pull yourself out of the squalid living conditions and at least live to fight another day.

Any children born in the Sectors were taken to be tested to see if they were strong enough to become part of the Commission's army. They would be graded on their intelligence and join different parts of the Commission's organisation. Basically, they were taken and raised in boot camps, where they would be brainwashed into believing that the way everything was run was for the good of the whole community. They would become soldiers with no feelings, just robots preprogrammed to do the High Commissioner's bidding.

Sadly, some of them had actually killed their own parents before without even knowing. Raised as soldiers and brainwashed to the will of the Commission, they saw anyone who lived in the Sectors as the scum of society. Happily shooting and killing anyone who tried to break free from their prospective areas. They had been brought up to believe that these people weren't worthy of any other life. They wanted anarchy to reign, and they threatened to raise it all to the ground. If they weren't controlled, they would jeopardise what little land and resources were left.

Some living in the Sectors had tried a sea born escape, but beyond the Last Isle there was nothing but more water. This was the last of the world's dry land and even though the living conditions in the Sectors were atrocious, they were better than a life at sea. Without proper boats, they stood no chance against the violent seas. The wood it took to build the rafts for this sea-faring escape was also much better used trying to keep the people warm in the winter.

Winter was extremely cold and if you wanted to survive, you really needed to win at least one Rabbit Run competition throughout the year. Without the extra supplies provided for winning this competition, death by starvation was a real and present danger, and if hunger didn't get them, the freezing temperatures would. The sea no longer provided any sustenance, the excessive increase in temperature boiled any life from the Oceans, so even if these people escaped, most would soon return, realising that there was no sanctuary to be found at sea.

A young girl who still had hope in her heart approached her mother. "I want to put my name forward for the Rabbit Run. We cannot survive another winter without the extra supplies. I have been training very hard and I believe that I can do it. The rest of the hopefuls in this Sector have no chance of bringing home the bacon. Please, mum, I'm ready to take it on. I don't want to watch any more of my friends die," Luna pleaded to her mother.

"No, Luna, I couldn't bear to lose you too. We have already lost so much. I just wouldn't survive if you were taken from me. We have to stick together. Your father and brother have already paid the ultimate price. I can't lose you too," her mother pleaded back.

Luna's mother had an injury which made her exempt from competing, and Luna had only just turned sixteen, so she could have possibly slipped through the net until she was tested. Most never wanted to face these appalling contests, and they would do almost anything they could to keep their age from being found out. Some could fly under the radar for maybe one or two years, but soon all who were eligible from that Sector would be discovered. However, with the rewards on offer for victory in these games being an extremely strong incentive, many also relished the chance to fight for their freedom and a better way of life.

The main purpose for the women living in the Sectors was to get pregnant. So many died each day that the flock needed to be constantly replenished. At any one time, there were hundreds of pregnant women across the Sectors. This not only gave them an exemption from competing, but an extra incentive for the expectant mothers was knowing that if they made it to thirty weeks, they would be transported into the Inner Sanctum to be cared for until their babies were born. This little glimpse at a better life saw many women getting pregnant soon after they had given birth. In the last stages of pregnancy, these women would be given more food than they'd probably had all year. So the pull of being pregnant was a great incentive. Very few made it to thirty weeks, however, but those who did have a chance to sample a better life, even if it was for just a short period of time.

Generally, only Sectors that had won the Rabbit Run, or survived the Predator Pit, would have enough nourishment to grow their babies to the required stage of gestation. Sadly, as soon as the child had been born, it was snatched away to be tested. If the child was shown to have strong genes, it would be taken away to become another brainwashed soldier in the High Commissioner's army, or trained to be a technical engineer for the company. If the child showed no strong attributes, it would return to the Sector with its mother. Either way, after the mothers had been transported back to the Sector from which they came, they felt sad and completely dejected. They either lost a child right there and then, or they would experience the pain of losing the child shortly after. Very few survived if they were thrown back into the Sectors. Babies needed constant nourishment, something the Sectors couldn't provide.

Most mothers actually wished for their child to be taken by the Commission, at least then they would get to live. The even sadder thing was that it took no time at all before these women wanted to be impregnated again, even if their child returned with them, and with a Sector full of horny suitors ready and waiting, another seed was planted soon after.

These people may not have enough food and water to survive, but they still had the luxury of sex, something the people living in the Inner Sanctum didn't. Sex was seen as an extremely dirty, germ-filled practice, and the High Commissioner outlawed the process for those living in the Inner Sanctum. He didn't want to risk disease spreading throughout his Kingdom. He also didn't want the city filled with expectant mothers who provided little contribution to this new society. They would just become an extra drain on resources. Most Inner Sanctum residents didn't want to defile their perfect bodies either, and have their lives of luxury tainted by the disgusting act. They also didn't have time between their lives of privilege and parties to look after a snotty-nosed little brat. The chosen children would live in military conditions. They knew nothing of a free life, but they were fed extremely well. The High Commissioner needed everyone in his organisation to be strong.

Although sex was outlawed in the Inner Sanctum, it's not like they didn't have ways to provide the pleasure received from this sensual act, but the risk of disease and infection was taken out of this new coupling process, which used technology to produce the electrifying, satisfying feeling that was even better than the sexual act itself. Technology pulled on every single pleasure receptor to produce an effect that was out of this world. Much better and a lot more hygienic than the real thing.

Most women in the Sectors, however, used their bodies as nothing more than mules, just vessels to carry a living, breathing mass of meat. Most would continue this until their bodies could no longer bear any more offspring. There was no love involved, no point in getting attached to the child, because there was a strong possibility that the child would be taken away from them as soon as it was born. Some who returned with their child felt happy for a while, but with the lack of nourishment required for a newborn baby not available, most never lasted long and any who did ended up deformed and in a lot of pain. Sadly, those who didn't die soon after their return would rarely make it to adulthood. Many graves had been dug over the years to cater for these poor souls. Death was seen as the most humane answer for most of the children who returned to the Sectors. They were just another mouth to feed and with supplies already thin on the ground, many poor little souls were put to sleep forever.

This actually turned out to be a much less painful experience for the mothers, at least if the children were killed straight away, they wouldn't have to watch the child suffer. Some women, however, wouldn't help to grow a tyrannical organisation such as the Commission and sought to find a way out from their greasy grasp. Hope, however, was extremely thin on the ground. These people had been drained of all their fighting spirit, and most found it easier to bow down and live by the rules imposed upon them.

Rule breaking brought its own special kind of punishment. Anyone caught doing something they weren't supposed to, were stripped naked and tied up in the street for everyone to see. They would receive an amount of lashes from a leather whip, depending on the severity of their actions. The huge Sector screens displayed this horrifying experience as a warning to anyone else who thought about carrying out such actions. After being beaten, they would be left to suffer at the hands of the other people in that Sector. Many weren't happy to have the spotlight of the Commission shining down upon their Sector, this brought with it nothing but discomfort and misery. Once you were in the Commission's sights, you could expect more pain and suffering to ensue.

Advances in lab-grown foetuses were improving, but until they perfected the process, the High Commissioner relied upon the people of the Sectors to continue producing babies for his ever-growing army. If it wasn't for their ability to produce mini soldiers and provide entertainment for the Inner Sanctum, the Commission would have no need for what they saw as little more than vermin.

Other than a sea-born escape, there was no way out of the Sectors. Huge walls guarded day and night kept them in concentration-camp-conditions. The only way in and out was via the cable car system that transported supplies into each Sector. Huge metal containers which were picked up and dropped off by a huge claw, was the only way in which supplies got in and people got out. High-tech scanners stopped anyone who shouldn't be aboard from getting a free ride. The people soon learned this was a suicide mission. Many who sneaked onto the containers believing they had fooled the system, were left devastated when the container had reached the top of its ascent, and any stowaways would be left screaming with blind fear and panic when the bottom of the container opened, expelling them into a two-hundred-foot free fall, of which none would survive. Still they continued to try, the pull of the luxurious lifestyle inside the Inner Sanctum saw many dropped to their deaths on a monthly basis.

With everyone gathered around the big screens, the High Commissioner's face appeared. "Hello to you all. It's that time again, the time to see who has what it takes to become a winner."

Forced cheers from some in the crowds reacted to his speech.

"Once again, we get to choose the budding hopefuls who have the chance to not only better the lives of themselves and their families, but also help their Sector as a whole. Those who have the strength to meet this battle head on will find that a better life awaits them. Before we spin the wheel of chance, I would like to thank Sectors three, five, six, and eight. You have provided a bountiful harvest and you will be rewarded for your efforts. Unfortunately, Sectors one, two, four, and seven have failed to meet their quotas. They will not receive their monthly discarded bounty package."

Some Sectors cheered, while others just looked at the floor, trying to figure out how they were going to survive the month without the discarded waste package.

"Now, if everyone is ready. LET'S SPIN THE WHEEL," the High Commissioner said, pushing down on a drastically oversized red button.

The wheel spun around displaying all of its beautiful colours. Some, however, only saw darkness. One big black spinning vortex that they wished to be sucked into. One among them would be chosen to face a very uncertain fate. It could be a loved one or a close friend, but whoever was chosen, it would affect the Sector as a whole.

"Please don't let it be me, please, I just couldn't cope," cried a young girl.

"Stop that. Just stop it now. You know that we have no choice, just be quiet before you get us into trouble," replied her mother.

The people living in the Sectors had become one big family. They had to work as one, or chances of survival were very slim. Everyone worked together to make their unbearable existence slightly less horrifying. If they didn't come together as one, they stood no chance.

This close-knit bond, however, brought with it a lot of pain when the contestants were chosen. They treated everyone like a part of their extended family, so whoever was unfortunate enough to be picked, would leave a stinging in all their hearts.

All names of those who were eligible to compete were loaded onto the wheel. Everyone followed the spinning wheel with wide eyes, all feeling immense fear and an anxious anticipation of who would be chosen. The clicking sound made by the selector as the huge wheel began to slow, resonated throughout everyone's ears like a jack-hammer. Each click was one click closer to hearing who would more than likely be sentenced to death. *CLICK, CLICK, CLICK, CLICK,* It continued until finally stopping on a name.

"Here we are. The first Sector picked is Sector three, and the person chosen to compete is .... Claire. Congratulations Claire, you now have the chance to fight for a better life for you and your family. Let's all give Claire a big hand."

Those who didn't clap had guns pointed in their direction which helped start the process.

"That's one name selected. Now who are going to be the other lucky contestants," the High Commissioner said, pushing down on the red button. "Round and round the wheel goes, where it stops nobody knows."

Before the wheel had the chance to select the next victim, screaming, shouting, and panic ensued when Claire, the recently chosen, took a knife and cut her throat. As blood began to pour from her neck, she fell to the ground out in the open for all to see. She didn't want to face either trial, the thought of being ripped apart by vicious animals was too much for her to contend with. She knew she wasn't the strongest of athletes and many better than her have failed in the past, so she saw no way of conquering either challenge. Deciding to take her life in a much less brutal way, was the only way she could see her way out of the misery she was facing.

"Murderers!" came the screams from her mother, who now cradled Claire in her arms.

Unrest among the rest of the Sector began heightening, people threw anything they had to hand at the big screen.

"Cut the feed," whispered the High Commissioner, giving a hand signal.

Each Sector could see the High Commissioner, but they had no idea what was occurring in the other Sectors.

With the feed cut, the High Commissioner gave the order. "Release the gas now," he shouted.

The people in the Sectors knew the gas was coming before they saw it. All the guards hastily putting on their gas masks was a huge clue, but soon after the gas descended like one huge, fluffy white cloud, rolling towards them like an avalanche. Many tried to flee the epicentre, but there was no hiding from this noxious substance. The whole Sector would be sealed off and gas would seep into every little nook and cranny. Some learned to hold their breath for a considerable time, allowing them to at least reach the safety of their homes before they'd fallen foul of the awful substance. Most got fed up waking with their faces in the dirt, so at least when they woke the next day with the most horrific pounding headache that felt like a hangover from hell, they would be in the relative comfort of their own homes.

The other Sectors were all wondering what was going on. Never before had a selection ceremony been cut off mid-transmission. With Sector three now suitably subdued, the big screen once again came alive.

"We are so sorry for that unforeseen interruption. Unfortunately, we had technical difficulties, but rest assured they have been rectified and the show will go on. Sadly, we have found out that Claire, our Sector three contestant, is pregnant, so she is unable to compete. Unfortunately, this information was late in coming, so her name wasn't removed from the wheel of chance. To save any more confusion we will move onto the next lucky Sector who will now provide two people to enter into the contest and because of this minor hiccup in proceedings, those who compete will have the chance of winning even more supplies for their Sector. The Rabbit Run contestants who survive will win twice the supplies than before. Better still for those who face the Predator Pit and succeed, they will have the chance to not only bring their family, but also one other family from their Sector into the Inner Sanctum. How about that?" the High Commissioner said, waiting for an applause.

"To keep everything in order, however, two people will be chosen from Sector four. We must have eight hopefuls to face the Rabbit Run. But with two chosen from Sector four, their chances of winning will be drastically increased, allowing them better odds of out running the Hunter Killer, THE KING OF THE HUNT!!" the High Commissioner always raised his voice when delivering this last sentence.

Some in Sector four cheered, others felt even sicker than usual. This was unheard of, it had never happened before, never has the High Commissioner offered such a deal. Raised stakes indeed, but with the survival rate being extremely low, it was more likely to bring more suffering to Sector four than anything else. Some, however, were wondering what was really happening. A mistake like this had never occurred before and for the High Commissioner to offer a greater incentive, many felt that they weren't being told the whole story. Sadly, as the cheers continued from Sector four, all the other Sectors felt even more hard done by than usual. There was still only the slimmest of chances that whoever competed in either contest would win, but this did up the stakes significantly.

"Thank you all for your continued support in keeping the last of this planet's land viable. It is your hard work on the ground and our continuing efforts in technological satellite advancement that allows us all to survive the terrible fate that has befallen the world. It's that show of effort from all of you in the Sectors that forces me into this next decision. Now, usually the wheel of chance gives the people of that Sector a fair and equal chance of competing in the Tourneys. However, now that there is such a huge prize on the line. I'm giving Sector four the chance to choose their own competitors. This means they can choose the best among them, giving them every chance to succeed. You have twenty-four hours to decide......... Choose wisely, this could be the biggest prize a Sector has ever won, and we all want you to succeed. Please enjoy the rest of the show, and remember if we persist and persevere, we will all prosper."

The High Commissioner disappeared from the screens, and the extravagant show continued, but no one was in the least bit interested. What they'd just heard was monumental. Maybe this selection process could continue, giving every Sector a better chance at surviving the Tourneys? One Sector had a lot of thinking to do, but all the other Sectors' minds were now on overdrive, dreaming of what could possibly be? If they could pick the best among them, their chances would be greatly increased. How different would life be?

CHAPTER THREE

Unexpected Find

THE HUNTER KILLER WAS a beast of the High Commissioner's creation. He'd somehow managed to fuse a Lion, a Leopard, and a Cheetah altogether to create the most vicious killer machine the world has ever seen. And this beast was always hungry for the hunt. With the attributes of these three already devastating predators, this beast had also been enhanced, like it was on steroids, making it even more powerful. Once in the jaws of this Hell-Cat, you stood no chance of survival. This creature tore through meat and bone like it was nothing, fully possessed for the kill, it gorged upon its victim's flesh. This jet-black beast now also had a row of spiky protrusions running down the length of its body. Tipped with fiery-red bristles which could be flicked from its tail. These poison darts could help to slow down any fleeing victim, however, they were rarely used as this creature's rapid speed was usually too fast to outrun.

The High Commissioner had control over this violent killing machine, as he did with all of his precious predators. He controlled them like a master controlling his pet dog. Most were left completely shocked when he paraded around with the huge beast's beside him, all totally loyal to their master. His powerful persona was cemented even further when he patrolled the Sectors with a Grizzly Bear on one side and a Siberian Tiger on the other. Both boarding his movements as he casually walked amongst the people like he was taking a quiet stroll in the park. Many wondered how he gained this type of control over the usually unruly animals. Some believed he used shock collars, but this was more than that, it was like he was in their minds, controlling their every move. These animals were totally subservient to him and no one had a chance to get within twenty feet of this Messiah before they were torn limb from limb by his mind-controlled pets.

It was these very beasts that the hopefuls in Sector four were now worrying about. The Predator Pit was still a lottery on which bone-crushing-beast you would be facing. However, some of these deadly beasts were favoured over others. If you had to face down a Lion, your chances of survival were extremely slim. A Crocodile, however, could be out manoeuvred, that is until the sides of the Predator Pit came closing in around you, but you did have a greater chance of survival. If you were unlucky enough to end up with a Tiger, Grizzly Bear, Lion, Polar Bear, or Wolf, your death certificate was usually already signed and in the hands of the coroner.

If by some miracle you managed to survive five minutes with one of these man-eating-creatures, you very rarely escape unharmed. The majority lost limbs and their bodies were usually damaged beyond repair. Even if they did survive and were moved into the luxurious lifestyle of wanting for nothing inside the Inner Sanctum, the pain they suffered couldn't be eased, and many begged for the mercy of death. It now became an act of kindness from the High Commissioner to end their suffering.

However, everyone knew who would be hunting them down during the Rabbit Run, and that was the Hunter Killer. This devilish creation's mightily powerful attributes from the animals that made it were already extremely deadly, but this creature power had been increased ten-fold. This beast was like a freight-train with a nitrous-oxide injection. It moved like lightning, was completely unstoppable and could turn on a dime. A deadly mix of power, speed and agility that few could escape from.

A group of people called the Tamer's used ancient methods from the Native Americans to find a way past the High Commissioner's hold on these creatures. They found a way to tap into their minds to calm the beasts that they faced. This ability was extremely rare, but a prophecy told long ago said that the true Wild Whisperer would come to save them all. This unique person could control the beasts, relinquish the High Commissioner's control over them. In turn, overthrow this tyrannical leader and save the people from having to live under his oppressive rule.

This amazing ability has been bestowed upon one worthy person every one-hundred-years. However, only the most deserving would be given this exceptional gift. The Tamer's unique abilities are what keep many people alive after most of the dry land had been flooded. They could help the animals, and in turn the animals provided them with sustenance. A fit animal was never killed, but an animal who was suffering would now welcome death, safe in the knowledge that their pain would be no more, but they also provided food for the people who would help to tend to their young, keeping their species alive. This circle of life saved so many from starving to death. Without the Tamer's, the population that was left on planet Earth would have been greatly reduced. The animal's unyielding nature to survive helped to save both species from extinction.

The High Commissioner had his own personal reasons why he disliked the Tamer's. He hated anyone other than himself being the one in complete control. After the Tamer's abilities were found out during the Tourneys, he found another way to keep control over his deadly creatures. Using technology, he managed to stop the Tamer's from influencing his beasts. Their only saviour now was the Wild Whisperer. This person could hopefully override any hold that the

High Commissioner possessed and convince the animals to fight alongside them.

Talk had already begun throughout the Sectors that the Wild Whisperer could be among them, but would this person use their unique gift to save the people, or would they be too scared of the retribution that might befall them from the Commission? The High Commissioner had also heard the whispers and he wanted nothing more than to stamp out this possible threat to all he had built. He would be the only one to have power over the animals, they were his safety net and also his greatest weapon, one which he planned to use to further his kingdom.

One young girl who was desperate to prove herself in the Tourneys was Luna Star. This small, scrawny waif of a girl, however, was more or less laughed at when the mere notion of her competing was suggested. From a very young age, Luna trained with her father and brother who both trained very hard to give themselves the best possible chance if they were ever to be picked. Both had survived the Rabbit Run, but they both lost their lives inside the Predator Pit, leaving Luna and her mother all alone. Luna had also only just turned sixteen, and even though in the random conventional method of this choosing, many would feel cheated and extremely unhappy if Luna was chosen. No one gave a second thought to this girl, whose dreams of grandeur would never be indulged.

Many young girls had lost their lives facing the Tourneys, and not one single female of the species had managed to survive the Rabbit Run, let alone conquer the Predator Pit. Most women didn't want anything to do with such cruel contests. Many got pregnant as soon as they possibly could, to prevent this eventuality from happening. So you can understand everyone's lack of faith in this small girl, but Luna knew that she could triumph, she just needed a chance to prove herself. Now that Sector four had the chance to choose two people who would face the Tourneys, Luna decided to put her name forward. She knew that this may be her only opportunity to get her voice heard and if their Sector ever needed a win it was now. They hadn't won in so long that the coming winter would claim many lives without the extra supplies from winning this contest.

Luna's best chance to get herself heard was to talk with the Elder. Each Sector had an Elder, this person was usually the eldest in that Sector and they would try to keep some kind of control among its residents. They didn't really have any power as that lay with the Commission, but they were looked to for advice and guidance. Due to their unrelenting will to stay alive they were seen as extremely tenacious, tough, resourceful and a great fountain of knowledge.

Sector four's Elder was a man named William Roberts and he was about sixty years old. He was in fact one of the eldest of the Elders that there had ever been. The conditions in which these people lived didn't allow for a long life. Once most had reached a certain age, their bodies no longer had the strength and endurance to survive this cruel existence. People who never worked, never got fed and when the ratios on offer weren't enough to feed a small child, broken bodies never got the nourishment they so desperately needed.

William saw Luna approaching and knew what she was going to say. In the past, she had even asked that a letter be sent to the High Commissioner himself, asking that a girl younger than the choosing age be allowed to face the Tourneys. Obviously William never sent such a letter, it was too much to stomach when a child of sixteen faced the Tourneys and lost their lives, he would hate for anything to happen to this sweet young girl. Luna had the heart of a Lion and an all-encompassing love for everyone and everything. She never moaned about her unfair existence and always tried to bring a smile with her wherever she went.

"Hello Luna, let me guess?" William paused as if he was thinking. "You want to face the Tourneys, am I right?"

"Please William. I'm the fastest and most agile out of everyone. I can win the Rabbit Run, I just know I can. Not only that, but I have been training so hard. Help me to make them see," pleaded Luna.

"My child, I know one thing for sure, you have more heart than anyone I have ever known. You could teach so much, to so many, but they don't see the strength that I see within you. To them, you are small and weak. I will try to fight your corner, but I feel that their minds have already been made up," said William, looking at her with forgiving eyes.

Anna grabbed her daughter's arm and led her away. "Luna, come now, it's nearly time for the Rubbish Rummage," called her mother.

Luna's mum was happy that the rest of the Sector saw her little girl as weak and pathetic. She knew of her true strength and heart, but couldn't bear to think about what would happen if she lost her. Both her husband and son had been killed inside the Predator Pit. Both who were strong and very capable had managed to survive the Rabbit Run and both were thought to have a good chance of winning in the Predator Pit. Sadly, their fate lay with so many others who had lost their lives to the sick games.

Luna's mother had sacrificed her own health to provide enough sustenance for Luna. After a pelvic injury during labour left her struggling to walk, she negated her recovery so that her little girl could live. She saw something special in her eyes the day she was born, they had a sparkle just like the stars in the night sky which contributed to her name. Anna, her mother, was so relieved when her child was rejected by the Commission and she would get to return with her. There was something special about this girl, something different from all the rest. She had an aura about her and a feeling of hope washed over you when you looked into her bright sparkly eyes.

Sadly, very few children survived when they returned to the Sectors, but Anna did everything she could to make sure her special little Luna endured. There was one activity that her mother wanted her little girl to partake in, and that was the Rubbish Rummage. She was perfectly sized to clamber through the pile of the Inner Sanctum waste that was gifted to the Sectors on the first of every month. She could get to the middle quicker than most and that was where the really good stuff usually was. Luna acted like a pig sniffing out truffles, clambering in and around the huge pile of leftovers to get the best supplies for her mother. This woman had gone hungry on many occasions to allow for her daughter to have the nourishment she needed to survive. Anna struggled to walk so she needed Luna for many of her needs now, but no matter how tight she held onto her beloved daughter, she could feel her slipping away.

Luna emerged from the pile of rubbish with a huge smile upon her face. It's surprising what can make a person smile when they have next to nothing, even rummaging through a huge pile of someone else's stinky, slimy, discarded waste. After she emerged from the stinking pile, she firstly ran due to her excitement, but soon after slowed to a walk, as she approached her mother. She didn't want anyone else to know what she had found. "Look, look what I've found," she whispered into her mother's ear.

After seeing a glimpse of what her daughter had found, they both slowly walked back to their hut. "Just act normal," Anna said, feeling the stare of many eyes burning into the back of her head.

Back at the hut Luna revealed her find. "Look at it. It's huge," she said, licking her lips. "Quickly hide it away. I will go back out and see what else I can find."

Anna took hold of the huge piece of meat that Luna had found. Meat was very rare in the Sectors, and the knowledge of such a find would see the whole Sector fighting to get even the smallest piece of this extremely elusive item. The monthly Rubbish Rummage usually produced some rotten vegetables, some mouldy bread and a truck load of banana skins, but meat of any kind was exceptionally rare. Sometimes you may find an odd bone that still had some meat clinging to it, but never a full, fat, juicy steak.

They decided to cook this lucky find at night when hopefully everyone else would be sleeping, although the smell of this rare delicacy cooking would probably wake the dead. Luna and her mother were like excited little school girls for the rest of the day. The thought of how the juicy steak would taste, saw their mouths watering. Before all of that, Luna had to have her monthly wash. Even the residents of the Sectors couldn't deny anyone the water needed to wash the smell of filthy rubbish from their skin and clothes. Sadly, with nothing in the way of soap, the smell often still lingered. The smoky smell produced after their clothes had been dried over a fire, however, was usually enough to mask the bad smelling odour.

As night fell the two women could hardly wait, but they would have to, if they didn't want to alert everyone else to their special find. "How much longer do we have to wait? My stomach is in knots," Luna asked.

"Just a little longer, we don't want to cause a riot now do we?"

Luna waited peacefully, looking up at the stars. She often got lost in the night sky. She loved to imagine what it would be like to fly away, soar up through the clouds, and follow the stars to another planet, where life might actually be worth living. Where everyone had the same amount of resources, and where they could be free from the Commission and its tyrannical rule.

When the time came they made their way down to the shore, hoping that the scent of the sea might help to mask the meat while it was cooking.

Using the sand and some rocks they made a little oven to cook the steak hoping to minimise the smoke being produced by the gently searing meat. Thankfully, there was an off-shore wind which would help to keep the delightful smell from reaching others in the Sector.

After only ten minutes it was ready to eat. Both of them were now drooling like dogs. Luna was first to take a bite. "Oh my god, it's delicious," she said between chews.

Anna looked lovingly at her daughter's face as she took another bite, it was so captivating, she looked like she was in heaven. After seeing the delight on her daughter's face, she could wait no longer and she too tucked into the meaty treat. After they'd finished off the last of the mouth-watering delight, they both lay on the beach looking up at the stars. With the feeling of a full belly for the first time in what seemed like forever, but not only that their tongues and taste-buds were still tingling from the intense flavours they had experienced. Their usually extremely bland diet never got the taste buds engaged, let alone tingling with delight.

Laying next to one another staring up at the night sky felt so good. Maybe it was the meal they had just eaten, the soft sand on which they lay, or the gentle breeze that brought a freshness from the sea, or maybe all three, but even knowing of the life that they had to return too, at that precise moment in time they didn't care, they were so happy, it made all the pain just melt away.

"Do you think that we will ever be able to live a free life again?" asked Luna.

Anna looked deep into her daughter's eyes. "Freedom can come in many different forms, even if you don't necessarily believe that you are free, especially if you're being controlled by others and feel shackled like an animal. However, when you have love in your heart, your mind can take you away to anywhere you want to be. No one can ever truly be held captive if they have enough imagination. Love for another helps us to keep hope in our hearts, and if we have that, we will always be free!"

Luna looked lovingly at her mother. She said some beautiful, but strange words sometimes. Unfortunately, all that awaited them tomorrow was more pain and suffering. Their hope had been slightly raised by the decision to allow them to pick their own competitors, and the fact that their Sector now had two people running the gauntlet, but could either one survive? Luna knew that her mother would struggle to survive another winter, and the only way that this would be a greater possibility was if the people from their Sector survived the Rabbit Run Tourney.

CHAPTER FOUR

Altered Animals

FILLED WITH MORE ENERGY than ever before, Anna and Luna returned to camp with a spring in their step.

"Why are you so happy?" asked a man chewing on a piece of rotten fruit.

"We are just happy to be alive," they both answered as they walked by.

They were looked at with disdain and suspicion, no one was happy to be alive in this place, animals were treated better than they were. However, it's surprising what a good meal can do for someone's outlook. With the brain and body fed suitably, it can bring a whole new level of awareness.

When they reached their hut, raised voices caught their attention. "Why does he get the chance? I am much stronger," shouted a disgruntled person.

"You don't have a chance of out running the beast," replied the person they were arguing with.

"Please calm down everyone. This is for the good of the whole Sector. We must be in agreement," said the Elder, trying to defuse the situation.

Raised voices ensued until a squeaky voice cut through the noise. "I should be the one who takes on the Rabbit Run. I'm better than all of you," Luna screamed.

"Shush Luna, now is not the time," said her mother trying to cover her mouth.

A man from the crowd walked towards Luna and shoved her quite forcefully which resulted in her being thrown across the ground and landing in a heap. "Stupid girl, you have no business here. You aren't even old enough to face the Tourney's. Go away before you get hurt," said the brute of a man.

Anna jumped to her daughter's defence, but soon bowed her head when she was looked at with malicious intent.

"Take that silly little girl home before she gets hurt," said another disgruntled person.

Anna helped Luna up off the ground. "Why do you push these people so?" she asked.

"I can win. I know I can. If they just let me, I will show them."

"Luna, my child, we live in extremely uncertain times. I have tried to keep you safe, but you are now of age, and if you continue to highlight yourself in this way, I will not be able to stop them from hurting you. Please, you're all I have left in this world," Anna sobbed. "I couldn't bear to lose you."

"I'm sorry mum. I just want to help. I want to win so I can pay back all the times you went hungry, so that I could eat," Luna sobbed.

"Your day will come my love, I'm sure of it, but please........ I can't lose you. I have already lost so much......... It would just break my heart."

"It's ok mum, I won't say another word about it."

After a loving embrace they decided to put their abundance of energy to good use. They collected firewood for the campfire. It was coming to the end of summer and the temperature was falling. Ever since the ice-caps melted, temperature extremes made surviving extremely difficult. The Commission's satellites could block out the worst of the sun's scolding rays, preventing everyone from being burned alive, but keeping the cold out was a whole other matter. The barrier could stop the harmful sun's rays, but it couldn't stop the land from freezing. The climate also shifted rapidly from a sizzling-hot summer to an icy-cold winter, leaving many not prepared for the sudden changes in temperature.

The people of the Inner Sanctum had no worries when the temperature dropped. With everything powered by a nuclear reactor, they had the power to heat the whole Inner Sanctum, as well as providing ample cooling in the sizzling-hot summer months. Most of their food was grown using the latest in technological advancement, so the changes in weather never had an effect upon their food supply like it did for those living in the Sectors. However, this lab grown cuisine lacked the flavour of land grown food, so they still had need for the Sector's harvest. Some also wondered if there was something else fuelling those who lived in the Inner Sanctum?

As night fell, Anna kept a close eye on her daughter, watching as she slept soundly. After a Rubbish Rummage Luna was always more tired, however, tonight the usually delightful thoughts she would have while watching her daughter sleeping, turned to fear. She'd noticed the way in which the men looked at her child. Now she is sixteen she would be expected to help repopulate the world. Even in these uncertain times there was an unwritten rule among the Sectors that no child under the age of sixteen would be used as a baby making mule. The punishment for such an offence was severe, so no one dared to interfere with someone who was underage. Most young girls would be protected by their fathers or older brothers, allowing them a few more years until someone got their greasy mitts around their waist. Sadly, Luna didn't have that little safety net, and her mother was in no fit state to offer the protection she required.

After having to watch your young daughter face either the Rabbit Run, or the Predator Pit, there was only one thing worse, and that was to see them struggle with the stress and strains of pregnancy while they were still so young. A long-drawn-out, painful process that usually had the same outcome as the Tourney's. Without proper nourishment their young bodies became too weak to carry on. They were just not rugged enough at such a young age to be able to carry a baby, and sadly the mother usually lost their lives along with the foetus, long before its due date. Anna would fight until her dying breath to protect her daughter, but sadly she knew that this wouldn't be enough. Sat with a shovel in her hands, Anna prayed that she would be left alone. Thankfully on this night no *filthy-fingered vilifier* came knocking!

Luna's dreams on this night would be filled with competition and conquest, not only for herself, but for all those who suffer under the tyrannical rule of the Commission. What if she could talk to the animals? To free them from the High Commissioner's control, maybe they could help the people overthrow the Commission and its satanic ways? She dreamed of being the Wild Whisperer, speaking to the animals and using their strength to put an end to the oppression and cruelty of her people. To help drag them out of the desperate lives they now barely existed in.

Before Luna had a chance to fulfil her dreams, the ground began to shake and her ears began to hurt once more when the alarm sounded signalling the start of their very long day. The day of the choosing would always bring dread and fear, but for some it also meant a day off from their usual tasks. The people in the Sectors were forced to work six days a week mining for Thorium, along with many other tasks. Thorium was a substance similar to Uranium, but much safer and a lot more powerful. Less was needed to produce the same amount of energy and it was a lot more abundant. People were expected to mine from sunrise to sunset. The Commission did allow them one day off a week which was Sunday, but this was more of a need than a kindness. Saturday was party time for the Inner Sanctum residents, although for the people living in the Inner Sanctum, everyday was like Mardi Gras.

Once a month on Saturday was also the day when the Rabbit Run would be showcased, and all the Sector guards would be pulled away from their posts to make sure that the event was well catered for. So the Commission also gave them the day off because the partying would go on until the early hours. The High Commissioner hosted everyone at his mansion during the Rabbit Run events and heightened security was needed.

Hector was a very suspicious man, and he was always worried that someone would be trying to infiltrate his organisation. He never showed this mistrustful nature, and he was always the most gracious of hosts and confident master of ceremonies. His presence alone commanded respect and servitude, especially owing to the fact that he was always accompanied by two of his vicious beasts, totally under his full control like little lap dogs, but playful puppies they were not. His favourite combination was to have a Lion on his right side and a Tiger on his left-hand side, but this combination of pet protectors varied, especially when the Rabbit Run was taking place.

These modified beasts were far from their original origins. The High Commissioner liked to experiment with cross species gene replacement therapy. Every animal in his Zoo had been changed in some way, even down to their colouring. He had Lions with fiery red manes, jet-black bodies and piercing red eyes. Blood-red Tigers with yellow zigzag stripes and piercing black eyes. This particular Tiger actually looked like it was on fire, its movement highlighting the colour of its coat which shimmered in the bright lights. There were Black polar bears and bright white grizzly bears. They had all been transformed in some way, and every single one of them was much deadlier than it was before. Many wondered how he had such control over these animals, they never wore shock collars, or anything that would suggest that he was controlling them in any way. Was he the Wild Whisperer?

Another thing that troubled many who lived in the Sectors was the fact that this man never seemed to age. Was he some kind of Vampire, or was it because he wanted for nothing, and had all the technological advancements to keep him looking so young and healthy? The growing of new body-parts and organs in a lab was now available to the richer in society and advancements in A.I. Technology helped make them much stronger and last a lot longer.

Sadly, even the young living in the Sectors looked old. They had to work so hard on very little nourishment that they never really developed properly. Many had child-like bodies, but they wore ancient looking skin. They could be easily out muscled by the guards who had been fed well all of their lives. The right nourishment can see sustained growth in an individual, but if you take that away, the body never grows to its full potential. Bones are weaker, muscles are smaller, every attribute of that person becomes limited and feebler than those who had been fed well. The people of the Inner Sanctum stood like all powerful gods, towering above the lesser people who lived in the Sectors.

One person who was still in fact a child, never had this feeling of inadequacy. Yes she was smaller and weaker, but she turned her lesser height and size into a person who was faster and a lot more agile. A lighter frame allowed her to climb and swing through the trees like a monkey, and her short stature allowed her to be fast and unseen like a Ninja. Luna embraced what she had to work with and never saw it as an inferior quality, she saw it as a gift. That's why she was so certain that she could triumph over the Rabbit Run competition. She had watched many over the years and most failed to outrun the Hunter Killer, but of the ones who did, they were usually much smaller and more agile, allowing them to stay one step ahead of the creature's snapping jaws.

If the people would just see her for the person she could be and not just a weak little girl, their Sector could be feasting upon more food than they'd ever imagined. With extra rainfall and sea defences they could continue to provide a healthy crop all year around. The biting cold winters would be much more manageable if they had enough food to keep their bodies fuelled throughout the colder months. The risk of losing their whole crop would be greatly diminished, saving time and energy that could keep them strong enough to survive the more demanding times.

Winning a Tourney not only provided more supplies, but it also provided hope, and if you have hope in your hearts, the lack of food in your belly doesn't feel so painstakingly hollow. People will always endure even in the most inhospitable of climates, but when your life's in the hands of an evil dictator, all the hope in the world, still may not be enough!

CHAPTER FIVE

Rabbit Run

THERE WAS HUGE ANTICIPATION for the next Rabbit Run competition for all who lived in the Sectors. Not only that, the High Commissioner and the people of the Inner Sanctum were also extremely interested in how different the performance would be when the people got to choose their own participant. Maybe it was the extra hope of winning that these people had, or just the fact that they thought they might just be gaining back some sort of control over their own lives? Whatever the reason was, production from the mines had increased across all Sectors. Letting the people choose their own fate had installed in them a greater work ethic. Reports from all Sectors concluded that since the High Commissioner allowed Sector four to choose their participants, less coercive control was needed from the guards.

The Commission didn't want every Rabbit Run or Predator Pit to end in victory, or they would run out of slaves to mine for the exceptionally precious Thorium. However, if they gave these people more hope by allowing them to choose a person who they believed could win, the increase in production would seriously outweigh any extra supplies that might be won. There was still only the slimmest chance of winning anyway.

The last three Rabbit Runs had all ended miserably. The competitors barely got started before they were hunted down and tore apart by the Hunter Killer. The High Commissioner had also

47

felt the discontent among his people and knew that if he didn't put on a good show, cracks may begin to appear in the organisation. No one just wants to witness a slaughter, even if that is how most of the Tourneys ended up. However, they wanted to see a contest where the outcome wasn't always pre-written. There was no fun if there was no contest at all, there had to be a greater chance of these people winning. Cash flow was also being affected by this lack of competition, who wanted to bet on a generally predetermined outcome when there was no sport in it?

Plus, when people are distracted by smoke and mirrors, they tend not to look too hard into any low-lying problems that might be occurring. If their minds are sufficiently engaged they carry on blissfully unaware of any issues. As long as they are being catered for they don't go looking for problems. A happy and blissful flock is easier to tend to than an inquisitive one, and what the Commission was building needed no extra prying eyes.

The day of the Rabbit Run had arrived and all were highly anticipating what might transpire. Of course as usual the huge elaborate show began. Usually most would be forced at gunpoint to sit and watch the entertainment that ensued, however, now everyone was sitting quietly, watching and waiting for the contest to begin. No one shouted out their little protests against the cruel games that were about to see another poor soul lose their lives. No, this time a Sector had chosen their competitors and hope in every Sector was at an all-time high.

Everyone in their own Sector knew who would be facing the Rabbit Run because the competitors would be transported to the Inner Sanctum a week before the event was to occur, to allow them a chance to familiarise themselves with the obstacles that they were soon to be facing. The rest of the Sectors all watched on with great intent to see who had been chosen to face the competition, but there was more scrutiny than usual over the Sector four contestants.

Everyone was keeping a close eye on who had been chosen, hoping to see in them a contestant that could win!

"Hello and welcome to the eighty-second Rabbit Run competition. As you all know the stakes are even higher than usual. One Sector has had the chance to choose their own contestants, and without further ado, let's meet the hopefuls who have a lot riding on their shoulders...................... Firstly I present to you Oliver," the High Commissioner said, shaking Oliver by the hand. "Now the next hopeful from Sector four is .... Thomas."

There wasn't a blinked eye anywhere when Oliver and Thomas were revealed. These chosen two, could be the people to change the course of these games forever! Oliver was a fit lad, at age twenty-two he was much larger than many who lived in the Sectors, so initial thoughts on the participant were positive. Thomas was slightly smaller, but still a strapping lad considering that they were from the Sectors.

The screen then showed the course that these hopefuls would be facing. Each section would be highlighted with numbers showing how many had fallen at each juncture. The vast numbers were a hard pill to swallow, especially when so many had only made it onto the second, or third section of the course. However, this was a new day, a day for the downtrodden Sectors to finally gain back some control over their lives.

The Rabbit Run course started with a huge wooden A-frame climb. This piece of apparatus was forty feet in height. Climbing it was tough, but time could be made up on the descent if you were willing to throw yourself from each beam rather than climb down. The second part was a suspended cargo net that spanned two-hundred feet across. Nimble feet were needed for traversing this piece of equipment with speed. This element of the course had seen the downfall of many poor souls, the unstable surface catching many whose feet slipped through the gaps, getting themselves tangled up in the netted structure.

Third was a rope swing, four ropes dangled above a muddy trench. Easy enough, however, increasing gaps between each rope made for a very daunting transverse. One error in judgement saw you falling into a deep pit filled with mud that there was usually no escaping from. The fourth section saw the competitors navigate the tunnels. A huge wall containing ten openings faced them when they arrived. Each tunnel was one-hundred-feet long and making your way through it was tough, especially for the larger person. However, not all the tunnels had an open end, a fact that was only found out when they finished the long enclosed scramble, which had more twist and turn than a roller coaster. It was a complete lottery of which tunnels would have these holes to freedom, and this pattern was changed every time the course was run. If you entered a tunnel without an open end, your Rabbit Run was usually over. You could still escape through these tunnels, however, the extra time needed to break through the blockage at the end, usually gave the Hunter Killer all the time it needed to pounce on its prey.

All the Sectors had tried to work out the formula of which the Commission used to select these dead ends, but it seemed as random as the weather and it came down to a total guess on the day. The tunnels were interlinked, so if you were quick enough you could back up and try again. However, the tunnels had claimed many victims and their horrifying screams echoed out even louder through the steel tubular openings. In the past, some had tried hiding out in the meandering network of tunnels, but once the Hunter Killer picked up your scent, your time on this Earth was quickly snuffed out. If you had made it this far then the obstacles got a little easier, but at this point in time the Hunter Killer would be snapping at your heels, so concentration was key to keep your cool and face down the last two sections.

The fifth apparatus was a long stretch of monkey bars. A strong upper body, and a lightweight frame was needed for this section of the course. The bars in this long transverse stretched wider towards the end, meaning that you would have to take a huge leap of faith to make it through. Beneath this horizontal metal ladder was a section of water, unfortunately for the participants this water was filled with snapping Crocodiles. One false move, one weakened grip could see you falling into the jaws of some very hungry beasts. Keeping your feet high was imperative, many had been snatched by their ankles and dragged into the waters below. That's if the Hunter Killer didn't pull your body up through the bars by your head and have his own little feast first!

Last up was a simple balance beam run to reach the end where salvation in the form of a cage would be waiting for you. Only after you had made it inside and shut the door to this metal box would the event be completed. After such an energy-draining, muscle-aching scramble for life, however, the simple task of keeping your balance wasn't easy. Tired, wobbly legs didn't make for a swift traverse of this obstacle, which was one-hundred-feet in length. This somewhat easier obstacle was made slightly more terrifying knowing that it was surrounded on both sides by hundreds of sharp-pointed, body-piercing poles that would turn any fallen person into a pin cushion. Not to mention if the Hunter Killer had also clambered onto the already unsteady surface. With the agility of a cat, or three cats to be precise, the huge beast had no trouble navigating the lengthy beam, but its presence alone upon the plank-like-pole was usually enough to topple off any who had made it this far.

The Commission used runners from their own security forces to demonstrate that the course could indeed be completed, but many wondered if these people were entirely human. Advancements in A.I. Technology were extremely progressive before the ice-caps melted, and some believed that humans being enhanced by technology was the next step in evolution. These demonstrators also never had the fear of god put into them by being chased down by the Hunter Killer. Maybe everyone in the Inner Sanctum was in some way integrated with this technology? It's not that no one ever triumphed over the Rabbit Run, and even fewer survived the Predator Pit, but it was possible, there was a chance to bring your family out of the trenches and provide them with a better life.

After the glitz and glamorous performance, Oliver and Thomas, along with the other competitors, were placed on the starting line. Each contestant would get a ten-minute head start before the Hunter Killer would be released. Ten minutes might seem like a good head start, however, the average time taken to complete this course was thirty minutes, but considering that the chasing beast could traverse the course in a little over fifteen minutes it left little time for any errors.

All of Sector four's inhabitants were on tenterhooks, there was so much on the line and these two people not only held the fate of their own Sector, but also the hope of all the other Sectors, who were hoping that this free choice may continue.

"Right, if we are all ready, let's begin," said the High Commissioner, pressing a big red button that sounded the starting alarm.

"I hope one of them makes it. Double the supplies, we will eat like kings," shouted one hyped up hopeful.

"Do you really think that they have a chance to win?" Luna asked her mother.

Anna looked at her daughter with hopeful eyes. "God knows we need a win, and I do believe these lads could have what it takes. All we can do now is pray," she said, crossing her fingers.

The huge screen now showed the eight hopeful runners. Their names which were highlighted in big black letters would turn red if and when they were no longer in the competition. All eight were attacking the first obstacle relatively strongly. Most had reached the top and were now descending. One, however, from Sector five lost their footing and were sent plummeting to the ground. His falling body shook the apparatus wildly, as it hit each rung of this huge ladder nearly toppling off a couple others who had to act fast to save themselves from the same free-falling, pancake-splatting experience. With one already down and seven to go, would anyone reach the end of this deadly gauntlet?

Many had worked out that for a hopeful to have even the slightest chance of winning the Rabbit Run, they would have to at least reach the tunnels, and also have the good fortune of picking an open-ended tunnel. Even then it was still a close race to the finish, but those who had reached this point in the contest would have the best chance of winning. The further people got in the course also helped greatly in the chances of someone winning. The Hunter Killer would take little time to kill any who he'd chased down if the hunt was still on. So those who fell early on were killed swiftly, but if more made it to the later stages of the course, especially if the contestants were bunched closer together, it got into a bit of a feeding frenzy and would take a little longer on each victim knowing that its next meaty treat was right around the corner.

Sadly, once you stood facing this course it was every man, woman and child for themselves. Any solidarity went straight out of the window and all were in a race for their lives. No one even thought about the prizes that were on offer, survival was the biggest prize of all.

Whether it was the extra hope that these people were feeling, or the fact that they knew that a much bigger prize was on the line for those who triumphed? Whatever the reason was, every contestant was doing much better than average. More had completed the second section than any race that had come before, but as the time ticked down before the release of the Hunter Killer, *KING OF THE*

HUNT, would any of them make it all the way to the end, to not just save their own skin, but to save many others in the Sectors who won't survive another harsh winter?

CHAPTER SIX

An Unexpected Sacrifice

IN THE HIGH COMMISSIONER'S mansion energy was at an all-time high. More money was being bet on the competitors than even before. There might just be something to this free choice situation he thought to himself.

"Hello, welcome. Hello, oh don't you look pretty," he commented as he perused his huge banquet hall.

A person nervously approached. "Hello, umm, High Commissioner, may I," she said, reaching out her hand.

"Of course, don't be scared. He's a little puppy dog really. He doesn't bite, only I do, RAAA!" he said, snapping at the woman then stroking the huge Tiger's head that was next to him.

This animal was massive, bigger than your average Tiger, but most of the High Commissioner's animals were a lot bigger than their natural size. They had all been tampered with in some way. He had even found a way to change the colour of these beasts, and you don't really know fear until you have faced down a jet-black Tiger with glowing red eyes. In fact, none of the animals in his Zoo wore their natural colouring, most had been transformed in one way, or another. This Tiger in particular was bright white with glowing blue eyes, which looked slightly less intimidating, but still 'shaking in your boots' scary.

"It's almost time my Lord," said his servant.

"Can I have your attention please," he shouted, but no one noticed.

Shortly after, the whole building shook when the Tiger let out a thundering roar, instantly grabbing everyone's attention. All eyes were now firmly pointed in his direction.

"Hello friends. Welcome to you all. I hope you are all enjoying yourselves. Now the time is nearly upon us. Who will join me in the countdown."

Everyone now counted down from ten. A huge digital timer that sat above the double sweeping stairway that led to a huge balcony where the High Commissioner was standing, started counting down. *Ten, Nine, Eight, Seven, Six, Five, Four, Three, Two, One.* As the clock struck zero, an alarm sounded, signalling the release of the Hunter Killer. Not many paid a great deal of attention to the first stages of the contest, other than those who had bets riding upon the contestants. However, once the Hunter Killer had been released everyone's eyes were glued to one of many big screens that were dotted about the huge hall. Everyone loved the chase and witnessing the slaughter of these slaves once the Hunter Killer had chased them down.

Before the Commission came to power and took control, the Last Isle was a savage place. People had to hunt to stay alive, and fights over hunting territory and food saw many lose their lives. Resources were limited and if you didn't fight you wouldn't survive. Although the Commission sought to stop this savage way of life, it seems that the violence was now ingrained into their D.N.A and most relished the chance to see the death of another. However, this controlled brutality still had many Inner Sanctum residents wanting even more.

Its loud ROAR let the contestants know that it was now on their tail.

"It's coming! The beast is coming. What do we do? What do we do!?" screamed one frightened competitor.

Most had now reached the tunnels, sadly the contestant from Sector eight slipped from the rope swing and was stuck in the muddy trench. Some had managed to claw their way out of the gooey substance in the past, but even if you got free, the extra weight that clung to your body slowed you down to a crawl, making it impossible to finish the course.

As the first exited the tunnels, fear was at an all-time high. Six remained, but only four had found the opened ended tunnels. "Help me, please help me," screamed a frightened individual who had sadly arrived at a blocked tunnel exit.

Three of the four who had made it through shot off to the next obstacle, but one was stopped in his tracks. The torture he could hear in their voice as this person struggle to break through the blockage resonated so loudly, they just couldn't walk away.

"What is this? This has never happened before, but I think, yes, I do believe that a contestant is risking their own lives to help another competitor," said the commentator.

The gasps of intrigue now resonated throughout the High Commissioner's huge mansion. Everyone started clapping the bravery of this person. This had never happened before, it was usually every man, woman, and child for themselves.

After eventually breaking through the blockage with the help of Oliver, the saved victim who happened to be a young girl from Sector seven embraced their saviour. "Thank you, thank you so much," she sobbed with relief.

Again this act of togetherness had the onlooking crowd thoroughly engaged. The short embrace was cut even shorter when the blood-curdling roar of the beast chasing them down had reached the tunnels. Its loud roar travelled throughout the tunnels and out the other side with such force that it almost took the pair off their feet, as the soundwaves rushed past their bodies.

"Go! GO NOW!" shouted Oliver.

The young girl took her leave, all the while looking back at her saviour who stood strong, ready to face down the chasing creature.

"There are even more unprecedented scenes unfolding here on the deadly gauntlet. It looks as though one of the contestants from Sector four has decided to face down the beast. Sadly, he has just bought himself a one way ticket to the afterlife, but could this help the rest of the contestants who are still running for their lives?"

The High Commissioner couldn't believe what he was witnessing. No one has ever helped another competitor before, and no one has ever given their lives to try and slow down the Hunter Killer. Obviously they had no chance of defeating this huge beast, it was definitely a death sentence, unless this person was the fabled Wild Whisperer, but this act might just help to slow the creature down enough to help the remaining competitors. He had never seen the room so alive, it was like electricity was coursing through everyone's veins, and the tension could be cut with a knife. Betting had increased ten fold and engagement in the contest was like nothing he had ever seen before.

As the Hunter Killer exited the tunnels, it came face to face with this foolish man who decided to face it down. The creature paced up and down snapping its huge jaws in the contestant's direction. However, it didn't engage right away. Even its mind was perplexed as to what was occurring. This was a predator and the hunt was its game, but this person just stood there waiting to be killed. This confusion might just give the other contestants the extra time they needed. The atmosphere was so tense, everyone was on the edge of their seats, especially those living in the Sectors. Could this be the Wild Whisperer that everyone had all been hoping for?

The beast actually looked as if it was starting to calm down. Oliver was a Tamer and a pretty good one. He tried to calm this raging beast, but after its body twitched, like it had been poked with something sharp, it let out a huge roar and pounced on top of the brave competitor. Soon after, the head was ripped from this poor man's body and the chase was back on. The High Commissioner's control over this creature was far too powerful to be overcome by just a Tamer.

This brave act, however, had allowed the final remaining competitors to reach further than any group before. Sadly, Sector sixes contestant slipped from the monkey bars and was snapped up by the crocodiles. That left two, Sector four's other competitor, and the saved competitor from Sector seven. Could any of these hopefuls make it to safety and provide their Sectors with enough supplies to see them through the winter?

The balance beam was all that stood in the way of the last two competitors now. Tired bodies and aching legs, however, wouldn't make this an easy task. One false move and you would be full of more holes than a colander.

"Two remain. Can any of them make it to the finish? Their lives and that of many others in their Sectors depend on it. A cold winter is coming, one that is sure to take many lives. Let's get back to the action," said an excited announcer.

"Go first."

"What? Why?"

"Please, we don't have time for this, just go, GO NOW," said the competitor from Sector four.

Once again a competitor has made the ultimate sacrifice. This showed these people still had hearts, they still had love and compassion, and they wouldn't let a poor innocent child die if they could do something to help.

Both competitors were now making their way across the balance beam. A huge shift in the already unstable obstacle alerted them to the fact that the Hunter Killer had joined them on this gang-plank of death. The end was in sight, it was so close now they could almost taste it. The young girl from Sector seven jumped from the beam and scrambled into an awaiting cage.

"Come on, run. You can make it," she shouted, willing her counterpart on.

Sectors four's last chance in this race was now within touching distance. After leaping from the balance beam, just missing the swipe from a huge sharpened-clawed-paw, he scrambled into the cage. Now inside, he pulled the lever to shut the cage door, encasing himself in a safe space.

He pulled and pulled at the lever, but it was stuck. "COME ON, SHUT YOU STUPID THING, SHUT!" he screamed.

A low trembling growl stopped him in his tracks, the Hunter Killer was now inside the cage and its hot breath felt like the blazing sun upon his face. This wasn't fair, he'd made it. He'd played this sick game and won.

As the beast tore apart the man's body, there was shock and outrage among the High Commissioner's guests.

"It's a fix."

"That's not fair!"

"He'd made it to the end."

"I want my money back."

As the room got more and more rowdy, the High Commissioner knew he had to do something. "Silence, Silence, please everyone listen," he shouted, but to no avail.

A loud roar from one of his pets, however, quickly got the room's attention. "My friends, please don't let this unfortunate event ruin what has been an unprecedented Tourney. The unfortunate demise of Sector four's contestant has saddened us all. However, I'm nothing but a fair man. All bets will be covered and Sector four will receive their care package, along with the lucky contestant from Sector seven. I hope you have all enjoyed this Rabbit Run competition. I think I can safely say that we are all looking forward to how this contestant will fare when they face the PREDATOR PIT!"

Music started playing and the show continued, but the usual party mood was anything but. This Tourney had piqued everyone's interest. This contest had it all, compassion, sacrifice, and a hopeful will to win. The High Commissioner had received the message loud and clear, the people didn't just want to see a slaughter, they wanted to see a fair contest. A contest where the odds of survival weren't fully stacked in the Commission's favour.

Things had to change, the people would no longer just be pawns in the High Commissioner's games. They wanted to strive for their lives, and he knew if things didn't change, he would no longer keep the level of control over the Inner Sanctum, let alone the Sectors, who wouldn't play his sick games any more, if they didn't have a fairer chance at winning.

The wheel of fate may no longer be choosing the contestants, however, more will still be required, but will the free choice that they have been hoping for cause more pain and problems? Why did the High Commissioner care? He'd still have his entertainment and many would still lose their lives facing the deadly games, and with a vast increase in the production of Thorium, they may be able to leave this doomed planet and the Sector vermin behind far sooner than he'd anticipated.

CHAPTER SEVEN

Secret Communications

A NEW DAY DAWNED, AND everyone woke with a renewed thirst for life. The latest Tourney had seen the Sectors gain back some control over their lives. They would now get to choose who will face the Rabbit Run and then hopefully go onto face the Predator Pit. Many still wanted the chance to drag themselves out of their destitute living conditions and strive to have a better life inside the Inner Sanctum. Some, however, could think of nothing worse. Of course they wanted a better life for their families, but even living in the devastating conditions they faced in the Sectors, they were still living, although many wouldn't perceive that to be the case, as most were only just surviving.

However, if you faced either competition, the chances of surviving were still very slim, and even now that they had the ability to choose who would have to face these cruel games, the odds were still stacked in the Commission's favour. Sadly, the people who lived in the Sectors were seen as nothing more than slaves to the High Commission. He controlled their ability to provide food for themselves. He decided if he would shield them from the blazing sun's rays that now reached scorching temperatures.

Not only that, but he controlled their water usage, and even now that the Sectors could choose who would face the Tourneys, he still made them compete. This wasn't an optional choice, one person from each Sector would be forced to compete in the Rabbit

Run every month for a chance to better their lives. If a Sector failed to choose someone to compete, another would still be plucked out to face the gruelling games whether they wanted to or not. Unfortunately, the Commission had control over everything. Even those living in the Inner Sanctum didn't have the freedom they desired.

The satellite shield that protected the Last Isle was powered by Thorium. Everyone knew that without the shield they would all die. However, it was only the people from the Sectors who mined for this precious substance. Forced to work day and night, they believed they were helping their families survive, when in reality only part of what was being mined was used for their protection, most was being stored, so it could eventually power the space shuttle that would flee this dying planet.

The Commission knew that it would only be a matter of time before the last of the land got swallowed up by the sea, or the blistering-hot sun's rays become too powerful for the satellite shield to deflect. Of course the people living in the Sectors would be killed first and that's what the High Commissioner was counting on.

They had built a huge craft to carry what's left of the human race to safety amongst the stars, however, the little resources that were left when the planet was flooded, were only seen as enough to transport those living in the Inner Sanctum. Especially if they wanted to be kept in the standard they have been accustomed to. They planned to leave all those living in the Sectors behind. Only the most esteemed and worthy would get to escape this doomed planet. There was room for all to take this life-saving flight, but no one wanted to be sharing a vessel with the scum of society.

The people living in the Sectors had no idea that this was the plan. Their hard work was never going to benefit themselves. They were providing the means for others to flee the planet, leading them to certain death. Once the satellite shield had been removed, there would be no escaping the blistering-hot sun's rays. The temperature would be so high that their blood would boil and their skin would blister, cooking their bodies like a lobster. If the sun's rays didn't get them, they would soon succumb to the rising sea levels, drowning what little land was left. Leaving nothing but contaminated seawater, which wouldn't support life.

The Sectors were obviously unaware of the Commission's plans to leave them all to die. Even if they knew of such a possibility, there would be little they could do to fight back against the organisation that commanded such power. Was there any way that the poor people of the Sectors could overthrow this tyrannical establishment?

A lot of the High Commissioner's power comes from his ability to control the animals. He had a kind of mind control over these beasts that made him untouchable. However, the news of the Wild Whisperer was starting to worry him. If true, this person could possibly relinquish the hold that he has over the beasts and then use that control to turn the animals against the Commission. With power over the many terrifying beasts, they could take down the oppressive order and free the people living in the Sectors from a life of pain and suffering.

Even if this person was real, however, the fact that they were still stuck in the Sectors would be of little use. Other than a monthly visit to the Sectors where the High Commissioner would be accompanied by two of his bone-crushing-beasts just to show off his strength and status, the rest of the animals are housed inside his private Zoo. To overthrow this organisation, they would require the combined strength of all his precious predators to complete such a feat. The only time that all of the beasts were accessible was during the Predator Pit. Housed in separate glass cages, they are used to scare the fear of god into the contestants that were about to compete.

The High Commissioner likes to see the terror building on the faces of the contestant as the carousel of blood-curdling-creatures rotates, before the choosing takes place. Each beast growling, snapping and clawing at the sides of their glass cage just trying to get out to feed on some human flesh. That would be the only time that such an action would be possible, but still they would have to have someone on the inside who could unlock the cages, releasing the many beasts all at the same time. The chaos that ensued by such an occurrence might just give them the opening they need to take down the Commission.

There may just be someone who might be able to help. Many of the successful contestants who had faced and survived the Predator Pit were used to tend to the High Commissioner's altered animals. Seen as too weak to join the security forces, not smart enough to help with the satellite shield, or spacecraft building and with no standing in this affluent society, these people still had to work for their new lives, which were a far cry from what they had been promised. Still looked upon as nothing more than slaves, they never got to live the lavish lifestyle of the Inner Sanctums residents. They would be used for all of the menial jobs and at the many parties thrown by the High Commissioner, they would be expected to serve the needs of the higher ups in society.

Yes, they were more protected from the sun's rays and the rising tides, but many felt like they had lost the little bit of freedom they did have when they were living in the Sectors. Eyes were everywhere in the Inner Sanctum, it always seemed that someone was keeping a close watch on you. Life expectancy in the Inner Sanctum was greatly increased, as well as the fact that you no longer feared the possibility of being picked for the Tourneys. However, life inside the Inner Sanctum wasn't all it's cracked up to be.

Yes, the sting of hunger was taken away and the smell of not having washed for months no longer invaded their noses, but they felt claustrophobic, like they couldn't breathe, or do anything without someone watching. Many now wished for the freedom to move freely throughout their territory without being judged or looked down upon. Even if they were always painstakingly hungry and completely terrified.

Everyone who lived in the Sectors were in the same boat, and that brought a level of togetherness that many who had left now yearned for. It was one of these previous winners that the Sectors hoped could join them in the uprising to take down the tyrannical establishment for good. A lad named Lance Moon was the youngest ever to face and triumph over both Tourneys. There was little hope when this scrawny teenager was chosen to compete, but after surviving the Rabbit Run, he'd impressed many.

After returning to his Sector, he was treated like a king, he showed such skill, determination and maturity of someone so young. It wasn't just his life that he was fighting for, however, but he had something a lot more powerful that was making him strive in such an unrelenting way, and that was love. Lance Moon was in love with Luna Star. They had been together for a year before Lance was plucked away to face the Tourneys. His love for Luna saw him survive both Tourneys and earn his place in the Inner Sanctum. However, this was the last place he actually wanted to be, he wanted to be back by Luna's side, but if he was dead, he knew he may never have the chance to see his beloved Luna again.

Talk of a coup had been going around the Sectors for a while now, but with no one on the inside willing to go against the Commission their plan wouldn't even get off the ground. This inside man had to be willing to risk everything to help those living in the Sectors. Lance didn't really care about anyone else, but Luna, and by default that meant that he would be willing to put it all on the line to help the Sectors.

First, however, they had to find out who the Wild Whisperer was. The Tribe Elders assured everyone that they'd sensed the signs that this legendary animal communicator was among them, they just didn't know who. It could be anyone who would possess this special ability, but would that person be willing to risk their own lives to try and take down the Commission?

It was well tending to the animals in the farm that Luna first believed she might be the fabled Wild Whisperer. A group of pigs were reluctant to get into their pen. Luna's mother had tried everything, but still they evaded her. The animals always seemed to know when it was slaughtering day, and they were much more difficult to round up. Luna used the power of her mind to get the pigs into the pen, or so she believed. Corralling a group of pigs, however, was one thing, but to control all animals was another.

Anna told Luna that she was being ridiculous. The legend of the Wild Whisperer was just a story. No one could have the power to control all the animals, and anyway it has always been a man who had become this fabled hero. She didn't want Luna's head filled with any more dreams. She already had her head up in the clouds and if she wasn't careful she would be brought back down to Earth with a very painful bang. Was this just a lucky coincidence, or was Luna on to something?

The farms were positioned just outside the perimeter walls. The animals smelled, they were noisy and they required a lot of upkeep, so the Commission didn't want them to ruin the Eden that had been created in the Inner Sanctum. Who better to tend to this flock, than the slaves of society. They would tend to the herds and fatten up these animals, all in the name of providing meat for the Inner Sanctum.

Advancements in artificially grown food were progressing, but it never seemed to have as much flavour as the real thing. On occasion a lame animal might be gifted to the Sectors, but with many mouths to feed, the tiny slither of meat they would receive hardly touched the sides. It was sometimes worse to receive this tiny bit of food. Your taste buds became so alive that anything you tasted after which was awful to begin with, now tasted even worse. Sometimes it's better not to know what you are missing out on, than be tormented by a glimpse of this tantalising taste.

This was another pull for those wishing for a better life. If they survived the Tourneys they would be able to eat meat every day. Their stomachs would no longer sing in pain due to a complete hollowness that felt deeper than a never ending void. The farm did, however, provide a chance for the Sectors to communicate with each other. Although they were watched closely by guards they could slip notes to each other, opening up communication between the Sectors. This was something the Commission didn't want, a divided society is a less threatful one. They knew that if the Sectors all banded together, they could try and overthrow the Commission, so keeping them separated was an extremely high priority. There is always strength in numbers of any group. If enough people join together to fight against the same enemy, there is little they can't achieve.

It was still no easy task, electrified fences, and guns trained on every movement made it difficult, but a few brave people would try to keep in contact with the other Sectors. Some had family members they wanted to check on, and some were just trying to keep hope alive. Knowing that their loved ones were still with them, gave them the strength they needed to carry on. Unfortunately, if caught passing a message, the punishment would be severe. Hands have been known to be removed from the paper-passing-people before, so it had to be done with the utmost discretion.

Each Sector was fenced off from the other, but with the need to share feed and equipment amongst the different farming sections, they were sometimes able to pass on a message. The only message going around at the moment was news of the possible Wild Whisperer being amongst them. Everyone had waited years to hear those words and if it was true then many believed that this person would be their saviour. They could fight back against the Commission and free the people from their lives of persecution.

The Sectors had been planning their rebellion for many years now, but without the Wild Whisperer they wouldn't stand a chance. All of the new-age weaponry was controlled by the Commission, so even if they got their hands on some they would be of little use. Guns were fingerprint activated. This could be overridden if given time, but many saw the only way to have any chance at a possible uprising was to control the animals.

The High Commissioner had made certain beasts so strong that it would take a literal army to bring them down. Bullets wouldn't matter if they had these beasts on their side. Many had been altered in one way or another, but all were a lot deadlier and more powerful than they were before. Still, unless they could get the Wild Whisperer into the Predator Pit competition they had no chance.

If this person did exist, they would first have to complete the Rabbit Run, and all were still unsure if this person could gain control over the Hunter Killer without making it obvious. If the Commission had any inkling that someone was this fabled creature coercer, they would be killed immediately. It had to be kept under wraps until the opportune moment.

After another long, hard day, all the Sector's inhabitants wanted now was to sleep. Some had been mining all day, some had been tending to the animals, and others had just been trying to survive this death sentence of an existence. The last thing that anyone needed was to hear the alarm sound, which meant that they had to gather around the huge screens and listen to whatever dribble the High Commissioner had to say.

"Hurry up! You heard the alarm," shouted a guard, at some very tired individuals.

"What do you think it's about? We have never had an announcement this late before," asked Luna.

"I don't know and I don't care. I just hope it doesn't last long," her mother replied, getting out of breath.

Luna put her arm around her mother's waist and helped her walk to the gathering area. She was often in so much pain that Luna couldn't bear to watch as she continued to struggle.

"Hello to you all. I hope I find everyone in high spirits tonight," said the High Commissioner.

A few moans and groans left the tired people's mouths, until the barrel of a gun was pointed in their direction, and the cheers began to reign out.

"Now it has been brought to my attention that some among you have been trying to pass information between the Sectors. The Commission makes sure that it informs the Sectors of all and any information that is required. All Sectors receive the same information, so there is no need to be passing notes like little school children, unless there is another reason for this information sharing?............ I believe that I have shown my gratitude and leniency towards all in the Sectors by honouring Sector four's care package. The Commission has nothing to hide and our recent decision to allow the Sectors to choose their contestants in the Tourneys is a huge show of good faith.......... But let me make this clear...........THERE WILL BE NO MORE SECRET COMMUNICATIONS. THE PENALTY FOR THOSE INVOLVED WILL BE SEVERE!!..........We must all play our part in keeping what's left of this precious world intact. Everyone must contribute if we want to survive. Your Commission continues to strive to provide better conditions for all, but we must all make sacrifices if we are to continue to keep order. Anarchy will only destroy what's left of this precious planet. We must persist, preserve, and then we will all prosper."

Most just cheered and clapped so they could get this over with and go to sleep, some of which will be lucky to get four hours before they were called back to the grind.

As everyone made their way back to their living quarters, many faces portrayed fear. They knew that the Commission could make their already terrible existence even worse, and no one wanted that. Survival was only just attainable now, and they knew that the Commission could kill every single one of them if they so wished. Most would now be thankful for what they did have, like air in their lungs and a beating heart. Living was the key, but with the High Commissioner acting as the Grim Reaper, were any of them really safe?

CHAPTER EIGHT

Kepler-186F

LUNA KNEW THE ONLY way she would get the chance to face the Tourneys, was if she could prove that she was strong enough to compete. She had to show the others that she was capable of winning, that's all anyone really cared about anyway. Twenty days before the next Rabbit Run was due to take place, she decided to train as much as she possibly could to prove to the rest of her Sector that she was indeed worthy of a chance.

Everyone in the Sectors were on their best behaviour. Life could still be made much harder for them if the High Commissioner wished. They had to prove that they did deserve the right to choose their own competitors. A luxury that could just as easily be taken away again.

With two Sectors receiving care packages from the recent Tourney, there was renewed hope. If they could just keep on winning, they may never have to watch someone suffer as they die from malnutrition, a most horrific way to go. This painful occurrence was more prevalent than anyone wanted, but with food and water rationed, many parents went hungry to give their children the best chance of survival. Many, however, would never live long enough for the lack of sustenance to kill them, most took their own lives when the pain became too unbearable, and they couldn't endure the suffering any longer.

Luna's mother was one of these people sacrificing their own health for the sake of her child. Anna also had a terrible injury that left her struggling to walk, so she never got the extra sustenance that the people working in the mines received. It wasn't a lot, especially considering how long and hard these people had been working, but it did take the sting out of being so hollow, which at times felt like you had a hole right through your midsection.

Now Luna had turned sixteen, she was expected to work in the mines. Mining was dirty, difficult and dangerous and conditions underground were cramped and particularly perilous. Some mines were hot and wet – others were hot and dusty, and underground workers often worked naked or semi-naked. Luna wanted to put all of her energy into training for the Tourneys, but after a day, or night shift in the mines, there would be little energy left, but she would try her best to get herself in tip-top Tourney competing condition.

The mines ran day and night to keep a steady production of Thorium feeding the Inner Sanctum. Everyone believed that this was required to maintain power to the forcefield that was stopping everyone from becoming as burnt as a crisp. In reality only a small percentage was being used for this purpose, the majority of this mined substance was being turned into fuel for the spacecraft that would carry them away from this dying planet. There was just one little problem, the people who put their lives on the line every day to mine for this precious material, were unaware that their seats were not booked on this life-preserving vessel. After all of their work, after all of their sacrifice, they would be left to a coffin-less cremation, once the sun-reflecting-shield had been taken away.

The Commission told the Inner Sanctum they only had room for half of the population, but there was room for everyone. Yes, it would be cramped and uncomfortable, but all could be saved from this dying planet if they so wished. Obviously the High Commissioner and his animals would be first, followed by the more prevalent in society. The rich and those who had the technological skill required to build a new home on another planet. Everyone who lives in the Sectors would be left behind. Even those who had earned their position in the Inner Sanctum by competing and winning the High Commissioner sick games wouldn't be getting this ride to a new planet.

A planet had been found that could support life, it was basically like another Earth, a planet called Kepler-186F. A relatively newly formed planet that was five-hundred light years away. However, space travel had become second nature, and with the invention of the new hyper-speed-propulsion-engines, space was no longer this far away place that many would only ever get to view through a telescope. Many actually took day trips to the Moon, like they were going to the beach for the day. You could now visit all of the planets in our solar system in under a week.

More powerful engines and more efficient fuel, along with stronger spacecraft's, meant that space travel was as safe as flying on a plane. Advancement in space travel has been the sole focus for every country on the planet for the last two-hundred years. Global warming had reached fever pitch and everyone knew that it was only a matter of time before the ice-caps melted, resulting in the seas swallowing up the majority of the land. The mega wealthy of society had already fled the planet for pastures new. Huge spacecrafts that were like cruise ships could be lived on comfortably while the journey to their new home took place. Sadly, these crafts could have carried more than double the amount of people they did, but as usual it was only the affluent in society who could afford such luxury.

Light years still took a while to travel, but using black-hole-portals meant that what used to take thirty-seven-thousand years to transverse, now only took about a week, give or take a few days. Still, the planet Kepler-186F would take years to reach, but with little land on planet Earth left, many saw this as the only way to save the human race. The planet Kepler-186F was where the Commission was headed, but as you can imagine it takes a lot of fuel to travel that distance. However, one ton of Thorium that has been turned into a propellant can produce the same power as that of five-million barrels of oil. Safer, cleaner energy that makes space travel the only saving grace for the human race.

Everyone in the Sectors was under the belief that everyone would be booked on this space-faring craft, which is why they worked so hard, mining the Thorium required to power the vessel, and why they tolerated the chastisement of their fellow human beings, who were forced to compete in the High Commissioner sick and twisted games. All were under the impression that they were all working towards the same goal and they would be making this trip together. Sadly, this was far from the truth, the people living in the Sectors would be left to a certain death, nothing more than insects left to fry upon a dying planet.

For now, hope had never been greater for the Sector's inhabitants. They would now get to choose who would face the Tourneys. Many believed times were changing and that better days were ahead. Winning the Tourneys meant more food and supplies for that Sector, and considering that most were struggling to survive on the scraps they were given, it was basically life-saving to win these events.

What everyone really wanted was to overthrow the cruel Commission and take back their freedom, but the only way that this might ever be an eventuality is if the Wild Whisperer was found. This folk-law hero would have the ability to control the animals. With control over the many flesh-tearing-fiends that the High Commissioner has dominion over, they might just be able to fight back against the all-powerful Commission, who had the latest in technological weaponry. They had laser guns that could turn a person into a pile of dust, which is what many wished for after they had been caught doing something they shouldn't do. It was far better to be vaporised, than stripped naked, whipped and beaten out in the open for the whole Sector to see. This punishment was usually dished out to those who had stolen Thorium, or those who had been caught passing information between the Sectors.

Thorium was a very powerful substance, and not only could it be turned into a very explosive fuel, it could also be used as a drug. After working in the mines the people started to realise that their clothes which had been impregnated with the substance could be used as a way to get high. Many spent hours scraping and teasing little bits of the substance from their clothes, so they could get enough to melt into a liquid, creating a drug that made you feel like all of your worries just melted away. You felt like you were already on another planet, and your meaningless existence was a lot more tolerable. Like most drugs, they are used to escape something, whether it be a persecuted home life, or a life that provided so much pain that any other feeling would be welcomed over their usual suffering.

Obviously this had been found out by the Commission, hence why everyone who worked in the mines had to be pretty much naked apart from underwear, and not just for the sweltering temperature. Inspections took place after every shift and with little clothes on their bodies, it was difficult to conceal the substance, but many still found a way, secreting it into bodily orifices, they still managed to liberate some of the substance for themselves.

If found with this substance, however, the punishment was severe and after a public lashing, many didn't survive long after such an offensive ordeal. They would be left tied up for a week with no food and only a small amount of water just to keep them alive enough to still feel the pain.

After such a degrading ordeal, many took their own lives to free them from the torture and torment they continued to feel long after the punishment had finished. Without proper medical supplies infected wounds would turn septic, leaving them with only one choice. If they had more supplies they may not need to risk taking this drug which gave them an escape from their miserable existence. So all Sectors had now devised training camps to help train those who wished to compete in the Tourneys, to have the best chance of winning. Survival was key and that was greatly increased by winning these competitions.

Much to the dismay of some, there were still plenty of people wanting to put their names forward to compete in these cruel competitions, but at least it was now their own choice, and they weren't being forced into a possible painful death at the hands of some very scary beasts. Even though death was the more regular outcome in these events, many still wanted to try. The pull of more supplies for their Sector and the chance to live a better life inside the Inner Sanctum, saw people lining up to join the training camps.

After the planet fell into chaos, many joined together to survive, and many living in the Sectors were like an extended family, so they knew that their efforts would also be helping out many more that they held dear to their hearts. With many lives in a constant precarious position, most just wanted to try, or at least die trying. It's better to go down fighting than to just roll over and expire.

Life may not be all parties and privilege for the people living in the Sectors, but they still wanted to live. While they still had a beat in their hearts, and air in their lungs, they knew they could keep striving for better days. However, if they all knew what the Commission's form of fate had planned for them, most would just give up now.

Hope, however, can be an extremely powerful emotion, and those who keep it in their hearts will always have a chance to do something about their own destiny. It was fight, or die and even though fighting for your life was about as difficult as it could be, many still wanted to be in control of their own futures. They would continue to fight until their dying breath, all the while still hoping that one day they would be free!

CHAPTER NINE

Perks of Pregnancy

THE NEWS OF TRAINING camps had one person excited, but another was left extremely fearful. Luna relished the chance to show everyone that she possessed the skills needed to survive the Tourneys. Her mother, however, wanted her to stay well away from anything to do with these vile competitions. She'd already lost a husband and son to the Commission's cruel games and she didn't want Luna anywhere near even the thought of competing.

Luna was thin and scrawny, not many living in the Sectors were very big. The lack of sustenance stopped them from growing to their full size. However, while everyone else saw their lack of muscle and size a problem, Luna never wished to be bigger or stronger, she embraced what she had and turned herself into a fast and wiry flash of lightning. She was so fast, she may even be able to outrun the Hunter Killer in a foot race. No one, however, looked at her as anything more than a little waif of a girl who shouldn't get involved in men's things. Now that she is of age, she should just get pregnant and keep her mouth shut like all of the other women in the Sectors.

Luna's mother was so worried about her daughter's lack of servitude and feared that her self-confident attitude would get her in a lot of trouble. Women were treated as nothing more than people who should be seen, but not heard. Life for women had reverted to the early nineteen hundreds, where they were seen as little more than play-things for the men. They had no say in anything that occurred, and other than providing the men with ways to enjoy themselves, as well as being baby making mules. Women should bow down, be quiet, and only speak when they are spoken to. They will do what they are told, or they will suffer the consequences!

Not all of the men were this way, but with most only wanting the one thing that could give them that certain feeling which could make this horror show of a life worth living, many were totally insatiable for the sexual act. It was the only activity that provided another feeling in this horrific existence, however, it was no longer about love and togetherness it was purely a savage physical act.

Luna no longer had a dad or older brother to look out for her, and a disabled mother, who desperately feared what might happen to her loud, out-spoken, confident daughter. Luna could get away with this gung-ho attitude while she was still underage, even though she had received some physical violence in the past. Now, however, she was fair game to every strung-out, ravenous man, who liked nothing more than fresh meat. The majority of the women living in the Sectors had given birth to many babies, and the act of love-making was now of little pleasure to either party, but a young girl who is yet to bear a child was a treat that almost every man wanted. A fresh-faced, untouched thrill-ride that had men lining up to take their turn.

Anna's fear only grew when witnessing the alluring looks that her daughter was receiving as they made their way to the animal pens. The first of the month was drawing near and the High Commissioner wanted some plumped up animals for his banquet. The Rabbit Run competitions were always a huge lavish event with more food on offer than the Sectors would receive in a year, even if they had won one of the Commissions cruel contests.

Although many in the Sectors got angry knowing that it was their hard work rearing these animals for others to enjoy. Most, however, realised that it would also be a huge source of food for themselves. Yes the food they would receive would have to be picked from a pile of rubbish and the juicy tender cuts of meat would have bite marks and be covered in some disgusting substances, but meat of any kind provided the Sectors with that little extra kick of energy, which made their dire existence a little more bearable.

Anna was one of the lucky people who would be slaughtering these animals for the High Commissioner's feast. She was injured and unable to carry out many jobs, but one thing she could do was butcher an animal. Before the Commission took over what was left of the planet, many lived off the land. They would hunt and gather anything they could to stay alive. So many were completely at home with slaughtering and dissecting an animal, as they were buttering toast. and Anna was one of the best! Skills passed on to her from her father were one of the main reasons they manage to survive the rising tides.

Although many people had lost their lives due to Global Warming, the animals and insects seemed to endure. They had an astonishing ability to read mother nature and her changes, allowing them to relocate and survive much better than the human race. If it wasn't for the animal's sixth-sense, the human race would have perished long ago. They provided a lifeline which allowed the species to survive.

Anna insisted that Luna accompany her to the slaughter sheds where she could keep an eye on her. She also wanted Luna to learn how to carry out this vital skill, plus she always felt a little more in control, a little more powerful, knowing that she had a variety of very sharp implements at her disposal. She may be slow and disabled, but everyone still bleeds when they are cut. Versed in the fighting arts, before she was rendered less-able, she was a great warrior. A weapon in her hand, especially a blade of any kind, was more than a deadly device. If she was close enough to an attacker, she could dissect a person with surgical precision. This was another reason why Luna had been saved from many possible deadly situations that may have befallen her in the past.

The slaughter shed was also relatively unguarded, not many wanted to witness the slaying of these animals, the noise they produced when being killed went through your ears like a red-hot poker. The sight, the sound and especially the smell was something most couldn't stomach. The people living in the Sectors were more used to this savage occurrence, but the guards who had been brought up in the clean, hygienic Inner Sanctum couldn't stand the process, so they didn't keep as close an eye on proceedings as they should have. This, however, gave Anna time to train Luna in the fighting arts. She needed to know that her daughter could defend herself, especially now she was sixteen and looked to be on pretty much every man's radar.

She didn't want her daughter to become a baby-making-mule and to have to deal with the heartache of losing a child to the Commission, or even worse, watch as that child slowly dies from malnutrition. Anna had lost many children over the years, thankfully they were all produced by her husband before his untimely death, but many living in the Sectors had bore babies for a variety of different men. The pull of the perks of pregnancy, saw many opening themselves up to be used and abused. Once pregnant, the women were more protected, they didn't have to face the Tourneys, and they also had the promise of a short luxury stay inside the Inner Sanctum, that's if they made it to the thirty weeks required, which was a very rare occurrence. The pregnant women would no longer have to work, their sole purpose was to grow the foetus to the required stage.

Repopulation was needed to bolster the Commission's army of mindless soldiers. The High Commissioner wanted a force that could reign supreme wherever they ended up. He loved the power and control he possessed over others, and certainly didn't want to lose everything that he had built when they arrived at another planet.

He planned on taking over upon his arrival on Kepler-186F, but to do so he would need to amass a huge army who were totally subservient to him.

This was also part of the reason why he planned on leaving those living in the Sectors behind. They would never follow him and when they arrived at the new planet, he believed they would flee to safety, or become part of any resistance that might be formed against him becoming the supreme leader. All he wanted to take with him was those who would do his bidding, no questions asked! Those who would give their own lives to protect him. With an army of compliant soldiers and a Zoo full of enhanced deadly predators at his disposal, he believed that there would be no force that could stand against them. Once on Kepler-186F, he would expand his forces and in time have control over the whole planet.

There were those, however, who were conspiring against him. A small group of people who resided in the Inner Sanctum had opened their eyes to the cruelty being dished out by the Commission. Alongside some of the fortunate winners of the Predator Pit, they planned on helping the people in the Sectors to form a rebellion against the Commission. They'd seen enough suffering to last three-hundred lifetimes, and they also knew that the High Commissioner's reign of terror would continue on at their future destination.

He had to be stopped before he sentenced so many more innocent people to a horrific death, and before he could enslave a whole planet. However, such an undertaking seemed impossible without the Wild Whisperer. He was just too powerful, especially with the plethora of bone-crushing-beasts at his side. That was the key to defeating this tyrant, they had to gain control of the animals, only then could they hope to defeat this iron-fisted dictator whose lust for power would see the end to all of their lives.

Even though the High Commissioner had an army of spine-shaking, blood-curdling, ready to tear flesh from the bone beasts, he still wasn't satisfied. He wanted a creature that was so powerful, so deadly, that no one would dare to stand against him. He needed a beast that couldn't be defeated by any means. If he had control over such a creature, he could never be stopped. This Hybrid of Hell would cement his position as the King of Kings, all shall bow down to his majesty. He would be worshipped like a God and engrain his name so deep into the history books it could never be erased.

While the High Commissioner had dreams of ruling it all, Luna was hoping and praying that she would get the chance to prove herself. She arrived to many disgusted stares. There were only men at this training facility and she definitely didn't fit in. "Go away you silly little girl. This is no place for a weak child," scoffed one man.

"Does this stupid child never learn? Next time we will have to do a better job," snarled another.

Luna tried not to take any notice, she believed that her actions would speak louder than her words. However, as she walked up to the first apparatus hoping to show these sexist men that she was as good if not better than them, she was tripped and ended up laying face down in the mud. Laughter ensued, the group of men all took great pleasure in putting this stupid little girl in her place. Luna was strong and she would fight as hard as she could, but fast and agile she may be, however, the bigger, stronger men would have eaten her for breakfast.

After wiping the mud from her face she decided to walk away. She would try again another day. A howling noise from a nearby tree, however, drew her attention.

"Ouch! What was that," said one of the group.

"Oi, who's doing that, STOP!" shouted another who had been hit by a stone.

Soon they were all screaming in pain as missiles continued to reign down from above. Luna knew who the thrower of these targeted missiles was, and it brought more than a little smile to her muddy face. The persistent projectiles were being thrown by Bella. Bella was Luna's best friend and she wasn't going to stand for this kind of attack on her friend. Totally camouflaged in the trees, Bella continued to throw objects at these vile men until they decided to remove themselves from the training area.

Luna's smile turned into laughter as she watched the men all running away with their tails between their legs. "Thank you Bella. You can come down now, the coast is clear," she said between chuckles.

"Are you ok? Those stupid men don't know what they are talking about, you would beat all of them in any competition."

The two girls hugged and squeezed each other tightly. "Thanks again, but you need to be careful, if they find out it was you, they will come looking," Luna said, worrying about her friend's actions.

"Let them come. Stupid men, I wasn't about to let them hurt my best friend now was I?" Bella said proudly. "You know what we promised each other and I want you to know that I will always be there for you, no matter what."

The two girls had grown up together and were more like sisters than friends. Each had helped the other when they really needed it and both took strength from the other to survive this horrible existence. Both girls also wished to be the Wild Whisperer. They both had the biggest of hearts and wanted nothing more than to help their fellow people living in the Sectors to be free. However, the fabled Wild Whisperer had always been a man. Stories passed down through hundreds of generations told of how this person could speak with the animals and how together they could overcome anything. It was the only way that the people living in the Sectors could fight back against the Commission.

Both girls came from a long line of Tamers and both had been taught how to connect with the animals, they couldn't control them, but they had the ability to calm certain animals if they were stressed. This skill helped greatly on slaughter day when the animal's sixth sense knew that they were about to become someone's meal.

Even though the Tamers had killed and eaten animals in the past, they only took the sick and injured, the ones who were already suffering. The people helped to stop the animal's discomfort and distress, and in return they would have a hearty meal. This relationship between the Tamers and the animals kept so many alive after most of the land was swallowed up by the sea. A unique coming together of two species that helped both parties survive. Without the animals the humans would have died out long ago. Sadly, many selfish and deluded people still never realised that this was the case. Would they be able to see the animals' worth before it was too late?

CHAPTER TEN

A.I. Advancements

A LOUD CRY IN THE MIDDLE of the night saw an army of people rushing to the High Commissioner's aid. His screams of pain echoed throughout the large hallways, bouncing off the lofted ceilings like a Powerball of terror.

"My Lord, what is it? What can I do?" asked his closest servant.

"Get the surgical team here NOW!" he screamed.

While panic ensued, the High Commissioner's wife arrived to be by her husband's side. "What can I do to help you, my love?" she said, cradling his tense body.

Within a matter of minutes the surgical team had arrived and they brought with them an array of space-age medical equipment. Their swift arrival, however, still may not have been quick enough. Not for saving the High Commissioner's life, but for saving their own lives. Every second of pain that he suffered would be seen as a direct attack upon him and he would have someone's head for their insolence.

"Quickly hook up the monitors. You get the injections ready. Don't worry it won't take much longer sir," said the head doctor whose hands were shaking violently.

His shaking hands were quickly brought still when the High Commissioner grasped hold of them so tightly, the sound of breaking bones could be heard. "Stop this pain NOW!" he said with a terrifying glare.

The reason for the High Commissioner's pain was due to a recent heart transplant that he'd received. His body wasn't the same body that he was born with. Advancement in artificially grown organs meant that a person's whole body could be fully rebuilt if they so wished. Not only were these manufactured body parts a way to rejuvenate and prolong a person's life, but many could also be enhanced using the latest in A.I. Technology. Why not have a more powerful enhanced body, superior in every way to a regular human being, if it's a possibility?

The High Commissioner had so many of these bodily upgrades that you could no longer figure out if he was more android, or human now. Many wondered how this man never seemed to age, and this is why. He was born with a weak heart which stopped him from being very active in his younger years, but after a successful heart transplant gave him more than just a stronger ticker, he started experimenting with enhanced organs. Some organs, however, were rejected by the body, there had to be a balance between the human flesh and artificially enhanced parts. The High Commissioner was always trying to push this to the absolute extremes. He wanted to be as powerful as the beasts he commanded and also prolong his life so that he could continue to rule as long as possible.

A heart enhanced with a Lion's D.N.A, alongside artificial upgrades was what was causing his pain. This heart was being rejected by his body, and there was only one way to remedy the situation. The heart had to be removed before it exploded inside his chest. Being much bigger than a normal human heart, you could visibly see his ribs being pushed so far outwards that his whole rib cage was as visible as that of a skeleton.

"What's taking so long? Get it out now!"

"It will be ok, my love. Just breathe," his wife said, kissing him on the forehead. "Hurry up and remove this now, or your families will SUFFER!" she screamed at the surgical team.

Unfortunately for the surgical team, the only wrath more deadly than that of the High Commissioner's was that of his wife. She was a cold, callous woman who liked nothing more than to see others suffering.

"Sorry my lady, we are about to start. We are just waiting on the antiseptic to take effect."

"DO IT NOW!" bellowed the High Commissioner.

The new heart was ready and waiting to be replaced. Unfortunately for the High Commissioner, he would have to have a regular human heart put into his chest now. After an experimental heart had failed, he needed to allow his body time to heal, but with many other artificially enhanced parts of his body requiring the extra strength of an enhanced heart to be fully functionable, he would be left in a weakened state until it was safe to try another enhanced heart.

The High Commissioner never got put to sleep during these operations. He wanted to be able to strike fear into the surgeons as they worked, making them well aware of what would happen to their families if something went wrong. His wife was also always by his side during these procedures to make sure everything went to plan. She was the only person that he completely trusted and because she was a notable surgeon herself, she could oversee the operation to make sure that no one tried anything stupid.

It was at one of these operations that the two met, locking eyes over the operating table after she had successfully saved his life. The High Commissioner's first wife died a few years ago. She became ill and didn't want anything of an artificial nature to be put inside of her body, no matter how much her husband pleaded. The loss of his wife hit him hard, and he never believed that he would marry again, but when the beautiful Sasha caught his eye during one of his many operations, the two fell madly in love and were married soon after.

Everyone was forced to watch the lavish event where money seemed to be no object. Many living in the Sectors actually hoped for this union to happen, not because they wanted to see the High Commissioner happy, or have another huge event that they would have to cater for, but most knew that there would be a huge amount of discarded food. There was always too much food at these gatherings, and the Sectors knew that they would eventually get the pick of the fancy food that was wasted. Ok, the food wouldn't be served to them on a silver platter, but after digging through a mound of stinky, slimy rubbish and after washing the worst of the smell from the many discarded treats, they would dine out like never before.

After the big day, Sasha took her place next to the High Commissioner, they were like the new king and queen and if worshipping them before was suggested, now it was visibly enforced. She now joined him on his visits to the Sectors like a couple of royals making out that they were there to help, but in reality, it was only about highlighting their own status and power. They didn't care about the poor people living in the Sectors, in fact, they actually despised them. Filthy scum who don't deserve a life, however, while they still provided the Commission with what they needed, they had to be seen to embrace the Sectors and keep them sweet until they no longer had any use for them.

When the surgery was completed the High Commissioner and his wife retired to their chambers to rest and recuperate. Advancement in surgical practices meant that operations were as quick and easy as pulling teeth. Almost everyone in the Inner Sanctum had been enhanced in some way, or another. Most had been altered from their original physical make-up. Some had robotic limbs which made them stronger. Some had a pigment in their hair follicles that could change the colour of their hair by just a thought. At times the Inner Sanctum looked like a blue-rinse convention.

From above, it looked like you had spilled a packet of skittles, multi-coloured-mops of all shapes and sizes were everywhere.

The most popular enhancement was to have a stronger heart. This enhanced the body as a whole, giving them more energy, strength, athleticism and a more advanced mind. These body improvements were also a great money making endeavour for the Commission, who were also trying to increase their finances. Money and power are the two things required when you wish to take over a country, and considering the Commission planned on taking over a whole planet, they would need both in copious amounts.

With the High Commissioner still feeling weak, it fell to his wife to make the next Rabbit Run announcement. This was it, all of the Sectors had chosen who would face this deadly gauntlet, so hope was at an all-time high. The training camps had all who would be competing in the best shape they could be considering their environment, but lack of sustenance can be replaced with hope, a hollow stomach can be fed with desire and a downtrodden mind can be lifted by dreaming of what could possibly be.

After the alarm sounded, the big screens came to life and many were surprised not to see the High Commissioner's face greeting them. However, his new wife was the huge face that now stared down at them with devilish intent.

"Hello to you all. I hope that we find you happy and well. My gracious husband has allowed me to address you on this occasion. He is currently working on a very important project that could mean a better life for us all. The Commission is always working to provide the best for each and everyone of us, but we all must continue to play our roles if we are to survive."

"What is she reading this from, a script? What a load of crap," said an unconvinced person.

"You know, I heard that she is even more sadistic than the High Commissioner. One evil bitch!"

"Yes she's a bitch alright, just look at her sour face," joked another.

A gun pointed in their direction zipped their lips while Sasha continued.

"As a kindness you all get to compete for a better life for you and your families, and I'm sure that you are all as excited as me for this particular Rabbit Run competition, because you have had the leniency afforded to be allowed to choose your own contestants. We would love for all of you to join us in the Inner Sanctum, but work must also continue if we are to survive. Each of us plays a vital role in saving our species. Without all of the cogs turning in this huge organisation, we wouldn't be able to endure. Now I believe I have the names of the eight hopefuls who will be having their chance to win a better life. The first name is Benis from Sector one. From Sector two is Darry. Sector three's hopeful is Flyn. Sector four will have Jono flying the flag for their Sector. Sector five will have Hexor making the run. Sector six's contestant is Kelo. Now, the last two hopefuls for this unprecedented Rabbit Run competition are............ Mison from Sector seven and our only woman competitor, Mavee from Sector eight............ I would like to wish you all the greatest of luck, and remember that your Commission strives to provide better conditions for us all. We must persist, preserve, and then we can all prosper!"

Sasha's face was removed from the screen and the over the top, outlandish display continued. There were two things that left the Sectors scratching their heads. One was why was the High Commissioner not making the announcement, and second, why had Sector eight chosen a woman to compete in the contests, especially when they had the right to choose who they wished?

Most, however, had little energy to think about anything at all, many had little sleep and now they would have to work in the mines, all the while knowing that soon another life could be taken from them, leaving them with an increased workload. Yes, there would be one less mouth to feed, but that person's contribution to the work that had to be carried out, outweighed any tiny morsel of food that they might receive after their demise.

One person was visibly buzzing about the announcement. Luna was overjoyed that a woman had been picked, maybe the Sectors were starting to realise a woman's worth? Sadly, this wasn't the case, it turns out that no one from Sector eight wanted to compete, they'd found out about the demise of Sector three's contestant Claire and they would no longer compete in these cruel games. However, knowing that this act would bring a lot more pain and suffering their way, Mavee decided to put her name forward. She had two children, a son aged six and a daughter aged eight. She didn't want to leave her children all alone, but she also wished to take them away from the poverty-stricken Sectors. Furthermore, she also knew that if no one stepped up to the plate the whole Sector would suffer, and considering survival was still very much a lottery, she knew that many wouldn't survive harsher sanctions.

Only once before has a Sector refused to provide a contestant, and the fallout from such an action caused immense pain for them all. To defy the Commission was to gamble with more than your life. After they'd used an array of different punishments, you only wished that you were dead, but the release of death wouldn't be granted. Those who defied the Commission would suffer like never before. The living conditions they faced in the Sectors now, would be like a walk in the park compared to the pain and punishment that would be dished out upon them for this defiance.

To save her children and the Sector a whole lot of agony and affliction, Mavee stepped up. No one thought that she had the slightest chance of winning and the other Sectors were quite happy knowing that while the Hunter Killer was tearing apart this sure to be slow and useless woman, they would be gifted an advantage.

Luna, however, put all of her faith into this woman, if she was to win, it might just change the Sector's outlook upon women competing. Many women have competed before when the wheel of chance unfortunately landed on their names, but sadly not one single woman has ever triumphed over the Rabbit Run, so hope in this female competitor was paper thin.

With the names announced, it would now be up to each competitor to get themselves into the best mental and physical condition that they could. Regardless if any of them actually won or not, they needed to show the Commission that allowing them their own choice of competitor, would be better for everyone involved. They had to perform better and give the baying crowds what they wanted to see. A more exciting contest where even though death was probably going to be the outcome, they would hopefully hold off this more than likely eventuality until the very end.

If they could prove that this was the best way, they would no longer have to watch the anguish and agony inflicted upon those who had been picked randomly. Many parents would sacrifice themselves to prevent their sons or daughters from having to face these cruel contests. There was no greater pain than having to watch one of your children die, however, the suffering was increased ten-fold knowing that it was as a result of these competitions. At least those who chose to compete now knew what they were signing up for. With training camps helping to get the competitors in the best possible shape, hopefully fewer people will die in these sick and twisted Tourneys.

CHAPTER ELEVEN

Show of Power

IT WAS THE SOUND OF screams that woke many in the Sectors, after a loud, ear-shattering roar was played into their homes. This stomach-churning sound let everyone know that they would soon be having a visit from the High Commissioner and his deadly animals. Each Sector would be greeted by the presence of two of his brutal beasts, walking beside him like tame pets. However, some of these creatures stood almost as tall as he did. He loved to see people's eyes grow in size at the sheer terror of what they were witnessing as he walked throughout their Sector with his cruel creatures who hissed, snapped and cracked their huge jaws together showing their flesh eating intent.

On this visit he would be joined by his new wife and both of them would walk throughout each Sector handing out a few scraps of food to the terrified people. This was all about a show of power, not a helping hand to the people. They threw pieces of stale bread treating them like they were nothing more than ducks in a pond. He needed to show who was in charge and what faced them if they didn't follow his rule.

In the past, some had tried to attack the High Commissioner when he carried out one of these power-parades, but with a group of highly trained snipers watching his every move, no one ever got close enough to strike a blow. Although these attacks were against him, he actually welcomed them at times, because after the foolish person had been shot, their bodies would be devoured by his predator-pets, creating an even more terrifying display which would help to bolster his dominance.

There were more than two new things that appeared when the High Commissioner did his parade throughout the Sectors. Firstly he had his new wife by his side, and he also had a new heart which actually made his body glow in the sunlight. However, what was walking beside him had every single person feeling startled, scared, shaken, but also totally captivated. A new beast had been created and this creature even made the Hunter Killer look like a little pussycat. This towering animal resembled that of a Tiger, but this particular big cat's body was jet-black in colour and highlighted with fiery red and yellow stripes that were so vibrant it looked as if it was being lit by a fire from inside. Its eyes glowed red and its huge teeth looked like they had been carved from metal. The shiny surface blinded on-lookers when it opened its huge jaw, displaying the metal mashers.

The ground began to shake as the beast walked by, hundreds of terrified people couldn't stop their bodies from trembling with fear. The beast radiated a dreadful desire, looking at the crowds of people like they were his next meal. One overly intrigued man got a little too close and the pulsating predator removed his hand from his arm with one swift bite and swallowed it whole. The strangest thing then occurred, the now one-handed man didn't start spraying blood everywhere, nor did he start screaming and shouting like a crazy person, which would have been totally justified considering what had just happened, however, the wound was automatically sealed and cauterised by the beast's scalding teeth. The wound never bled, or caused him any pain. It was only when the too curious man saw that he only had one hand did he start screaming and shouting.

Quickly taken down by the High Commissioner's guards, the one-handed man was removed from making a scene. This creature, whatever it was, was on another level to anything that had been created before. If this was the continuing trend, then the people in the Sectors could have chosen Superman to face the Predator Pit, and they still wouldn't win. This new creation had everyone worried except for one little girl. All she felt was sorrow for the brute of a beast, she could feel the pain that it was experiencing, it just wanted to roam free, free from the shackles that bound it.

During Sector four's visit, his wife had decided to take a little walk around by herself, to show that she was here for the people. She wanted to talk to them and portray that she was a sympathetic person who wanted to help the people living in the Sectors. Wanting to show that there was a togetherness for all who lived on the Last Isle. Obviously armed with a terrifying creature by her side and an army of guards, however, the High Commissioner was happy to let his wife roam alone.

It was the Blue-eyed-beast that accompanied Sasha on this visit. Its bright white fur and piercing blue eyes made this creature look rather tame compared to the rest, but this beast had a special attribute, one that turned it from a pussycat into a hell-cat. This animal had an extendable jaw that could open up like a snake, revealing a mouth full of serrated-edged teeth that would tear flesh from the bone and devour humans like they were being fed to it on a conveyor belt. In fact, it could have probably swallowed a person whole, but where is the fun in that.

Sasha also likes to watch as unsuspecting people look at this creature with a gentle eye, that is until it opens its mouth and the terror upon their face builds quicker than a tidal-wave at sea. Some were so horrified that they couldn't hold onto their bodily functions, resulting in a dirty protest to the fear that they were experiencing.

Unaware of the Wild Whisperer prophecy, she found it adorable when a young girl came over and petted the huge beast, she wasn't afraid and the grunting, growling creature went as docile as a puppy.

If the girl had thrown a stick, the creature was sure to run after it. No one else was around to witness this chance encounter other than Luna's mother, and this interaction sent shivers down her spine like she had been hit in the back by an iceberg.

"What is your name child?" asked Sasha.

Thankfully, before she could answer, her mother came rushing over. "Move away child. I told you to collect the firewood, go now!" Anna said, ushering Luna away. "Sorry my lady, that one is a bit too curious for her own good."

Sasha moved on with her visit thinking little more about the interaction.

Out of earshot Anna scalded her daughter. "What on Earth are you doing?"

"What's wrong, the poor animal was in so much pain. I could sense its misery, I wanted to try and help ease its suffering. They shouldn't have to suffer in such ways."

"Don't you understand what will happen if this news gets back to the High Commissioner? He will kill any threat to his control. They are killing anyone who might have the old Tamer ways within them. He will not hesitate to destroy whole Sectors if he believes that the Wild Whisperer might be among them. You have to think, Luna, think!"

"What, do you think that I am the Wild Whisperer?"

"Don't be daft, child. We come from a long line of Tamers. Yes our people contain a connection with the animals, but to be able to control them all, it's just a myth. I don't want to see you get taken away from me, so no more stupid behaviour. Stop talking with the animals, stop highlighting yourself and just stay quiet and unseen, please Luna, I can't lose you too!" Anna said, completely breaking down and crying.

"It's ok mum, It's ok. I will try to be less visible, please don't cry."

Luckily for Luna, Sasha was uninformed about the prophecy of the Wild Whisperer and she never took any notice of this unusual occurrence, and for Luna's sake they better hope that remains the case.

With the fanciful, false parades over, everyone could once again breathe a sigh of relief, however, some of those who previously wanted to face the Tourneys were now questioning their choice. This new bright-blazing-beast had scared stiff, and everyone knew that if this was the creature he decided to display, who knows what other massive monstrosities he had just waiting in the wings for the unfortunate few who might make it into the Predator Pit.

Although Anna believed in the legend of the Wild Whisperer, this fabled person has always been a man, but after witnessing Luna's actions she became slightly worried. However, all those who descend from the Tamer blood-line had the ability to connect with the animals on some level. The Tamers could anticipate the animals and use that ability to bring order and calm to certain situations. The Native American Tamer's abilities were passed down through generations. Everyone was blessed with this unique ability, but very few learned to master the talent.

Tamer's might be able to connect with mother nature's animals, however, but the drastically changed, enhanced beasts that the High Commissioner had produced was a whole other matter. These creatures were far from what they were to begin with and worse still they were being controlled by the High Commissioner himself!

So many people were putting their hope into this mythical person, but even if they did exist, would they be able to control animals that were now more machine than meat. One thing that Anna knew was that she didn't want her daughter to have anything to do with all of this nonsense. She was all she had left, and as long as they were together, they could weather any storm and survive anything that was thrown at them. She knew that Luna was special in some way, but being special only brought more scrutiny down upon them. If they stayed unseen and did their duties to a good standard, the Commission usually left them alone.

They may not have much, and living really wasn't what they were doing, but surviving this miserable existence was a lot easier if they kept their heads down and did what they were told. The Commission was too strong, they held all of the power and to go against them was extremely foolish and would definitely result in not only death for those involved, but a lot more pain and suffering for all who lived in the Sectors.

Most believed that their salvation would come when they reached Kepler-186F. Hoping the planet would already have a system in place that the Commission couldn't possibly fight back against. The already colonised planet would be able to repel any attack, especially if all the people in the Sectors joined beside them. Little did the people of the Sectors know that their seats weren't booked on the spacecraft that would be blasting off as soon as they had mined enough Thorium to get this huge vessel into the sky.

The only hope for the Sectors was to fight back against the Commission, before they were all left to die on a sun-scorched planet. Without the Commission's satellite shield keeping out the roasting rays from the sun, they would be cooked alive. After years of persecution and pain, they would be left to die a slow and agonising death. Blistered skin and dehydration would leave them all wishing for an axe to the neck to bring a quick end to their lives of torment and torture.

There was no hard and fast proof yet that had been obtained about the Commission's upcoming betrayal, but whispers started to be heard throughout the Inner Sanctum that had given some pause for thought. Most of the Inner Sanctum residents couldn't care less about those who lived in the Sectors. Many believed that they should be exterminated like the vermin they are. However, there were still some who sympathised with these poor people and although they would never risk their own lives to help them, some just couldn't stand by and give these people no chance of survival. They wouldn't join the fight, but they would try to inform the people of what was to become of them. Many would love to take down the High Commissioner, even some inside the Inner Sanctum, but he was just so powerful and his zoo full of spine-splitting-savages kept everyone living under a dark, gloomy veil of terror no matter the side of the divide you ended up on.

Everyone feared the High Commissioner, and not just those living in the Sectors. This man would kill you at a dinner party if you sip your coffee too loud, or opened your mouth when you were eating. Believing these were the actions of savages, and if you wanted to keep your place with the highest in society you would act appropriately. He expected his people to act in a sophisticated manner, they were certain standards to adhere to and if you didn't maintain this level of sophistication you would be thrown out of the Inner Sanctum, and into the Sectors where you would probably be eaten alive. They wouldn't pass up the chance to get some revenge upon someone from that place, and when you have nothing, even the thought of a gently seared human limb can have you licking your lips!

CHAPTER TWELVE

Triumphant Woman

AS THE DAYS CONTINUED, Luna kept her promise to her mother by keeping a low profile. She zipped her mouth and stopped getting involved in things that were none of her business. With Luna now of age, however, even her best attempts to stay under the radar weren't enough and she had caught the eye of many amorous admirers, all wanting to sample some fresh meat.

It was while working in the farm area when a group of young men decided to pounce. "Hey beautiful, when are you going to give me some sugar?"

"Yea, if you supply the sugar, I'll supply the spoon to stir it."

There was a lustful laughter from the group of men who all had unsavoury thoughts of what they would like to do to this pale-skinned girl.

It wasn't just Luna's outspoken voice and curious nature that put her on everyone's radar, but also the fact that she was pale white. Everyone else had tanned skin, the blistering sun's rays would bake the body to a golden brown with the slightest of exposure, so pale white skin was a thing of the past, but Luna's was still milky white. This made her stand out like a sore thumb and also made her extremely desirable to many. Everyone else was either very tanned, or just dirty from working in the mines. And because they had very little water to waste upon things like personal hygiene, many had years of ingrained dirt, the type that only some sort of soap and a good hard scrub would clean, but when most usually only get a quick hosing down, the dirt clung to their bodies and seeped into their pores, leaving their skin forever coloured.

Anna also noticed the extra attention that her daughter was receiving and wanted to keep a close eye on her. Luna was often in a world of her own, lost in daydreams, she was also very naive, she never really read the signs. She was a happy soul, which was extremely rare to find in the Sectors, but her loving nature might just get her into serious trouble.

"You there, they need you in the slaughterhouse," shouted a guard at Anna.

"Luna, come with me."

"No, just you, the girl stays here."

"Luna, I have to go to the slaughterhouse, they want more meat for the party. Stay here and make sure that all of the goats are fed and watered before you put them back in their pen, and no wandering," Anna said with glaring eyes.

"Yes, yes, I know. Just go, I will be fine," Luna replied, trying to ease her mum's tension.

Anna hated leaving Luna alone, but you never questioned an order from one of the guards, to do so could bring down various punishments upon them, each one more horrifying than the last. Whilst the guard was transporting Anna to the slaughterhouse, a group of men decided to take their chance to harass the young girl. Although her mother was disabled, her skills with weapons of any kind still kept many at bay.

"Luna, Luna. Hello there sweetheart, how's about me and you take a trip into the forest," said a lad named Blue.

"Go away, I find all of you repulsive. Leave me alone," Luna replied, trying to sound confident.

"Not so fast, little lady. Grab her lads," shouted another.

"Get your hands off me NOW!" Luna screamed.

Luna was now being forcefully led from the farming area by a group of five men. There was no way she could fight back against this group of much stronger males. Her friend who saw what was occurring rushed to her friend's aid, but this group had also been looking for this young girl who had left many with deep wounds after the missile throwing incident.

"Leave her alone, you bunch of animals," screamed Bella.

"Ow, you little bitch," said a lad after being kicked in the shins.

"Get that other little cow, NOW!"

"I think it's time that we taught you both a lesson. What do you say lads?" *A harmonious agreement was heard that sounded very sinister.*

The two girls tried to escape the clutches of this group of young men, but they had no chance against the much stronger males. It was at that moment when one of the males went flying through the air like he had been hit by a train. Soon after, another one was thrust through the air at great speed.

The three remaining males let go of Luna and Bella and started backing off slowly. Neither girl had a clue what was happening, but when they turned around to run away, they saw a line of goats snorting and scraping their hooves across the ground. As the remaining males turned heel and began to flee, the line of goats gave chase, bucking and bashing them out of the pen. The girls laughed watching the men being ungracefully shoved out of the farm area. Bella gave her friend a huge hug and left. She was already late for her work detail, but she would never walk on by when her friend was in trouble, even if it meant possible punishment for herself.

After the initial adrenaline had worn off, Luna was very shaken up by the incident and she fell to her knees. When the goats returned, they huddled around her in a protective shield and began to nuzzle her body trying to comfort the frightened girl. It all happened so quickly that no one really knew what had occurred, and when Anna returned she found her daughter on her knees crying, surrounded by goats.

"SHU, SHU, you silly creatures. Luna, what's wrong? What happened?" Anna probed.

"It's nothing, I just, well, what happened was.... I fell and hurt my back. It was so stupid of me."

"It's ok, my love. Come here, we will use our water rations for you to have a nice hot bath later."

"No, I will be ok. Look, it's not even hurting that much any more," Luna said, jumping up trying to reassure her mother.

There was no way that Luna could disclose the true events that took place. Her mother was already a worrying mess and she didn't want to add to her feelings of woe. The thought of a bath sounded delightful to Luna, it was very rare that this now luxurious event took place. Usually it was just a quick hose down, to get the worst of the filth from their bodies. Luna knew, however, that her mother would go without to provide this opulent experience, as she's done many times in the past, so she had to convince her that she was ok. Anna sensed she didn't know the whole story, but she hoped to bring a smile to both their faces, when she revealed what she had acquired from the slaughterhouse, a nice piece of meat for them both to enjoy.

With a laborious and constant work, sleep, work cycle, it never seemed to take long until once again it was time for the Rabbit Run competition. As many tired and weary bodies made their way to the big screens, most had genuine hope in their hearts, but this definitely didn't show on their downtrodden faces.

This competition was it, the one in which the people's choice of participant would be racing. Every Sector was full of a faithful optimism in their chosen competitor, all except for Sector eight that is. Mavee from Sector eight was the only woman to be running, and ever since the contest began, not one single woman had managed to complete the course. They were soon hunted down, and the odds of this woman getting very far were next to nothing. No bets would be placed upon this female competitor, who was sacrificing herself for the sake of her children and the Sector as a whole.

Mavee was small and skinny, a mere waif standing next to the huge brutes of men that had been chosen by the other Sectors. Surely she had no chance of succeeding?

While everyone waited for the razzle-dazzle show to be over, some tried to sneak a little sleep. Production in the mines had been stepped up and everyone was working longer and harder. Tired bodies and exhausted minds saw many drifting off into the world of dreams. A world where their lives weren't such a tortured existence. After a short stay in this place of hope and happiness, their eyes were opened wide by the sound of gunfire whizzing past their heads.

With everyone's attention now refocused, the High Commissioner appeared on the screen. "Hello and welcome to the Rabbit Run competition. I know that we are just as excited as you all to see what your chosen contestants will do. My beautiful new wife being the loving, caring and absolutely humanitarian person she is, has another little surprise for all of the contestants. My love," he said, handing over the stage to her.

"Hello to you all. Can I just say, the love I felt from you all as I walked around your homes was touching. I felt accepted and cherished. You all welcomed me with open arms."

"Yea, open arms and a gun to the head," said a disgruntled onlooker.

"What did she expect when she was accompanied by one of those cruel creations?" added another.

"To say thank you for your most gracious welcome. I have managed to convince the great High Commissioner, my husband Hector, to allow the runners an extra minute before the Hunter Killer is released," Sasha paused for the applause she was expecting.

There was a short pause before pointing guns, harsh stares and overriding fear started the crowds clapping and cheering.

"Thank you, thank you, oh please, it's the least I can do. We all know that the extra production needed from the mines has stretched your resources thin, but rest assured that everyone is working longer and harder to get everything ready for our departure from this dying world, and we shall all benefit from the hard work that is being put in by us all."

"Is this chick for real? We work our asses off while they put their feet up and have parties. What a joke," said a tired and angry person.

"Yea, what good is an extra minute against that lightning-fast feline?"

"We must all sacrifice for the good of the future. Remember that your Commission is here to make life better for us all. If we continue to persist and persevere, we will all prosper," Sasha said, walking away and waving.

"Thank you my dear. Let's all have a huge round of applause for my ever loving wife. We are all excited to see who will triumph over the Rabbit Run and get their chance to fight for a better life inside the Inner Sanctum. With an extra minute, this competition is now wide open. Good luck to you all."

Now that the High Commissioner and his new wife had stopped babbling, everyone was more focused than ever. The siren sounded and the contestants raced out from the starting line like greyhounds chasing after a rabbit. All of the competitors completed the A frame and moved onto the cargo net. Landing at the same time, it was the lighter and more nimble Mavee that took an early lead, leaving the huge strapping men trailing behind.

Mavee was first to reach the rope swing and she sailed across the array of ropes in record time. One of the contestants got their foot stuck on the cargo net while the rest continued trying to catch up with Mavee. Even with an extra minute before the release of the

Hunter Killer, still it seemed to come all too soon, and shortly after it had already claimed its first victim. Sector three's contestant couldn't free himself from the cargo net and was first to fall to the mighty beast.

With the sound of blood-curdling screams reaching the other competitors' ears, their fear began to grow rapidly. They were now being hunted down, and the grim reaper was hot on their tails.

Mavee had now reached the tunnels and her shorter stature allowed her to almost stand up straight which allowed her to get through at quite a fast pace. Sector four contestants had fallen from the rope swing and after managing to release himself from the pit of claggy, sloppy mud, he was too tired to escape the jaws of the Hunter Killer, who with one swift bite removed the poor man's head.

Even though these competitors had an extra minute before the Hunter Killer was released, it seemed to take a lot less time killing its victims, seeing it on the rest of the contestants' arses in no time at all. The harrowing screams continued as the Hunter killer slayed its next three victims, who were all caught in the tunnels, leaving just three to continue on.

"There are unprecedented scenes unfolding in this tantalising Rabbit Run gauntlet. Mavee, our only woman contestant, has already defied the odds and made it further than any woman before her. Could she be the first woman in history to triumph over this Tourney?" said the over-excited commentator.

The High commissioner was beside himself, not that he showed it. His mansion was now full of respectable people acting like excited school kids on Christmas Eve. This woman wouldn't make it to the end, would she?

Mavee was first to finish the monkey bars, sadly the crocodile pit beneath them claimed another victim, leaving just Mavee and two others. As they made their way to the balance beam all three were extremely exhausted. Sector seven's competitor couldn't go on any longer. He was done, his lungs burned like fire and his legs wouldn't take another step. He knew that he would soon be dead, he just hoped that his death would give the remaining two the extra time they needed to complete the course and evade the Hunter Killers' jaws. However, while he waited for the pain and suffering he would be experiencing, he was knocked off his feet as the Hunter Killer raced past. Not even a swipe from its deadly claw befell the man, which left him, and everyone else scratching their heads.

The remaining two had now reached the balance beam, but the tremors produced by the Hunter Killer's presence saw the contestant from Sector six become frozen with fear. His body wouldn't move, no matter how much he willed it to.

Mavee turned to see the man frozen like a statue. "Come on, you can make it. It's not far now," she pleaded.

Seeing the terror in the man's eyes she knew he was done. At least this man's obstruction on the beam would slow down the chasing beast. Sadly, soon after his legs were moving rather swiftly as the Hunter Killer removed them from his torso with one swipe of its huge claw. Propelling his legs in one direction and his body in the other, while racing through like a train trying to catch up with Mavee.

Mavee was the only one left, and as she leapt from the balance beam into the cages, she shocked just about everyone. Wide gaping mouths were everywhere, this was the first woman ever to win the Rabbit Run. Shortly after, huge cheers rang out from all Sectors at this amazing occurrence. Even though all the others had all failed, this win alone gave so much hope to everyone. A woman had won a Tourney, a WOMAN! What would this mean going forward?

There was outrage and upset among the High Commissioner guests. Not one person had bet on this weak woman to win and they had all lost a lot of money.

"Please everyone. This rare occurrence has shocked us all, but has this not been the most exciting Tourney to date. Competition is what you wanted and competition is what you got. Maybe you will all think a little differently when the Predator Pit takes place?"

Everyone was left dumbfounded. What did this mean? Would women now be seen as more than just baby making mules? One could only hope, however, this was the first and probably the last, so would anything really change?

However, this woman's actions had inspired another, who not only wanted a better life for herself and her mother, but she also wanted a better life for all who lived in the Sectors. Luna was overjoyed that Mavee had triumphed over the Rabbit Run. No one had put any hope in this woman winning. Now maybe the Sectors will see that women can be strong, fast and resilient.

All of the Sectors had chosen their best competitors, but all had failed. It looked like there was something more than just physical ability that was needed to win these cruel contests. Love, hope and relenting nature to survive also played a huge part. People have been known to be able to achieve amazing things when they put every single fibre of their being into the task at hand. Adrenaline, hope and fear can combine to become a very powerful cocktail. One that could see anyone find the strength that they believed had been starved and beaten from them. This woman's actions may just be the extra incentive the Sectors have been looking for?

There was just one act left, but no one stuck around to witness it. Many were left so shocked, outraged, or completely dumbfounded that they didn't even want to watch the Hunter Killer devour his last victim. This person could have tried running, or hiding, but there was nowhere left to hide once the brutal beast had picked up your scent. This last victim just lay on the ground looking up at the sky, trying to free his mind before the final act, all the while knowing that his pain would finally be over.

CHAPTER THIRTEEN

Night Time Torment

EVERYONE WAS STILL reeling from the last Rabbit Run competition, but whilst one woman returned to her Sector to cheers, praise and adoration. The other women in the Sectors were quickly shown that this one woman's actions wouldn't change a single thing. If anything, life got harder for them now. How dare a small, skinny, useless woman win a competition over men? Especially hand-picked champions, this didn't go down well with many and they sought to put the women in their place.

Sadly, whilst the small, skinnier-framed women might give them an advantage in the Rabbit Run, it did little to protect them from the much bigger and stronger males. Soon screams resonated from all the Sectors after men forcefully assaulted the women to put them back in their place. The savagery of this world now saw a woman's triumph as a threat, and not the amazing achievement that it was. Even though this could mean more chances for a Sector to win, in turn providing more supplies for everyone.

In the light of day this brutal chastisement wouldn't be allowed, but in the dead of night, sparsely guarded Sectors were left open for actions of a depraved nature. Most weren't stupid enough to leave any visible marks that might be seen by the guards. This kind of cruelty wasn't tolerated by the Commission, and those responsible would be punished. It seems that the only one who could inflict pain and suffering onto the people living in the Sectors was the Commission themselves.

Regrettably, women never came forward after these diabolical attacks. With less men working in that Sector, quotas were harder to reach, and unmet quotas meant more agony and affliction for them all. So many kept quiet to protect family members and children from even worse sanctions that would be imposed upon them by the Commission.

Having the Commission's spotlight shining down upon your Sector was never a good thing. An increase in guards meant that the little bit of freedom they did have would be gone. There was nowhere to hide once your Sector had been highlighted. Although these despicable men deserved to be severely punished for their actions, keeping quiet about these attacks was sadly the lesser of two evils.

It seems even when the women won, they lost, but this did little to stop one girl from dreaming of a better life. Inspired by the actions of Mavee, Luna was more determined than ever to face the Tourneys, but now that the choice was in the hands of the Sectors, would a woman ever get the chance to face them again?

Even though this winning woman's actions would provide more supplies for her Sector, many would rather go hungry than be upstaged by a weak, pathetic woman. They would cut their noses off to spite their face, rather than embracing this achievement that had given them all a little more in their lives of nothingness.

The next morning should have brought with it a greater feeling of hope and a more united society, however, it brought more downtrodden faces and battered bodies. Although the majority of the woman's injuries were hidden from view, their faces highlighted their pain and suffering like a full moon on a clear night. They couldn't hide their torment and tenderness as they made their way to work. Many faces had meandering white lines resembling tiny rivers where their tears had cut through the dirt to leave another telling sign of the distress that they had suffered.

Surprisingly spared from an attack during the night was Luna and her mother. Anna knew that she was a long way past being desirable to the opposite sex, although desperate acts have happened in the past. However, she was more surprised that her daughter hadn't got the attention of these groups of despicable humans. It seems that Luna's little farming incident the other day had spread throughout the Sector, and no one wanted to touch this girl who many now feared could be the Wild Whisperer.

They would never feel safe knowing that this person could turn any animal against them. Even Goats, Pigs, Cows and Chickens have the ability to cause serious damage, or even death, and any injury was like a death sentence in this place. Lacking enough nourishment to keep an uninjured body alive was just about attainable, but unless you had a special skill that the Commission could use, you risked dying a very slow and painful death.

Only the strongest would survive in this new world. If you didn't contribute in some way you didn't receive any food, unless you had a family who were willing to ration their own supplies to keep you alive, but that usually only made that family unit as a whole much weaker and more susceptible to illness.

Thankfully for Anna, she was about the best butcher around. Her injuries left her unable to do most things, but she could slice up any animal into a feast fit for a king. Her special skill also allowed her a chance to sneak some of the waste products out of the slaughterhouse for Luna and herself. Only the finest cuts of meat would be served to the Inner Sanctum residents, so livers, heart and even intestines would all be chopped up into animal feed, but they could also be used to provide some extra nourishment for herself and her daughter. However, if Anna was caught stealing this meat she would be severely chastised, but in a world where you had very little, sometimes the only way to survive is to break the rules.

Being a single mother had many challenges. To provide and protect a child was extremely difficult without a male presence in the family. In the past Anna had endured many awful experiences to protect her child from coming to any harm. Sometimes it's better not to put up any resistance, you tend to get hurt even more if you try and fight back. Most women had now realised that this was the easiest way, and they put up little struggle to these degrading attacks.

Although Anna was happy that her daughter had been left alone, she would be even more scared if she knew the reason why. If the High Commissioner found out about a possible Wild Whisperer, he wouldn't hesitate to put an end to their lives. Even though there was an unwritten rule among the people living in the Sectors that this information would be kept quiet, if someone believed that this information would help to make their own lives a little bit easier, would they still keep tight-lipped about such a revelation?

Many had been tortured in the past, if the Commission thought they were hiding something. For now Luna's secret was safe, everyone was still hoping that one day the Wild Whisperer would be the one to set them free, but now that women were being seen as a threat, would the masculinity of some be happy to be saved by a young girl?

There was only one thing on most minds at the moment, and that was the coming winter. The winds had changed and there was a cooler feeling in the air. Thankfully, in the winter, there was more togetherness among the Sectors, everyone had to work together if they were to survive the cold snap. During this inhospitable time, many pulled resources to help keep as many people as they could from succumbing to the freezing conditions. Keeping the majority of people alive was the only way they could hope to maintain a Strong Sector. Sadly, there would always be some who wouldn't survive this colder time of year. Usually it was the injured and the elderly who succumbed to the harsh winter conditions.

The Commission didn't care if one Sector lost more people during the winter than others, the quotas stayed the same no matter how many people they had, so it was in the Sector's best interest to keep as many people alive as they could. There was one saving grace for the people living in the Sectors, and that was the extra supplies they would receive after the Predator Pit competition had been completed.

Christmas was definitely not a tradition that the Sectors could be involved in, they didn't have enough for themselves let alone any extra to be gifted to others. However, those living in the Inner Sanctum had more than the Sectors could ever dream of having. It was this abundance that would result in much more waste around this festive time, allowing the Sectors their own little present. Yes, it would have to be dug from a huge pile of rubbish, but while the fat and full people in the Inner Sanctum had eyes bigger than their bellies, it resulted in more for the Sectors. I suppose this was kind of a gift, although it wasn't really given, and it definitely wasn't gift wrapped, however, when you have become so hungry that your body begins to eat itself, a huge pile of any discarded food was seen as a banquet to many.

It was always first come, first served, and this event became like a Black Friday sale, people pushing and shoving, fighting and clambering over each other to get to the best bits. This was when Luna's small-framed, wiry body came into its own. She was like a mole, tunnelling through the huge pile to find the most nutritious food for herself and her mother. Considering the fact that Luna and her mother were all alone and they didn't have the protection of a male figure in their lives, they did quite well. Each supporting the other when things got really tough. They both had skills that were helping them to stay alive, and their smarts and tenacity saw them surviving over many who were deemed to be stronger.

This, however, still wasn't enough for Luna, she wanted more for her mother who had sacrificed so much to look after her when they lost her father and brother. She protected her child and made sure that she would never go hungry, even though she herself had on many occasions. Luna had also heard her mother's painful cries during many degrading assaults in the dead of night. She wanted to give her mother a better life, one where she didn't have to sacrifice, one where she didn't have to put her body through such pain and agony to work for an organisation that treated them like slaves. She wanted her mother to have so much food in her belly, she might just pop!

Luna wanted to care for her mother as she had cared for her and at least make her last years of life as comfortable as she possibly could. There was only one way to achieve this dream life and that was to win both Tourneys. After the first woman in history had just won, this gave Luna more hope than she'd ever had before, and there wasn't anything that would stop her from completing this goal. She would train day and night, that's when she wasn't forced to work that is. Although, she wouldn't let a little thing called sleep get in her way.

Although this lucky woman along with seven others had triumphed over the Rabbit Run, they still had to survive in the Predator Pit if they were to get the lives of luxury they had been promised. However, with the High Commissioner creating more and more deadly, enhanced, hybrid killing-machines, would anyone be able to triumph over the Predator Pit and pull themselves out of poverty and persecution?

Many in the Sectors, also wanting to guarantee their place on the space-saving-ship, knew that they would have to win the Predator Pit competition. Although no one believed that the Commission planned on leaving everyone in the Sectors behind, some knew that there may be a real possibility that there wouldn't be enough space for everyone, and the only way to make sure that had the best possible chance of leaving this doomed planet was to be a resident of the Inner Sanctum.

The people living in the Sectors knew that their trip to this new planet would be a lot different from those living in the Inner Sanctum. While they would have a luxury travel experience, the Sectors would be transported like cattle, caged and cramped into dark spaces, being kept worse than animals. Considering the fact that this journey might take years to complete, no one wanted to spend that amount of time cooped up like a battery chicken. They'd already suffered so much that the thought of this was another reason why many still wanted to try.

Yes, one woman had won, but in the ten years that these brutal contests had been running, only one woman had triumphed, which didn't give the best odds of another managing to win. Unfortunately, as the time to blastoff got closer, any solidarity was being washed away. It was every man, woman, and child for themselves, but would this now cause even more pain and suffering as people fought with each other to claim the right to compete?

CHAPTER FOURTEEN

Deadly Message

A HUGE EXPLOSION SHOOK the Last Isle in the early hours of the morning. Flames could be seen dancing above the barrier wall surrounding the Inner Sanctum, and considering this wall was one-hundred-feet in height, the explosion must have been pretty catastrophic. Panic ensued as people ran about trying to put out the flames.

"We are so sorry to wake you High Commissioner, but there has been an explosion in silo C. We need the override codes to save the other storage silos," said an extremely nervous and scared young man.

"Get me the head controller, NOW!"

"Yes sir, yes sir, yes I understand. Right away sir," said the head controller on the other end of the phone.

The only person who had access to the storage silo codes was the High Commissioner. In fact, he had the only mainframe access. Different areas would be allowed access to certain sections, but not one other could access the whole mainframe that controlled the Last Isle. He didn't trust anyone and he was making sure that no matter what happened, he would always stay in complete control.

After the Thorium had been turned into fuel, it had to be stored in cold conditions. Each silo was monitored to make sure that the temperature didn't exceed 10^0c. There are many different levels of protection, but if something goes wrong it can be devastating. Luckily, each silo is encased in steel reinforced concrete which is about three feet thick. However, if this radioactive material is not contained quickly enough, it could destroy what's left of the planet.

"Who is responsible for this?" the High Commissioner shouted.

There was complete silence in the command centre.

"WHO IS RESPONSIBLE FOR THIS FUCK UP? I WANT THEIR NAMES NOW!" he screamed, slightly spitting as he did.

The silence ensued while the High Commissioner walked around the room with wide, angry eyes that were like tractor beams to anyone who got caught in his stare. No one wanted to own up to this major mistake, they knew that their lives would be on the line. The High Commissioner had made it very clear on several occasions that protection of the precious Thorium fuel was of the utmost importance.

Everyone knew that if the person responsible didn't own up to their mistake, the whole control room of staff would be punished and possibly all banished to the Sectors, which most saw as a fate worse than death. People from the oppressive Inner Sanctum weren't kindly welcomed into the Sectors, for obvious reasons, so most would rather die than be given such a fate. The people from the Sectors would love nothing more than to inflict untold pain and suffering upon these stuck-up Sanctumers.

"Do you people not understand how important this is? The Thorium fuel is to be protected at all cost. I want a name now, or everyone will suffer. I'm running out of patience!"

A person got up and handed the High Commissioner a note. After reading the note he looked around for the person who had been named. Once locked onto their position, he stared at them until he saw the beads of sweat drip from their forehead. "Blake Markson," he said rather nicely.

"Sir, it wasn't me, it was, I mean, I just got confused. I'm sorry it will never happen again. Please, it was just a mistake," Blake pleaded.

The High Commissioner gave the nod to two guards who grabbed hold of the man who was about to experience pain like never before. This devastating mistake wouldn't be tolerated, there was so much riding on this, and the person responsible would be made a very visual example of.

In the Sectors, everyone was still wondering what had occurred.

"What do you think exploded?"

"I'm not sure, but I hope it's the High Commissioner mansion," said one optimistic person.

"Yea, I would love to see that go up in flames, with him and all of his freak show animals too," said John, laughing at the thought.

Sadly for the hopeful people in the Sectors, the big screen was illuminated and the High Commissioner was ready to address them. "Please let me start by saying that the incident that occurred, is now under control. Everyone remains safe and the precious Thorium fuel has been saved from disaster. This mistake caused by one of the Inner Sanctum workers, has put not only all of our lives at risk, but also our chance to flee this dying planet and make our way to a new life on Kepler-186F....... This kind of reckless oversight will not be tolerated. We must all work together if we are to save ourselves from this dying planet," the High Commissioner paused, "Blake Markson will be punished for his massive failure to us all."

The big screen then displayed the Predator Pit, inside of which was Blake Markson. Blake was only a lad of nineteen and had just been promoted to the job of night control commander. Sadly, the person who had promoted this young lad to the position was also standing inside the Predator Pit next to him, as he was seen just as culpable. They both looked so frightened, neither knew what would await them, but after being forced into this pit of doom, they both knew that it didn't look good. They just hoped that this was just a scare tactic and they weren't in any real danger. Just being inside this

Grim-reapers-glass-box was enough to scare the living daylight out of you.

The High Commissioner's face appeared again. "We cannot afford to make any mistakes, especially now that we are so close to our goal. The people in the Inner Sanctum are also governed by the rules. We must be united as one, or we will be doomed to fail. These people have let themselves down, they have let the Commission down, and they have let us all down. The punishment must fit the crime. Accountability for these actions will be severe. This complete disaster will sadly affect us all moving forward. Hopefully some of your pain will be mitigated by this chosen action. The wrong doers will now face their punishment............ Remember, if we persist and persevere, we can all prosper!"

The screen once again displayed the Predator Pit. An illuminated glass box that was so clear you couldn't miss anything that occurred inside. Unfortunately for these unlucky people, the show that was to be displayed was a slaughter. This was no competition, these people had no chance of helping hand, or being set free. They would remain inside until their bodies had been torn into little pieces.

Harrowing screams invaded everyone's ears. It was like the volume had been turned up to maximum, you could hear every single gory second of this massacre. It was the Hunter Killer that was afforded this meal of flesh and bones. As the huge beast paraded around the perimeter of the Predator Pit, its tail produced a noise like that of a rattlesnake as it vibrated its tail bristles. The High Commissioner wanted these men to suffer and he wanted to show everyone what they could expect if they jeopardised the planet fleeing mission. This wouldn't be a quick and easy demise.

The Hunter Killer continued circling its victims, it wasn't used to this kind of occurrence, his victims were always running away from him, but these two stood completely still, other than their shaking bodies and knocking knees which now produced a similar sound of their own, the sound of complete and utter fear.

Their eyes continued to grow in size until it looked as if they might pop out from their heads. With a swipe from its tail, both men were impaled with blood-red-bristles. The poison carrying projectiles were quickly removed, but once they had pierced the skin, the pain began swiftly. Both men started clawing at their skin, the stinging heat produced by the poison was causing immense pain. Blood poured from the wounds created as they gouged into their limbs, tearing skin from their own bodies like strips of wallpaper.

Screaming ensued as they continued to rip skin from the infected area like they were peeling a banana. Many couldn't bear to watch the self-inflicted mutilation, their harrowing screams almost made many onlooker's ears bleed from the high-pitched audio being produced.

Only after the men had dropped to their knees and the base of the pit looked like a bloodbath, were these men afforded the painful experience of being torn limb from limb. Again many couldn't watch the bodies being ripped apart by the vicious beast, but even if you didn't watch, you couldn't get away from the awful sounds being produced, *screaming, snapping, tearing, roaring, gorging.* All of this noise, however, created an even more sickening vision in their minds. This was a warning to everyone, regardless of where you lived. Anyone who jeopardises the mission to leave this dying planet would be dealt with severely. A message to all that the High Commissioner wouldn't tolerate failings from anyone.

If they didn't create enough fuel for the journey to Kepler-186F all would be lost. This Last Isle was soon to be underwater with the rest of planet Earth, and they certainly didn't have time for any mistakes. Although it was someone from the Inner Sanctum who made the huge error, it would be the people living in the Sectors who would also suffer. They would now have to mine more Thorium to replace what had been lost and with time running out, already battered, bruised and broken bodies were about to get even more damaged and downtrodden.

The Predator Pit slaughter of those who had caused the explosion did little to bring any hope to those who would soon be trying to survive for their lives. Even though they wouldn't be facing the Hunter Killer, they would be facing one of the many other corpse-crushing-creations that were in the High Commissioner's altered-animal zoo.

As expected, the Sectors were forced to work even longer and harder in the mines to replace the precious Thorium that had been lost during the explosion. The extra pain and suffering started immediately and the first mining shift could feel this extra burden. "My hands are so sore. Please, look, I can't carry on," pleaded one overworked soul.

"You will work, or you have no use to the Commission," said a guard, pointing a gun in the poor soul's direction.

"Come on, it's ok. I've got him, he will be ok. GET UP NOW!" said a helpful friend, who scooped up the broken man.

"No, I won't do this any more. They work us until our hands bleed, our backs break and our skin blisters, and for what. We never get what we deserve. It's all for them. I won't do it any more," the distressed man screamed.

"Stop it now, or they will kill you. Just get up and move along," said the helpful friend.

Sadly, it was too late, this person had been given his one chance. His disruption had already wasted precious time. There was a new order issued to all the guards that time was of the essence and any disruptions wouldn't be tolerated. Thankfully, he wasn't killed on the spot, but he was carried away kicking and screaming like a toddler having a tantrum. The disgruntled man would soon wish that he had been killed where he stood, because he was about to become a nice meaty meal for the animals in the zoo.

To keep his zoo of altered animals hungry for human flesh, many had been plucked from their homes in the dead of night to become the next meal. With the majority of the animal meat required for the greedy Inner Sanctum residents, the High Commissioner had to find another way to feed his growling flock of cruel creatures, and what better than the scum of society, the slaves that nobody would miss.

He'd been feeding his animals on snatched up humans for a while now, making each one more insatiable for the taste of human flesh. These missing people were without any families, so they were never really missed. Those who did notice the thinning of their Sector's inhabitants were told that they had killed themselves. They could no longer survive, so the Commission granted them a way out of their pain and suffering.

Unfortunately, with less people and a heavier workload would anyone be able to find the time and energy to prepare for the Tourneys. Most were already running on empty, it was only the promise of a new life on Kepler-186F that kept them going, but if they knew that the Commission's plan was to leave them all behind, most would look to end their suffering now. They didn't have the fight left in them to challenge the powerful Commission, and they certainly didn't have the fight to face down the High Commissioner's deadly beasts. Weakened and drained of all hope, could the people living in the Sectors continue to fight for their survival, or was the extra torment and torture just too much to handle?

Winter was here and many had already succumbed to the frosty-freeze. Some had been lucky enough to lose just one, or two fingers or toes, but some who had lost their fight with the icy-chill took their own lives, rather than suffer any more. The High Commissioner's new one-strike rule was in full effect, and many knew that taking their own lives would be much less painful than what would happen to them when the Commission got hold of them.

The hope that some had was quickly being washed away by the rivers of tears that ran down their faces on a daily basis. Even removing the small frozen globes that settled on their cheeks caused more pain, tearing skin from their faces. If it wasn't for the fact they all still believed their saviour was coming in the form of a new life on another planet, where hopefully they could all rebuild their lives and get out from under the Commission control, they would have nothing left.

Everyone knew that the Commission could leave them to die if they so wished and there was nothing they could do about it. For now, they would have to play the games, bow down and do what they are told, and hopefully if they keep themselves in the Commission's good favour, a new life may still await them. Others, however, knew that no matter how hard they worked, how good they performed and how subservient they were, they would still be left to die a coffin-less cremation on this planet. Word had reached many sectors that it was a real possibility that they would all be left behind. While some took the stance to fight back, others wouldn't believe such an outlandish notion.

The rebellion had been set up shortly after the first unfortunate people were killed during the Rabbit Run competition. This was the first contest of many and these people knew that they were now viewed as nothing more than slaves by the Commission. Their hard work had helped to make the Last Isle a safer sanctuary for all, but once they were tossed aside like rubbish, many knew that this was just the start of a life of pain and persecution.

The rebellion knew that they had no way to fight back against the Commission on their own. The Sectors would have to unite as one, but also to stand even half a chance, they needed the help of the Wild Whisperer. Many Tamer families were in every Sector and the leaders had assured them the Wild Whisperer would come to save them, but after many years of suffering, so many had lost hope. However, with little else to pin their hopes on, the fabled creature communicator was now back on everyone's radar.

The Commission's heightened chastisement of the people had many now praying for this fabled person to come and set them free. Some would still not believe and/or put their faith into an old Tamers tale, but even those who didn't descend from Tamers were now hoping for this hero to save them from the cruel Commission.

Life for those living in the Sectors had never been more of a struggle. They were worked till their hands bled, killed for nothing and beaten if they stepped one foot out of line. This extra cruelty had many signing up to join the rebellion, but with many still wanting to believe that the only way to survive was to play by the Commission's rules, would there be enough of them to mount an attack even with the Wild Whisperer was on their side?

Whichever way you looked at it, everything was relying on this legendary person to first exist and secondly want to join the fight. If this person did exist, the rebellion was sure that they could convince the non-believers into taking up arms against their oppressors. However, there were still many cogs that had to line up to even entertain such an action. The Wild Whisperer's presence had never been more needed, and without it the people living in the Sectors were doomed.

CHAPTER FIFTEEN

The One Beast's Eye

Anna had just finished a long day in the slaughterhouse preparing for the upcoming Predator Pit feast. She shed tears witnessing the huge amounts that would be eaten on the day and even more tears about how much would be wasted. Although the Sectors would benefit from the leftovers, it always left her infuriated by how much some have and how little they had.

She left with a smile on her face today because she had managed to steal a couple of livers for Luna and herself to have on a cold Christmas morning which would hopefully make the pain of being forced to sit in the freezing weather and watch the Predator Pit competition a little bit more comfortable.

All she wanted to do now was get home and finish the day with a loving embrace from her daughter. As she made her way through the forest, she was stopped in her tracks by a group of people who all had hooded cloaks that secluded their faces. Automatically going into defence mode, she was ready to do anything to get back home to her child.

"Anna, it's ok, there's no need to be afraid," said a familiar voice.

"William, what's going on?" a startled Anna replied.

"It's ok, no need to fret. We would like you to accompany us into the forest. Please, there really is no need to be scared," he said in a gentle tone.

A few more of the group now removed their hoods to show the faces of people she knew and trusted. Feeling slightly more at ease, she followed the group deeper into the forest. The majority of this forest had been fenced off. The Commission told them that it was unstable due to the Thorium mines that ran beneath. However, a few curious people wanted to know what they were really hiding. It turns out that in the mountainous area at the far end of this forest was a natural spring. This fresh and abundant water source was the real reason why the Commission had fenced this area off. They controlled the Sectors' water rations, along with everything else so they could stay in complete control.

Anna had wondered for a while now how many people in her Sector seemed to have a lot more water. These people weren't foolish with their actions, or it would be easily found out, but the extra fresh water had helped many survive when they would have perished. The spring, however, wasn't the reason that they wanted to speak with her.

After leading Anna deeper into the woods and into a run-down shack William approached. "Anna, you know about the legend of the Wild Whisperer. You come from a strong Tamer family, and it's fair to say that at one point you believed that your son might be this fabled person."

"Yes of course who doesn't know about that tale, but it's not true. It was my husband that thought that our son may have this power, but I never gave it a second thought. He wasn't this person and nor will anyone else be, it's an old wives tale. We told it to our children to make them behave. The legend of the One Beast, ruler of all the animals. Its magical eye could be used to tell if they were lying. If they were found to be lying, the creature would invade their dreams and keep them awake with the cries of the animals all throughout the night until they told the truth. My children were told the same story. Although they didn't really need any more stories of fear after trying to survive in this horrible place."

"What if the stories were true. Not the child's tale, but the legend of the Wild Whisperer. The One Beast's Eye has the ability to unlock the full power of this person, allowing them to be the controller of all animals," William said with a heightened tone.

"The One Beast's Eye, if it ever existed, was lost long ago. No one knows of its whereabouts."

"What if I told you that it was real? What if I told you that we know where it is? If this was possible, would you want to help the Wild Whisperer to save our people from the Commission. You know what they have planned for us. It's time that we make a stand. We have been forming a rebellion for years now. All of the other Sectors are involved, but we need the Wild Whisperer on our side if we are to stand any chance. The only way to take down the Commission is with the High Commissioner's zoo full of precious predators on our side. If we could control those creatures we would be able to fight back. We would be able to save ourselves from impending doom."

"A rebellion? Even with all of the Sectors on board, we will not be able to take down the Commission, they are just too strong. What if this Wild Whisperer doesn't want to join the fight? Do you really have the One Beast's Eye?" Anna's interest had been piqued.

William gestured to someone who came towards them and handed him a package. "This is the One Beast's Eye. It has been kept safe and secure for thousands of years. Passed down through generations of Tamers, all hoping that one day it would reveal the Wild Whisperer. Two have shown that they could possibly be this legendary hero, but one has already been tested and they are not the one. Only one other may possess this special gift and only with their help can we hope to defeat the Commission."

"That's great! Take the eye to this person, let's find out if they are the one person who can help set us all free," Anna's fast-paced speech showed her growing excitement.

"Would you concur that whoever this person is, they should join us and fight back against the Commission? They should put their lives on the line to help save thousands of innocent lives?" William's tone was probing.

"Of course, this person will possess great power. If the rumours are true, then yes we must fight back, We must save our families from being left to die on this planet!" Anna said, getting charged.

"What if this person was a female?"

"The legend only tells of men who have become this fabled hero in the past......... However, male, or female, they have a duty to help protect their people."

William handed Anna the One Beast's Eye. "Look into the eye. Look deep into its wonder. Feel the connection with its power."

Anna held the eye up to her own. The One Beast's Eye sparkled with delight. It looked like it held a whole universe of stars inside. The pull from its power transported Anna to the wilderness plain. She saw a time when people and animals lived together in peace and harmony. The lands were lush and fruitful, with plenty for everyone, man and beast.

Suddenly she dropped the eye and gasped in horror. "No it cannot be, not my little girl. It had always been a man, she is still so young, no, no no," she said, dropping to her knees.

There was silence while everyone waited to give Anna time to come to terms with what she had just seen.

"Why? Why? Why does it have to be my Luna? She is not ready, she is not strong enough. You have to find someone else. She cannot do it." Anna was extremely emotional.

"There is only one. One person who can become the Wild Whisperer. There will not be another for one-hundred years, and we don't even have another year, let alone one-hundred! The One Beast's Eye is never wrong. Luna has been chosen, she must help us, or we will all die."

Anna picked up the eye and shook it like a can of spray paint. Once again she looked into its mystery hoping to get a different answer, like it was a magic eight-ball, but her special little girl's face was as clear as a full moon, beaming back at her with a luminous glow.

Once Anna calmed down from the initial shock the rebellion laid out everything they knew and how they planned to fight back. This plan was about as complicated as a Rubik's Cube and would need more cogs turning than a town clock, but if it all came together, they may just be able to save thousands of people from certain death.

Her walk home was long and thoughtful, when she finally returned she found Luna sleeping like a baby. Her small little girl looked to be no older than ten, how could she possess this power. Anna was still hoping that her daughter wasn't the fabled hero. She knew of Luna's strength and knew she would definitely want to help save her people. How could she stop her head-strong child from becoming the person she was always meant to be. She always knew that Luna was special, but this revelation had come as an almighty shock.

Tomorrow they would find out if Luna was the Wild Whisperer. From then on Anna would just have to pray that this rebellious plan worked. Without the Wild Whisperer's help they were all doomed to die, however, that didn't stop Anna's heart breaking every time she thought of what her only remaining child would have to do.

That time of year had come again. It was time for the show of all shows, the competition everyone had been waiting for, the Predator Pit.

On a cold Christmas morning, Anna woke Luna before the usual mind-numbing alarm sounded. "Luna, Luna, please wake up, I have something that I want to show to you," she said nervously.

A tired Luna was confused, it would usually be the awful sound of the air-raid siren alarm that woke them, this was unheard of, everyone needed to get every single last second of sleep that they could. They were all working longer and harder, and they all needed every single second of rest.

"What's going on? Why have you woken me so early?" Luna's tone was slightly sharp.

"I wanted to give you something. This object has been passed down through generations of Tamers. It was believed to have been lost, but it has been kept safe for when it would be needed. I think

I have known for a long time, but I just hoped that I was wrong. However, it would be selfish of me to deny your true-self. You are very special to me. However, I must not allow the suffering of thousands of people to continue if they can be helped."

"Mum, what is it, you're scaring me now?"

"The legend of the Wild Whisperer is true."

"But you said it wasn't."

"I never said it wasn't true, I said it was just a story and that I don't believe that you are this folk law person."

"Ok, I don't understand? So there is a Wild Whisperer, but you don't believe that I am it."

"Well, yes and no. I mean, I was hoping that you wouldn't be the one, but - I have a strong feeling that you might just be. I have witnessed a true Tamer spirit from within you, but the only way to know for sure is to see if the One Beast's Eye accepts you. Please don't feel pressured in any way. This is a lot to take in, trust me, I'm still coming to terms with what I have just witnessed."

"What's the One Beast's Eye?" Luna quizzed.

"The legend goes that the first animal to roam on this planet was called the One Beast. This huge animal was the most powerful creature there has ever been. Stronger than an Elephant, faster than a cheetah, deadlier than a Lion, and as intelligent as a human being. This creature ruled the lands and made sure that this world stayed plentiful for all who inhabit it. Humans, however, got greedy. They started cutting down the trees in the forests. They polluted the streams, rivers and lakes. Furthermore, they created fire that pushed thousands of animals from their homes............ The destruction that the humans brought to this world was getting out of control. They got greedier and greedier. They bred faster than rabbits and soon became a massive problem. The One Beast and an army of animals tried to fight back against the human plague that had descended upon their lands, but their numbers were great, and they used weapons and fire to kill without remorse. After the One Beast fell, the rest of the animals fled for their lives. The One Beast had control over the animals and his dying pain and suffering struck fear into them all. The One Beast was to be cooked over a fire and eaten. This was to show the animals who was now in charge of the land. The night before the roasting, a young lad wandering in the moonlit sky noticed something sparkling. On closer inspection he could see that it was the huge creature's eyes that still shone brightly, even though its life had been taken. The boy moved closer and saw a world of wonder through the fallen creature's eyes. More stars than in the night sky sparkled back at him, drawing him closer. As the boy touched the eye, he was connected to all of the animals. He could hear their thoughts, see what they saw, he could also feel their fear of the humans. The boy knew that these special eyes had to be saved. He managed to cut one eye out of the huge head, but before he could take the other, he was disturbed. Sadly, the next day the One Beast was roasted over a fire destroying its other eye. The young lad took the eye deep into the forest where the animals still roamed and he realised that he could communicate with them. As long as the eye was in contact with his body he could talk to the animals. He could warn them when hunts were taking place and help them to survive the human plague..............This young boy was called Domitor and he was the first ever Wild Whisperer. The One Beast's Eye and the knowledge of how it came to be has been passed down through generations, and each person swore to use its power to protect the animals. This object can give those who are worthy the power to control all animals. Only someone with a pure heart and a commitment to help all living things will be bestowed with its power. Many have used the eye to help the animals throughout the generations. They have become the Wild Whisperer and they fight on the side of all animals. I hoped that you wouldn't show the signs. I didn't want you to have to carry this burden. Now I see that it might be the only way we can survive. In the panic of the explosion, our people on the inside found plans and documents relating to the spaceship and its journey to Kepler-186F. The people of the Sectors are not booked on this life-saving flight, we will be left on a dying planet."

"What, they plan to leave us behind, after all of our hard work and sacrifice? No, they cannot do this, it's an outrage. We must fight back!" Luna screamed.

"Shush, keep your voice down. A straight-up war against the Commission would be suicide, and it may only force them into leaving this planet sooner, leaving us all to a very uncertain fate. The only way that we can hope to take down the Commission is to gain control of the animals. With the High Commissioner's predators on our side, we may just be able to fight back against this oppressive organisation," Anna said, pausing after seeing Luna's expression change. "I know it's a lot to take in, and I wished that there was another way, or that another person would be the Wild Whisperer, and not you, my sweet little girl, but I cannot stop you, if you wish to pursue this calling. You may now hold the hope of every single person living in the Sectors," Anna said, crying and revealing a leather wrap with an eye stitched into it.

"It's ok mum. I want to help, I want to save our people, and if I am the Wild Whisperer, I'm the only one who can help. I don't want to see people suffer and die any more. We have lost so much to the cruel Commission. They need to be stopped, we must fight back and stop the cruelty, we must stop their reign of Terror. We must save our fellow inhabitants before we are left to burn on a dying planet. We must free the animals from the High Commissioner's control. I felt their pain when I touched one of them. They don't want to kill, they want to be free, they want to be able to roam the land once again. I'm ready mum, I have always been ready. Please, I can do this? I want to do this. I want to save us all," Luna said, also crying.

Anna wrapped the One Beast's Eye around Luna's leg and tied the back. Her shaking hands struggled with the string as she tried to make a knot. As soon as the eye touched Luna's skin, all of the animals in the farm started going crazy. They *howled, baaed, clucked, oinked* and made such a racket that it alerted the Inner Sanctum guards.

A noise above their heads drew them outside where they saw hundreds of birds all perched nearby like they had heard the call. Luna also felt a power coursing through her veins. She had visions through the animal's eyes, and she could now hear their thoughts. At first, it was painful, the tsunami of noise saw her drop to her knees and hold her head in pain.

Anna went to her daughter's side and helped her to her feet. When Luna opened her eyes they glowed like cats' eyes caught in a bright light. She stood tall and proud, raising her arm in the air. Luna was the Wild Whisperer, she was the Tamer of all animals. She was now their protector and they were hers. She could feel the strength pulsating from within them and an understanding that they were now one and the same, joined by heart, body and soul.

In the High Commissioner's residence, the noise coming from his own animals woke him from a deep sleep. While asleep the High Commissioner had no control over the animals. He required an active mind and a connection to the A.I chips that had been implanted into them all. Shortly after opening his eyes, the Zoo full of beasts went quiet. The High Commissioner used pain to control these creatures. An implanted chip could control their minds, but also inflict unimaginable pain if they didn't do as commanded.

This type of control gave Luna and the others hope. The animals still had their own minds in spite of the changes that have been made to their bodies, and that meant that the Wild Whisperer could hopefully still connect with them. However, unless they could find a way to remove the microchips that had been implanted into the creatures, or at least find a way to electrically short them out, Luna still may not be able to gain full control over the mass of blood-curdling-creatures.

Luna was left completely shocked by this revelation, but she was also filled with purpose. Before she wanted to compete to save her mother from this life of doom and destitution, but now she would be saving thousands of people's lives, and hopefully damning those who carried out and allowed this persecution of the people to happen.

This revealing news had to be kept under wraps. There were still those who spied for the Commission and they couldn't be trusted. Over time they would have to coordinate and plan this elaborate attack, all the while staying off the Commission's radar. If there was an inkling that this folk law person existed, the Commission would be sure to torture every single person in the Sectors until the name was revealed. No one knew for sure what would happen to this legendary animal communicator, but it was most definitely going to be hateful and horrid.

However, this power would take time to learn and perfect. Some animals are harder to reach than others, and just because Luna could now talk to the animals, it doesn't mean that they all want to listen. She would have to gain their trust and work with them to enhance her skills.

Years of human enslavement and cruelty have seen the animals become very fearful of human beings. Maybe they won't even want to help a person who is seen as part of the problem? However, their lives of persecution by the High Commissioner would hopefully see them eager to help. Without the animals on their side, the Sectors would have no chance of saving themselves from a fate worse than death. Left on a scolding planet to blister and burn before they would be cremated while they were still alive and kicking.

The Sectors knew that the Commission was cruel and calculating, but they all believed that their hard work would see them saved from this dying planet. They were working towards a better life on another destination. This revelation wouldn't go down well, and the fallout from such devastating news would see tempers flare faster than a lit firework, but an all out war would just bring more pain and suffering to them all. They had to be smart, they had to bide their time and wait until the opportune moment, or the last hope to save their people would be lost forever!

CHAPTER SIXTEEN

Complete Shock

AFTER SUCH A MIND-BLOWING revelation, Luna went to lie down. Her mind was now full of so many questions, not to mention the thoughts of about a thousand animals that came flooding into her mind the second the One Beast's Eye touched her skin. She could feel their pain and suffering. She could feel that their minds were being controlled and the torture they experienced if they didn't obey their master. They wanted to be set free, they wanted to help anyone who could make this a possibility.

Firstly, she needed to bring peace to her own mind, she needed time to think. Obviously she would fight, she'd always wanted to take the fight to the Commission, especially after the loss of her father and brother. However, she knew that alone she would have no chance. This was part of the reason why Luna was so desperate to face the Tourneys. She obviously wanted a better life for her struggling mother, but she also knew that the best way to take down an organisation is from the inside. If she was in the Inner Sanctum, she may be able to find a way to bring an end to the tyranny.

How dare the Commission treat the Sectors in such ways? After all of the sacrifices they have made. To say Luna that was mad would be a massive understatement, she was totally incensed, every single bone in her body wanted to fight! She wanted to march into the High Commissioner's mansion, tear his head from his shoulders and feed it to the animals that he has tortured for so long. However, she knew that without proper control over her new powers and help from the animals, she would just be handing herself over to the Commission on a silver plateau.

She was the person that everyone had been waiting for, the person who could hopefully set them free. It was at this point that Luna began to realise the gravity of who she had become. Everyone would be looking at her now. She would have to be strong and resolute, but would the people accept her as this fabled hero? A small waif of a girl who they didn't even want facing the Tourneys in the first place. Many would still rather die than follow a woman into battle, let alone a young girl. Luna would have to convince these people this was the only way that they could survive.

Anna was now visibly shaking with worry. Should she have revealed all of this to her daughter? She knew that Luna had the strength to take on any challenge, but when all of the cards are stacked in the opposition's favour, could they manage to keep their heads and really achieve what most saw as an impossible task?

To have any chance of getting the right people into the right places for this elaborate plan to have even the slightest likelihood of working, they had to first find out who was on their side, who they could trust, but they also had to make sure that a certain woman triumphed over the Predator Pit first.

Even if they could get some to believe in the fact that Luna was the fabled Wild Whisperer, most would still not want to see another woman face the Tourneys. However, if a woman was to go on and survive the Predator Pit, not only winning themselves and their families a place in the Inner Sanctum, but also providing vital sustenance for the rest of their Sector, most would have to swallow their macho-manly pride for the good of their fellow people.

Still, it would be hard enough in itself to convince the rest of the Sector that they should allow a young girl this opportunity.

That, however, was a problem for another day, first they had to make sure that Mavee survived the Predator Pit. Luna couldn't just tap into the creature's mind and try to control it. This contest had to be believable, if not the High Commissioner would become highly suspicious. Luna had to make the creature pull its punches while still making it look as though this rampaging beast was thirsty for the kill. If the High Commissioner believed that there was anything fishy going on, he would torture ever single person until the Wild Whisperers name was revealed. Sadly, many would break quicker than a plastic garden chair when pressured. Everyone was on such a tightrope walk with their own survival, they would do just about anything to stop their punishing existence from getting any worse.

There was a lot of intrigue and second guessing going around the Sectors at the moment, because the alarm to gather everyone to the screens for the annual Predator Pit contest hadn't sounded as usual. It was now long past the usual time of this seasonal event, so everyone was left wondering what was happening?

"Do you think that they have cancelled the Christmas Crucifixion?" asked a young lad.

"Please don't call it that," replied an older woman.

"Why not? That's what usually happens. It's just a slaughter. No one ever comes out alive."

"I don't believe that it has been cancelled, but something is going on. I'm sure we will find out soon enough."

Many now referred to the Predator Pit Tourney as the Christmas Crucifixion, because it was very rare that anyone made it out alive. The cross had been erected and their hands had already been impaled before they had even stepped foot inside the grim-reapers-glass-box. No sooner had the words left the woman's mouth, the alarm sounded and everyone was escorted to the big screens.

"Hello everyone, Merry Christmas to you all. We have an announcement to make. The Predator Pit competition will not be taking place today as usual."

All sorts of noises came from the perplexed crowds. This competition was like having turkey at Christmas, a staple that had become tradition. Like turkey, nobody really likes it, but it is what you had on this day.

"Now, I know you will all be wondering why this event is not taking place today. Due to the pit's recent use as a punishment chamber, the cleaners are working tirelessly to get it sparkling clean for our hopeful contestants. It's not fair to the contestants, or to you the viewers if the pit is not cleaned properly. This tradition needs to be treated with the utmost care and attention, so that we can all enjoy what is going to be an amazing show. Due to this oversight, the Predator Pit competition will now take place tomorrow."

Many heads dropped upon hearing this news. This was the one day out of the entire year that they wouldn't have to work. After the Predator Pit had claimed its victims, they would be allowed to have the rest of the day off.

"Now because this oversight has delayed the competition and as a show of good faith to your continuing hard work, no one will have to work today. Your production from the mines has increased, but we must all strive to replace what was lost in the explosion. I know that you will continue to work as hard for your Commission as the Commission does for you. We are all in this fight together and if we continue to persist and persevere, we will all prosper....... Now I know that this explosion has set us all back, and maybe it's my new wife's influence, or maybe I'm just getting soft in my old age, but as an added thank you for all of your hard work, each Sector can take one animal from the farms and roast it. I want everyone to be full of energy for tomorrow's competition. Please accept this meat as a way of our alliance going forward. We need to replace the lost Thorium and I know that you will all strive to work harder than ever before. Please fill your bellies and enjoy a day of rest. Together is the only way that we can hope to survive long enough to flee this dying planet."

When the screens went blank, most were just standing around looking completely dumbfounded, others rushed towards the farms quicker than their legs would carry them. Almost everyone, however, was feeling rather cheerful, like a little fire had just been lit inside of them, warming their hearts. This joyous feeling even showed on the faces of some, as the thought of a whole roasted animal made their mouth water like never before.

Maybe this was a new era, one where the people living in the Sectors are seen as more than just slaves? They had never been given the right to choose who competes, and now they had been given food that doesn't need prising from a pile of rubbish, and to top it all off an actual day off. Many felt like Christmas had finally come to the Sectors, their hard work and sacrifice was finally paying off.

The more sceptical knew that this was just a buttering up exercise. They may have one day off, or even two, but to replace what was lost during the explosion, and to keep up with demand they would have to work twenty-four hours a day. Shifts would be increased and the little time they had to sleep would be squeezed even further. This man wasn't showing clemency and solidarity, he was keeping the people sweet so they would work harder. However, in an existence as terrible as this, any little ray of hope can be seen as a huge deal. Some even had their heads in the clouds dreaming of a time when the Inner Sanctum and the Sectors would live side by side, all together as one big happy family.

Unfortunately, for those who knew the Commission's real intentions, it would now become much harder to convince the people that they were all destined to be doomed! No matter how hard they worked. Like throwing a dog a bone, this little incentive would have some believing the Commission's lies, and if they couldn't be convinced to join the fight, they might just become the enemy.

Who they told about this deceitful occurrence and who they trusted to join them in the fight against the Commission would be a deadly game of chance. Like spinning the Predator Pit wheel where usually all roads lead to pain, suffering, then death, they would be gambling with many lives, not just their own. But if they didn't make a stand now they might never get the chance again. They had to bring their plan into action, or everyone, believers, or not would all die a most horrific and painful death.

The High Commissioner's sneaky show of support for the Sectors couldn't have been by chance. His plan to rule it all was also becoming compromised. If he didn't have enough fuel to take a sizable army with him to Kepler-186F, he may never get the total planet domination that he so desperately desires. Thermal Sensors had shown an eight degrees increase in the outside temperature, making it a very feverish sixty-eight degrees. With the satellite shield beginning to degrade from the constant battering from the blazing sun's rays, it was only a matter of time before it no longer provided protection to any who were left on the Last Isle.

A steady increase in temperature had been felt throughout the Sectors. This slow rise was due to the breaking down of the satellite shield, but while the Inner Sanctum had air-conditioning throughout keeping everyone nice and cool, the people living in the Sectors had nothing but the sea breeze, but this was more like a oversized hair dryer blowing warm air around, however, it did take the edge of the sweltering conditions. The sea still provided a slightly cooling release when bathing, but with no water to wash the salt and contaminants from your body, it actually made things even more uncomfortable.

Worse still was working in the mines, in the middle of winter when it was freezing cold outside it was still hot inside the small tunnels that made up the mines. A lot more people have also been dying of late due to the increasing temperature, which was another reason why the High Commissioner was keen to replace the precious fuel that was lost.

Before the silo exploded, they had collected enough fuel for the huge spacecraft to make the trip to Kepler-186F. However, space travel of that distance can be tricky and unexpected, so the High Commissioner really wanted to be taking a lot more fuel than was required for this journey, just in case anything threw the spacecraft off course. With the temperature rising, time was definitely not on their side, so he had to keep the Sectors happy. Mining the precious Thorium that was needed, was the most important task now.

His thirst for more power and control was growing and he would do whatever it takes to become the leader of it all. His rash judgement, however, was being calmed by Sasha. She knew that sometimes you have to throw a dog a bone to get what you desire. Sometimes a show of clemency and compassion can be a better persuader than that of fierce and forceful nature.

Sasha was probably more dangerous than the High Commissioner. She knew how to manipulate people into getting what she wanted. At least with the High Commissioner, the people knew what to expect. Ok it was a lot of pain and suffering, but they knew there would be no surprises. It can help people to deal with a certain situation when the attack is coming head on, but when it comes from behind, it can leave them feeling more frightened than ever before. With Sasha by his side, it looks like the people living in the Sectors are doomed, unless they find the strength and solidarity to fight back. But with a more kind and forgiving nature coming from the Commission, would the people be able to see past the smoke and mirrors, and believe in the deceit that this more compassionate Commission had planned for them?

Many still held onto the hope that all of their suffering was necessary for them to all start again on another planet. The Commission had their best interests at heart and everyone was in this together. After seeing two people from the Inner Sanctum killed inside the Predator Pit, they were more convinced than ever that the rules and suffering they must endure is felt by all. If they continue to work hard and do what is expected of them, they may get more leniency awarded to them, fewer sanctions, less pain and suffering for all who live in the Sectors.

The Commission was only doing what was necessary to protect what was left of this planet and to provide everyone with a way to flee before they all died. They would already be dead if it wasn't for the Commission's satellite shield. What's wrong with losing a few people to the Tourneys when so many other lives have been saved? Unfortunately, many would still believe this bullshit narrative. If only they knew the truth.

The Commission would have nothing if it wasn't for the hard work of those living in the Sectors. They risked their lives every day to mine the precious Thorium fuel required to get the spacecraft in the air. Without their back-breaking, hand-bleeding labour and sacrifice, the vessel would be of no use, just a huge useless lump of metal. It was the people living in the Sectors that would make this journey possible, and the Commission knew this only too well. The explosion had given them a little more time, but once the lost fuel had been replaced, the Commission wouldn't hesitate to leave this dying planet along with all of those living in the Sectors who would quickly see an end to their lives.

CHAPTER SEVENTEEN

PREDATOR PIT

AFTER A DAY OF REST and the succulent meal of meat, everyone living in the Sectors had never been happier, some were even looking forward to the Predator Pit competition. It's surprising what a decent rest and a not so painstakingly-hollow belly will do for some. Let's be fair, after the gifted animal had been shared out, it was little more than a slither of meat each, but even that tasty little morsel was like a full Christmas dinner to many and they had never been more content. Everyone was already at the gathering spot before the alarm sounded, all standing quietly, waiting to hear the announcement.

"Hello and welcome to you all. I hope that you have all enjoyed your day of rest and the extra sustenance has helped to give you more energy. Mining for Thorium is now the most important task that must be carried out. With that being said, the Sector that provides the most Thorium at the end of the Month will receive a highly enhanced care package. This will contain more food and supplies than ever before. You will also be able to pick two animals to roast. Your bellies will be ready to pop after the amount of food you will receive. All other jobs will now be put on hold until the lost Thorium has been replaced. Our continued efforts in the Inner Sanctum to keep everyone safe is holding out for now, but the satellite shield continues to degrade. Our only hope of survival is to flee this dying planet. We will continue working day and night to make sure everyone on the Last Isle is kept safe, but we are all in this fight together. Only together can we hope to save the last of planet Earth's population from doom."

Everyone looked at each other with watering mouths, after experiencing the taste of succulent meat they all wanted more, some were ready to head to the mines now, but the barrel of a gun kept them contained.

"My ever loving wife also has a gift for the Sector that produces the most Thorium. That Sector will be exempt from the next Rabbit Run competition. They can still face the Predator Pit if they so wish, but this will also be a choice, not an imposition. To keep everything fair, if they wish to face the Predator Pit at the end of the year and earn their place in the Inner Sanctum they will firstly have to triumph over the Rabbit Run, but the enhanced care package will hopefully sustain them throughout the year, so participation shouldn't be necessary. This gift is to show our appreciation for all of your hard work. Together we will be able to make the journey to the new planet possible. If we all work together, we can flee this dying planet and start new lives." As the High Commissioner paused, he received a round of applause. People were clapping, shouting and whistling, but this was done of their own accord, no gun barrel encouragement was required this time.

The High Commissioner looked to his wife who was the mastermind behind this show of encouragement and gave her a smile followed by a little nod. It was her idea to start using bribery to get more work from those living in the Sectors. He had used the fear of pain, suffering and death to encourage the Sectors into work, but sometimes all you need is a little carrot dangling on the end of a string. Sasha knew this only too well, and she was now gaining her place at the top of the mountain, alongside her husband Hector. She'd felt the alluring pull of having power over others and she wanted more. They would be the overlords of the new World, both holding all of the cards. Together they could never be stopped and with all of the A.I enhancements on offer they could possibly live forever more!

"Thank you, thank you, you're too kind............. Please, oh thank you once again," he said, taking a little bow. "Now is the time for what we have all been waiting for. This Predator Pit contest is the first in history to have all of the Sector's own choice of competitors. We have seen some very promising Rabbit Run performances, so I have a feeling that this year could be the most successful yet. Eight lucky hopefuls have made it through to this chance that could see them achieve a better life for themselves and their families. Without further ado, let's meet our eight hopefuls."

Everyone knew who the competitors were, so no one paid much attention when the High Commissioner was listing their names. They were all waiting for when they would get to spin the wheel of destiny that would reveal which spine-splitting-specimen they would be facing. Hope that all of these Sector-selected competitors would survive the Predator Pit was higher than usual, but chances are none of them would. However, there was one who must survive, this was a vital part of the Sector's rebellious plan.

Mavee had to survive to make it possible for another woman to be allowed to face the Tourneys. Many were still despondent at the fact a woman had even made it this far, but if they could see a woman survive the Predator Pit, they would know that it was no fluke that she had come this far. The survival rate of this gruesome competition was extremely low and a woman has never survived a Rabbit Run competition before, let alone triumphed over the deadliest contest of all!

Even though Luna, her mother and the people of the rebellion in Sector four hoped that they could convince the rest to let Luna compete, her chances of being allowed to compete, however, would greatly increase if Mavee was victorious. Sometimes people need to see it with their own eyes before their minds will let them conceive a certain action as a prosperous one. The only way that this could become a reality was if Luna could use her power as the Wild Whisperer to control the beast that Mavee would be facing. This possibility would still be a very uncertain occurrence due to the High Commissioner's control over these beasts, but as long as they still contained their original animal D.N.A, Luna should be able to have some influence over them.

Seven had entered, but none had made it out alive. Among the cruel creations that these unfortunate people had to face was a Crocmodo, a mixture of the strength, power and bone-crushing jaws of a crocodile combined with the speed and agility of a Komodo dragon. In contests before, landing on either a Crocodile or Alligator was a relatively good choice against all the other possibilities, that is. These creatures were a lot slower and less agile than that of a Lion, or Tiger, so out manoeuvring them was easier, that was until the side of the Predator Pit began closing in around you, but facing one of these creatures usually gave you the best chance of survival, especially if you have been gifted with weapons by the Inner Sanctum elite.

Obviously the High Commissioner wasn't happy enough with the already deadly attributes of the world's top predators. The original purpose of creating these hybrid animals was to make an animal that provided more food, or make an animal that required less sustenance, but provided more of a bounty, however, who wants to have a larger cow that can feed more people when you can have a Grizlion, a huge Grizzly bear and Lion Hybrid. Two already deadly beasts combined to make a colourful killing machine. Red fur and black stripes made this creature look like it already had the blood of many victims upon its skin. Other beasts included the Polar Wolf, two already deadly predators that combined the power and size of a Polar bear with the savagery of a Wolf which created a creature that had claimed many victims. There were also many others who were still in their own animal form, but all had been changed and enhanced in some way. Just staring into the burning red eyes of a jet-black Lion, or Tiger was enough to send shivers throughout anyone's spine.

"Luna, are you ready?" asked Anna.

"I think so, but I struggled to connect with the other animals before. What if I can't do it?" Luna said, sounding very defeated.

"You must Luna. Everything is riding on the outcome of this competition," Anna said, extremely worried about her daughter.

The world around them seemed to be in slow motion as the wheel of destiny spun around. The ticking of the selector got louder and louder as it slowed. *Tick........* *TICK......* *TICK...* *TICK...TICK.*

As the last TICK resonated like a countdown to doom, Mavee's deadly opponent was selected. She would be facing off against the Black-Striped-White. A huge Liger, a Lion and Tiger combination that saw a bright white coat and thick bushy mane of a Lion broken up with black stripes from a Tiger. Its jet-black eyes also made it all the more menacing. This creature's cynically clean white coat wouldn't stay that way for long after it had torn apart its victims, adding a splash of red into the mix. The bloody patterns changing with each torn off body part as it splattered around the Predator Pit. In fact, by the time it had finished tearing apart its victims, it could have been called the Black-Striped-Red.

This beast was one of the deadliest, a huge creature that stood almost five feet tall. No one stood a chance against this beast, especially not Mavee, a woman, however, the Inner Sanctum had also got behind this woman competitor who had defied all the odds, and with the array of weapons that could be gifted to her, she may not even need Luna's help. Everyone wanted this woman to succeed it seems, but against such a deadly foe, would all the assistance in the world help her to survive?

It looks like it was time to find out. Mavee stood in the centre of Predator Pit, looking out at all of the eager faces that stared back at her through the crystal-clear glass structure. This translucent box allowed for the spectators to get extremely up close and personal to the gory action. Like a fish in a tank you were there for another's entertainment. You could be eye to eye with a contestant and watch as life drains from their body. This unique perspective was what the hardcore fans loved, watching as a person helplessly claws at the sides of the sleek surface trying to pull their bodies from the jaws of death.

The buzzer sounded, this was it, the beast had entered the arena. There was so much riding on the outcome of this contest, that everyone was on tenterhooks. The huge beast circled Mavee, snapping its huge jaws in her direction. The anticipating eyes watching on were all left looking surprised when the floor opened up and revealed a spear. Someone had gifted Mavee a weapon. This was unheard of, most liked to see a limb removed, or at least a deadly cat and mouse chase before giving any help to the contestant. It looked like someone really wanted Mavee to survive.

This weapon, however, was still of no use to Mavee if she couldn't reach it, and at present a huge creature was standing in her way. Mavee moved left, then to the right in quick succession to try and predict the beast's movements, but the creature never moved a muscle, its eyes remained trained upon its victim. What was she going to do? At least the time was ticking away. Five minutes, that's all she had to survive.

All of a sudden the creature leapt towards Mavee like it had been pricked in the arse with a sharp object. This was the High Commissioner's controlling nudge to the animal to get on with the killing. Mavee was extremely agile and she drove out of the creature's path. After sidestepping the huge beast she reached the spear and now had a weapon in this fight. The beast attacked again, this time brandishing its huge clawed paw. The claws on this animal looked to be twice the length of its counterparts, and they were still in the retracted position. When the full length of its claws were revealed, Mavee nearly passed out right there and then.

Using the spear she managed to keep the beast at a distance, but it soon slipped past her defences and had its mouth mere inches from her face. Mavee struggled to keep the snapping jaws at bay with her hands. She could sense that the beast was going to lunge, so she let go of its huge head and slipped beneath it. As she went in one direction, the creature went in the other, but its proximity to the perimeter saw it smash into the glass wall with such force the onlooking crowds fled in fear of it breaking through.

The creature was stunned, but again its eyes lit up like it had been prompted for the kill. The High Commissioner was furious, how dare this woman defy one of his animal assassins? The beast grabbed the spear in its mouth and broke it into little pieces. Mavee was left defenceless again. She knew that she could endure a couple of bites, or strikes due to her protective suit, but the way in which these beasts attacked it was of little comfort.

Outside the Predator Pit there were scenes of distress and dismay. Many who were betting upon the outcome of this fight had tried to give Mavee more weapons to help her survive, but the system controlling this contest wouldn't let them.

"What's going on? I'm trying to help the poor women. I've got a lot of money riding on this," shouted one disgruntled onlooker.

"What is this? Stop the contest," shouted another.

Soon the whole place was in uproar.

"Please everyone, we are trying to fix the problem. Take your seats and my engineers will have it sorted shortly," said the High Commissioner, trying to calm the situation.

Little did everyone know, but this was his own doing, he didn't want this woman to survive. A WOMAN! Surviving against one of the most deadly beasts there was, NO WAY, not on his watch. However, with a stadium full of angry people all shooting daggers in his direction, could he carry on with his plan of sabotage?

There was so much riding on a unity with the Sectors that this action alone might cause a riot. If they found out that this woman didn't get a fair chance of surviving, would they still be as willing to work harder to replace the Thorium. The High Commissioner's own hatred towards those living in the Sectors might just be his undoing. Not to mention that he had a disgruntled audience who were all asking questions. Would Sasha need to come to her husband's aid again before he threw away all of their hard work just for his own repugnance to the situation that was occurring?

CHAPTER EIGHTEEN

Mavee Must Survive

MAVEE WAS STILL MANAGING to evade the jaws of the Black-Striped-White Liger. Although the High Commissioner's attempt to sabotage this event by stopping the gifting of weapons and defences, it also meant the Predator Pit itself couldn't be altered. The narrowing area is what was responsible for many deaths inside this glass structure. After every minute passed, the sides of the pit were enclosed by a metre. This left the fighting area very up close and personal, and little room to evade the jaws of death. Some had used an athletic skill and intelligence to out manoeuvre their deadly foe, but once the surrounding walls began reducing the area that they had to manoeuvre, most were left with only one fate.

The system controlling the Predator Pit was one entity and if the sides of the pit began moving inwards everyone would know that the system itself was not malfunctioning, but being restricted by an outside influence.

"Please my friends, we have our best and brightest engineers working on the problem, it will soon be fixed," the High Commissioner said, trying to calm things down.

"Stop the contest. It's a fix. We will not stand for this deceit," shouted an angry onlooker.

With the room getting more and more rowdy the High Commissioner had to do something. Within seconds, a roar that pierced through ears and shattered glass reigned out as the Hunter

Killer presence was announced. A line of now champagne soaked people holding glass stems meandered throughout the large hall. The High Commissioner would regain control and restamp his authority. He would not tolerate this kind of unrest among his people.

Meanwhile, with his attention on the rowdy crowds and control over the Hunter Killer, Mavee's deadly foe had stopped attacking. Luna had managed to get inside the creature's head and was slowly calming the beast down. They both now looked at each other with an uneasy stare. Mavee was exhausted from the chase and the beast continued snarling and grunting with evil intent. However, without the High Commissioner's direct control over the beast, the Liger seemed to be slightly lost.

With order restored, everyone's attention was taken back to the contest, which the High Commissioner sought to bring to a quick end. With his control now focused back on the Liger, the beast became more aggressive than ever. Lunging towards Mavee, it swiped its claws like it was aggressively chopping up salad. It looked like this was it, four minutes had elapsed, Mavee only needed to survive one more, but her tired body had little left and as the huge beast pounced upon her, she resided herself to the fate that was about to befall her.

The creature's breath was like a roaring fire, scolding the skin on her face. Its teeth were like kitchen knives, all sharpened to a razor-sharp, flesh-slicing edge. Just the weight of the beast alone was crushing her body. The Liger snapped its jaws towards her face, getting closer each time to finishing the deal. However, no matter how hard the High Commissioner willed the creature, it always just missed its intended target. Yes Mavee was dodging its attacks, but was this something more?

In Sector four, Luna was struggling to keep the beast under control without making it look so. This was her first real test with the

One Beast's Eye and her sweaty forehead and the painstaking look upon her face was telling.

"Breathe Luna, breathe. You must control yourself. There are eyes everywhere. We cannot be found out," said Anna, trying her best to hide her daughter's distress from the guards.

Back inside the pit, the pressure this huge creature was exerting on Mavee's chest was telling, and her breathing got significantly shallower, she was now gasping to take even the smallest of breaths. A cracking sound indicated that she had broken many ribs. If this didn't end soon the creature may not need to strike the finishing blow. Mavee stopped breathing and her eyes closed for what she believed would be the last time.

That was all she remembered, other than an annoying ringing sound that continued long after she believed that she was dead. Mavee, however, was still in the land of the living. The High Commissioner tried with all his might to make the creature strike the finishing blow, but Luna had managed to get inside the beast's head and was stopping it. In Fact, the animal got so confused from being pushed and pulled in different directions that it began running around the Pit like it was crazy.

Before anything else could occur, the buzzer sounded signalling the end of the five minute allotted time. Mavee was unconscious and she had many broken ribs, but as she was pulled from the Predator Pit, she was still alive. She'd survived and after some lengthy recovery time she would live a new life alongside her family who had all won themselves a better life inside the Inner Sanctum.

The High Commissioner was furious. He tried everything to dispose of this woman and the hope that she would give to those living in the Sectors, but with the Wild Whisperers influence over the animal he'd failed. Although Luna's actions had saved this woman and vitally completed step one of their rebellious plan. The High Commissioner was now in no doubt that this folklore legend was true and he would do everything he could to find and kill this person who could not only ruin his Tourneys, but also jeopardise his plans of becoming the supreme leader on Kepler-186F.

A week had passed and everyone was waiting for the welcoming ceremony. It didn't occur very often, but when it did, it gave the people living in the Sectors a chance to celebrate. One of their own had triumphed over the Predator Pit and they would now be welcomed into the Inner Sanctum. The ceremony was nowhere near as lavish as the Tourneys themselves, but it still brought with it hope. This ceremony in particular brought with it more hope than ever before. A woman had triumphed over not one, but two Tourneys and they along with their families would get to live a better life.

Mavee had two children who she loved dearly, and before she left them to face the Tourneys, she had given them a farewell that most who face these competitions did, and that was, I probably won't see you ever again speech, but now she had won, she could provide her children with a better life and that all that she wanted.

It was Sasha who once again took the lead on this ceremony, the High Commissioner's own hatred towards this woman who had defied not only the odds, but also his own actions to see her dead. With his anger boiling over, Sasha thought it best that she perform the ceremony. Now was not the time to show anything but welcoming and solidarity.

"Hello to you all. Thank you for joining me on this special occasion. Now, this ceremony has only ever seen the male of the species receive this amazing reward for their skill and tenacity in overcoming the Tourneys, especially the Predator Pit. I think you will all agree that Mavee has shown an amazingly high level of both these qualities and more to achieve what she has done. This woman has shown us that true strength lies within and anyone can earn their place alongside us in the Inner Sanctum. Your path to a better life remains inside all of you and Mavee is testament to that. Without further ado, let's speak to the woman of the moment Mavee."

It was clear to see that Mavee was still in a lot of pain as she rose from her seat, but the smile across her face helped to ease her burden. "Thank you to the High commissioner's wife."

"Please call me Sasha, we are all as one here."

"Thank you Sasha. This is a dream I never believed would become a reality. It was by an unhappy coincidence that I ended up competing in the Tourneys, but now, I am so grateful to have had the opportunity to compete. If I can do it, anyone can," Mavee said, beginning to well up.

"Oh, look how happy she is," Sasha said, pausing for applause, "Now it's not only you who gets this better life, but also your beautiful children. Who do we have here?" she asked, looking down at their smiling faces.

"This is Jules and this is Justina. My two beautiful children."

"Ahh, so sweet, look at their smiling faces. Well now is the time to take your first step into a better life for you all. Let's all give them a round of applause. Our newest residences of the Inner Sanctum. Watch as they walk towards a better life........... I think you will all agree that this is a huge step forward for the Tourneys. Each and everyone of you has the chance to join us here and live a better life. Mavee has proven that anyone can triumph over these contests, and I hope to be carrying out many more of these ceremonies. Remember, if we persist and persevere, we can all prosper."

There was elation in the Sectors, a woman had won herself a better life. A WOMAN! Many still couldn't believe this had occurred, but it was true. Luna was over the moon, she knew she could triumph over the Tourneys before she had this power over the animals, but it would still be a hard task to convince the rest of the people that this was the right thing to do.

The rebellions numbers were growing by the day and almost every Sector now had some who were willing to take the fight to the Commission, but after the recent kindness from the High Commissioner, many peoples views were changing. They were sadly buying into this buttering up exercise by the Commission and many didn't want to rock the boat, and some would actively try and stop such an action from occurring. Little did they know, but all of their lives were at risk.

When the Commission and the people of the Inner Sanctum blasted off from this planet in their spaceship, they would also take their technology with them, leaving the people living in the Sectors to a horrifying end. They would be cooked alive when the satellite shield had been removed. They wouldn't survive long in the seventy degree heat that would blaze down upon them, boiling their blood and blistering their skin. Left to become charred corpses whose bones would be the last signs that there once was life on this planet.

Even if this shield was to remain, the rising sea level would soon swallow up what was left of the dry land. The seas no longer provided any sustenance and with nowhere for animals to graze they would soon starve to death, that's if they didn't take their own lives first. The only way to survive was to flee this dying planet. To blast-off for pastures new, but with only so many spaces, it would be the cruel Commission's final devastating blow to all those living in the Sectors. A final two fingers up to all of those who had sacrificed so much, still dreaming of better days.

The High Commissioner would probably hover above the Last Isle, watching and taunting the poor people who had been left behind as one last knife piercing their hearts. The rebellion was their last hope, but with many people all willing to work harder than ever to replace the lost Thorium, would the rebellion have enough time to put their plan into action? There were still so many questions around this plan and many cogs that required turning, not to mention the fact that a certain young girl still had to survive a deadly gauntlet. Yes, Luna may have this unique ability, but she couldn't use it against the Hunter Killer. It would be as clear as a slap in the face, and the High Commissioner wouldn't hesitate to kill everyone in the contest, just to be sure he had stamped out any threat.

Luna would have to use her own speed, skill and agility to complete the Rabbit Run. She was certain of this fact before, but that was when she was just doing it for her mother and herself to live a better life in the Inner Sanctum. However, now there was so much more riding on this, she had the fate of thousands of people now weighing heavy on her shoulders. The stakes had been raised significantly, but would this extra pressure be just too much for one young girl to handle?

CHAPTER NINETEEN

Suspicions Raised

A WOMAN! HAD TRIUMPHED over the Rabbit Run and the Predator Pit Tourneys. Mavee was a true inspiration to all, but would her family receive the life of luxury that they had been promised? Many who have won the competitions to earn themselves a better life inside the Inner Sanctum were never seen again. The divide between the Inner Sanctum and the Sectors was one that couldn't be breached, so friends and families who had been left behind never got to communicate with their loved ones who had supposedly made it to a better life. Were these triumphant people still alive? Had they just been taken from sight and killed?

Resources were running low and many of the affluent Inner Sanctum didn't want to mix with those who had come from the Sectors, regardless of their amazing achievement. Sadly, no amount of washing can clean years of toil from their broken bodies. The blood, sweat and tears was as ingrained into their skin as the pain across their faces. Years of malnutrition had left them much smaller and weaker than their Inner Sanctum counterparts, so you couldn't hide where you had come from. Many had taken their own lives after being belittled and looked down upon like they were no better than the slaves they used to be. What was the point in winning if you are still treated like scum?

Yes, maybe you don't have to put your life on the line everyday mining for Thorium, or competing in the High Commissioner's deadly games, and yes your stomach never sang that most hollow, painstaking tune any more, but you had lost your whole identity. Before you had friends, you had a purpose. Ok, the main purpose was staying alive, but there was no comradery inside the Inner Sanctum, everyone was just out for themselves. They didn't care about each other, so they certainly didn't care about those who they had marked forevermore as scum.

The sad fact was, many who had made it into the Inner Sanctum wished they were back in the Sectors. Yes they had more food than they could eat and they never got scolded by the sun's blistering rays, or lost any fingers or toes to frostbite, but they had hope in their hearts and a feeling of love from the others around them. They never got looked at with disdain when they walked down the street. Some had even been spat at by those who believed that they should have stayed where they came from, in the dirt where they belong, along with the rest of the Sector scum.

These people expected to be welcomed as one of the higher in society, to fit in and live the pampered and privileged life. However, those who had triumphed over the cruel games still had to work in the Inner Sanctum. They never lived a life of parties and privilege, they still had to earn their keep, pay their way, or they would have little more than they did before. Ok, it wasn't as deadly and dirty as working in the mines, or as satiating and smelly as working in the farms and slaughterhouses, but it was usually a lot more degrading. Used as servants and pot washers, they still got given the most menial jobs, and their efforts were never appreciated by anyone.

At least when they were working in the Sectors, everyone helped each other, your hard work was valued and everyone felt a sense of pride in what they were doing. They were all working towards something bigger than themselves, all striving for a better life on another planet. A place where they would be able to start again, a place where they would be seen as equal to the rest of society. No longer would they be under the control of the cruel Commission, the chastisers of everything they know, the militant leaders who use fear and retribution to keep everyone in line. They would finally be free to choose their own paths.

Unfortunately, this new life that many have been dreaming of was just that, a dream that would never come true. They would go from expendable to extinct overnight, when they were left behind to die on what was left of planet Earth. The fate of all of these unfortunate people lay within the hands of a young girl. Luna was the Wild Whisperer. The legendary animal communicator, who could unite the people and with help from the animals they could overthrow this oppressive organisation.

However, to pull off this extraordinary rebellion, many others also had a huge part to play. One of which was a lad named Charlie. Charlie was a Predator Pit winner, but because he scored so high when he was tested, he was given a place in the technological department. His skills were too great to be wasted as a servant, or a general dog's body like many of the other winners. He was actually smarter than most people in the Inner Sanctum, and he was responsible for minimising the damage caused by the exploding Thorium.

While others panicked when the Thorium silo exploded, Charlie's years of living in the Sectors gave him calmness and strength in this distressing situation. He had dealt with so much more, but many posh and pampered people from the Inner Sanctum couldn't hold it together, and they completely melted down. They'd never needed to be strong in a crisis before, the worst calamity that had occurred for them up until now was breaking a nail. So, while most ran around like headless chickens, Charlie stayed calm and collected and rectified the situation before it got out of control.

Due to his excellent handling of that very dangerous situation he was promoted to head controller, however, after seeing what happened to the last head controller inside the Predator Pit, he didn't really want the job, but what he wanted didn't matter. The High Commissioner himself appointed him this role and saying no, isn't an option.

"Charlie, I want all of the footage from the recent Predator Pit Tourney. Inside the Pit itself and the view of everyone in the Sector when it was occurring," Hector asked.

"Yes Sir. Why do you need the footage of the Sectors looking on?"

"That's none of your business. I expect to have it all sent across within the next hour."

"The next hour, but that will."

"Within the next hour!" Hector said with wide eyes glaring in Charlie's direction.

"Yes Sir, that won't be a problem."

Never before has the High Commissioner asked for the footage from the Sectors. He always wanted to view the Predator Pit footage again so he could rewatch the gory games of cat and mouse before the unfortunate soul was torn apart. He loved to see his creations at work, studying how they performed and looking to see if there was anything he could do to make these killing machines even deadlier. The view of the Sectors watching on, however, had never been asked for. What was he looking for?

Thankfully, Charlie was part of the rebellion and he would find out anything he could to keep those living in the Sectors safe. He had to speak with Lance. Lance worked in the High Commissioner's Zoo of killer creations, he also had access to the farms and the slaughterhouse and could communicate with those living in the Sectors. His love for Luna had always seen him on the side of the rebellion. He wanted nothing more than to be back in the arms of his one true love. However, he was still unaware that Luna was the

Wild Whisperer. Would Lance still want to fight, knowing that the girl he held so dear to his heart would be put into the firing line?

Lance loved Luna with every inch of his being. They had grown up as children and when many others perished around them, the two grew a strong bond that turned into more than just a friendship. Not many children survived in the Sectors due to the lack of nourishment available, but Luna's dad, mum and brother had all sacrificed in some way to give her what she needed to stay alive. Luna's father was a great warrior and not many would want to mess with this man who many feared. This powerful persona kept Luna and her brother safe in the early years.

Calder also helped to train everyone for the Tourneys. He hated seeing death after death and decided to help train the people in his Sector to have at least half a chance of surviving. Many also believed that this man was the Wild Whisperer. He could speak to the animals, he could get them to follow his instructions, however, he only possessed the skills of a great Tamer, but he wasn't the folklore hero they all needed him to be. His long ancestral line pointed to this fact, but after his demise inside the Predator Pit, many lost faith in the legend of the Wild Whisperer. Some still held on to the fact his son, Baron may hold this special power, however, after his death inside the pit even the strongest of believers began thinking that this fabled person was just a myth.

Only every one-hundred years is a person given the power to control all animals. Throughout history, the Wild Whisperer has always been a man. Never before has a woman become this powerful animal influencer. Everyone, however, was definitely certain that the small, scrawny, pale-white girl called Luna wouldn't be this famed person.

For now, life in the Sectors was as good as it has ever been. Some had received their care packages, and all had received an animal to roast. Due to the extra celebrations, the monthly Rubbish Rummage had been a lot more fruitful. The Inner Sanctum's discarded waste provided more than ever before, so no one was lost during the winter period and as the temperature began rising so did the hope in people's hearts. No longer would they have to suffer the debilitating fear of whether they would be picked for the Rabbit Run competition. They at least had a choice of who would compete, and while there were many who wanted nothing to do with either competition, there were still so many who actually wanted to face these cruel games. It still wasn't a bed of roses living in the Sector's, but some who now no longer lived in fear of competing, actually wore a smile upon their faces, something that hadn't been seen in an extremely long time.

Sadly, this momentary occurrence was quickly wiped from many faces when they were forced to work longer in the mines. For now, they could survive this extra pressure that had been put onto them because they had received enough sustenance, but how much longer would this gravy train keep chugging along? And what good would any of it be if they were to be left to die? They had to get the word out about the Commission's plan.

The rebellion feared that once the Thorium had been replaced, it wouldn't take long before they fled this dying planet and its soon-to-be dead people. The huge spacecraft that would be carrying the people to their new home had been finished. The materials needed to build this craft were limited, however, parts of the satellite shield that protected the Sectors had been pillaged for parts, leaving the temperature slowly rising.

The huge vessel had enough space to take every single person who lived on the Last Isle to safety. Yes they would be cramped in tighter than sardines, but all could take the life-saving journey. The people of the Inner Sanctum, however, didn't want to share a space with what they saw as scum. Dirty low-life people who don't deserve to live. Not everyone in the Inner Sanctum thought this way, but if you were seen to be a sympathiser in any way, you risked backlash from those around you. It was a simple fact there were two races of people, the have and the have-nots, and many were more than happy to see the continued chastisement of who they saw as lesser creations to themselves. They harboured no bad feelings towards the fact that they would all be left to die.

This kind of hatred was the reason the world ended up in this way. People were always wanting more and not caring about the cost. Even after the ice-caps melted and millions of people lost their lives, they still continued to pillage the land, taking vital resources away from those who got left behind. Even when the cause has been realised, the people of Earth didn't try to rectify the situation; they just jumped ship rather than trying to save the planet on which they lived.

The sad fact is that the human race is a greedy and infesting creature and given enough time they would eventually destroy their new home, the planet Kepler-186F. No one ever learned from their mistakes, they would just carry on until another planet had been stripped bare for their greedy needs. The people living in the Sectors would be the best kind of people to populate a new planet. They would respect the land and only take what was necessary, but they would also help the land continue to grow. Planet Earth always had enough of everything to keep human beings and all other lifeforms alive forevermore, but the quest for power and greed by some left it in tatters.

CHAPTER TWENTY

Underground Tomb

THE HIGH COMMISSIONER had now received the footage from the Sectors, and if his suspicions were right he would see who the Wild Whisperer was. Fearing what the High Commissioner was looking for, Charlie scanned through the footage before he handed it over. His own fears were realised when he witnessed Luna's body convulsing, despite the attempt by her mother to shield her from view. Anna was successfully shielding her daughter from the view of the guards, but with many cameras dotted around each Sector, it was hard to conceal anything from the spying eye of the Commission. Many had been caught out by the cameras in the past for all manner of violations, and they were dealt with accordingly.

Charlie knew that not only would Luna's life be at risk, but the whole rebellion would be over if these images were seen by the High Commissioner. Unable to erase the footage altogether because it would raise too much suspicion, Charlie cut the video with the feed from another Sector. As long as the High Commissioner didn't pay too much attention, they may just get away with it. After handing over the footage, Charlie rushed to speak with Lance. He had to get the message out that the High Commissioner was aware of the Wild Whisperers presence.

As Charlie made his way to the Zoo to speak with Lance, he was stopped by a guard. "Stop, where do you think you are going?" asked the guard, pressing the end of his weapon into Charlie's chest.

"I have a very important message for the Zoo team."

"Let me know what it is and I will pass it along."

"I cannot do that. The High Commissioner sent me with this message, and only I am to deliver it."

"What's so important?" probed the guard.

"Look, I haven't got time to be messing around. I am the head of the technology department and I have things to do. If you don't believe me, speak to the High Commissioner, but I assure you he won't be happy with the interruption," Charlie said, starting to sweat.

He had committed now, he had to follow through, he just hoped that these meat-headed guards wouldn't check.

"Give the High Commissioner's office a call. Let's see if this former slave is telling the truth?"

What was he going to do now? If the High Commissioner found out about him lying, he would have his head and considering that Charlie was a key part in the rebellion, without him the plan was doomed to fail.

"Yes, hello, I have a Charlie. Wait a minute. What's your last name, boy," the guard asked.

"What, my last name?" Charlie asked.

"Yes, your last name. Do you see me looking at anyone else? Stupid slave."

"Umm, It's Watts, yes Charlie Watts."

"Watts. Yes, I have Charlie Watts here asking to have access to the Zoo."

Charlie was now shaking in his boots, what if he was found out?

That would be it, all of their hard work to free the Sectors from the Commission's control would be wasted.

Charlie looked desperately at the guard who was now receiving the information. "Yes, Ok. Yes I understand...... But what about protocol? Ok," the guard put down the phone and turned to his colleague. "Let him through."

Charlie was totally shocked to hear those words, but also extremely relieved. Luckily for Charlie, the High Commissioner's secretary spoke to the High Commissioner who was thoroughly engrossed in the Sector footage and told her that he wasn't to be disturbed, and if they couldn't sort it out for themselves, heads would roll. The secretary thought to play it safe. If this was important information and it didn't reach its intended recipient, she knew that there would be trouble. After what had happened to Blake Markson everyone was making sure that they didn't make any mistakes. They all now lived in fear of the retribution that could be placed upon them.

In the past, Charlie had little difficulty getting past the guards with a made up story, but everyone had been put on high alert after the Predator Pit contest. The High Commissioner was worried about what this may mean to his Kingdom. He was the only one who would control his Zoo full of flesh-tearing-fiends. He knew they would be key if he wanted to take over when they reached Kepler-186F.

Charlie quickly found Lance and explained everything that he knew. The High Commissioner was on the war path and he would do anything it takes to stop a threat to his majesty. Even though Lance was part of the rebellion, he was under the understanding that Luna would be safe from harm, and not part of this rebellious action. He loved her so much, that's why he was doing all of this in the first place. To save his precious Luna from a life of torment and torture. To save her from being left to die on a doomed planet.

He knew that they would need the Wild Whisperer if they were going to have any chance of defeating the Commission, but he never knew that the one he loved would be right in the middle of all the conflict. Worse still was the fact that she now had a target on her head, and she would be hunted down. The High Commissioner wouldn't stop until this threat had been neutralised.

Lance was beside himself with worry, the one he loved, the one he was trying to save, may just be the one who would save them all. He knew of the strength that Luna possessed, but he still feared for her life. If she was to die, life wouldn't be worth living for Lance. He had to find out if this was true. Hiding some of the animal's food so that he would have to go into the slaughterhouse to collect more. Each of the High Commissioner's prized beasts would only be fed with the finest cuts of meat. He needed them to be hungry for the taste of flesh and ravenous for the red stuff.

Anna was in the slaughterhouse when she heard someone saying. "psst, psst, overhear," the voice whispered.

After checking where the guards were stationed, Anna made her way to the whispers.

"You there. Where are you going?" shouted a guard that she didn't originally spot.

"The mincer. The High Commissioner wants more minced meat for the pies."

"Ok, move along."

Thankfully, after the terrible fate that had befallen Blake Markson, just the mention of the High Commissioner's names had people shaking in their boots. Many didn't question your actions if it was on the High Commissioner's order. Thankfully, the sad death of one person may just give the rebellion the freedom of movement they needed to put their plan into place.

Luckily, the mincing machine was out of direct line of sight from the guards tower. It's not to say that it was completely obscured, especially if the guards walked the raised platforms that encompassed the whole building, but while they were chatting in the control tower Anna and whoever was calling her were safe to talk.

"Lance, it's so good to see you," Anna said, moving in for a hug.

"No time for that now. Is it true what I heard?"

"Is what true?"

"About Luna. Is she? .... Is she the Wild Whisperer?" Lance's expression changed when he said the words.

"Yes, yes I'm afraid it's true."

"But, you said........... You said!"

"I know, I hoped with all of my heart that it wouldn't be her, but the One Beast's Eye has chosen her. Luna is the Wild Whisperer."

"NO, this can't be happening. You said that she would be safe while we fought back against the Commission. How can I fight knowing that my one true love is now in danger," Lance said, breaking down.

"She is in no danger. No one else knows yet and I will not be revealing that information until the very last moment."

"She's already in DANGER! The High Commissioner knows that the Wild Whisperer has been found and he is already on the lookout."

"How does he know? We were extremely careful," Anna's voice now portrayed fear.

"Not careful enough. I think we may have thrown him off the scent for now, but he will not give up until this threat is dealt with."

"What's taking so long back there," shouted a guard after noticing Anna's disappearance.

"I have to go."

"Tell Luna, I love her."

Lance was beside himself. He was doing all of this to keep Luna safe and provide her with a better life, but she wasn't supposed to be involved. He had to find out what the High Commissioner knew. Now, more importantly, he would have to make sure he didn't get caught. The High Commissioner was a smart man and he could tell a lie like a fart. The Sector's rebellion had only just got off the ground, however, it may be the shortest rebellion ever if the Wild Whisperer's identity was found out.

Anna decided not to tell Luna about her conversation with Lance. She knew how much Luna loved him and to know that he was worried would just add to the ever-growing pressure that had been placed upon her daughter's shoulders. Like Lance, Anna was totally gobsmacked when she found out that Luna was the Wild Whisperer. This fabled person had always been a man. Maybe no man living in the Sectors had the courage and fortitude to become this legendary hero?

Luna was so strong and capable considering her size, and she never let anything stop her from achieving what she wanted. However, at present this young girl was lost in the tight, twisting, tortuous tunnels of the mines. Luna's relative newness to mining Thorium had left her exposed. Because of her small stature, she was used to crawl through small exploratory tunnels to see if there was a cache of Thorium on the other side. These small investigatory tunnels would be made bigger if there was a decent amount of Thorium to be mined, but if not they would move to another area.

Unfortunately, Luna was on a shift with the group of lads who had tried harassing her in the past, on more than one occasion. Luna had milky-white skin which was extremely desirable to almost every man. Now that she had turned sixteen, she was seen as fair game and many wanted a piece of the milky-white delights that were on offer. Many had tried and failed, due to Luna's speed, tactical movements and a helping hand from her best friend. It was this incident that was still tormenting this group of lads. They had been shown up by two young girls and they wanted payback. Down in the mines, there were no trees to be ambushed from, no animals to come to her aid. She was all alone and they knew it.

In the dark sweltering tunnels the men sought to put their plan into action, "Luna, this way darling."

"Come on love, we ain't got all day."

Luna wasn't too worried at this point, because she had done this same exploratory journey many times before. She didn't like having to squeeze her tiny body through the smallest of gaps, but it was better than some of the other jobs they had made her do. Still, she had no idea what these people had in store for her. After she had made it to the other size, she checked her body for any scratches and scrapes. She couldn't risk getting any kind of infection, luckily her silky-smooth skin allowed her to glide across the rough edges of the rocks.

"I'm here," she shouted through the tunnel. "Right, let's have a little look around," she said to herself.

Thorium glowed a shiny-white colour, so it was generally easy to find, but sometimes you had to dig away the surface rubble to reveal its alluring glow. After a thorough search Luna decided that there wasn't enough of a Thorium deposit to warrant digging any further in this direction.

"There is nothing much here, I'm coming back now," she shouted down the tunnel.

"NO! Not yet. Umm, I mean, have you had a proper look," said one of the men.

"Take all of the time you need."

"Yea, and shortly you will have the rest of your life to look," sniggered another.

Soon after, Luna heard banging. "What's going on?" she screamed.

As she got closer to the tunnel she was met with a face full of dust followed by a load of rubble. The men had collapsed the tunnel leaving her trapped inside.

"Find your way out of that, you skinny little bitch."

"Not so clever now, are we?"

"Come on lads, let's get out of here."

Now in complete darkness, Luna screamed hoping to get her voice heard. "HELLO, IS ANYBODY THERE. HELLO, CAN YOU HEAR ME. Hello, hello, help, help me. Please help me."

At first Luna believed this to be an unfortunate accident and she would soon hear the pickaxes and shovels trying to dig her out. All alone in the dark she began to get scared. It was so dark that she couldn't see her hand in front of her face. Being new to the mines, Luna had never found herself in such a predicament. No one had individual lights, they were only issued to the group as a whole. Some who had worked for years in these dark enclosed spaces had actually evolved a sort of night-vision. They couldn't see like they had a light, but they could see enough to navigate their way out of the mines. Sadly for Luna she hadn't gained such vision, and for her it was the darkest nothingness she had ever witnessed.

After a while, she realised that she had been left behind and that no one would be looking for her. Nine times out of ten, the numbers who entered the mines in the morning were not the same amount that exited them later. Many had lost their lives in the mines and the guards didn't care. They never performed a head count to keep an eye on numbers. There was nowhere to escape to, and no one would risk their lives to go back in and look for any who hadn't made it out. Sadly, if you got stuck in the mines your time was limited. Poor ventilation and long exposure to the Thorium deposits usually meant if you didn't return after your shift, you wouldn't be returning at all. Some seasoned miners had been known to make their way out after, but this was a rare occurrence. The skeletons of those who died were a constant reminder of how important it was to stick together in these murky depths.

Was this the final nail in the coffin for Luna Star? What would this mean for the rebellion? Without the Wild Whisperer, they stood no chance against the Commission. Luna was the key to it all, if she died thousands more would shortly follow when the

Commission left the planet, leaving those in the Sectors unprotected from the blistering sun's rays.

CHAPTER TWENTY-ONE

Unexpected Saviour

LANCE WAS A BUMBLING mess after his conversation with Anna. How could Luna be the Wild Whisperer? They'd all been told the stories as children. Stories passed down through the generations. However, not once in the god-knows how many years that this legend has been occurring has a woman been this fabled hero, let alone a young girl. How could this be?

Yes Luna's family held a strong Tamer gene, but so did many other families. The One Beast's Eye only chooses one person, just one who will unite the animals and save them from suffering. These animals, however, were far from their original origins. All of them had been altered in some way, especially to make them even deadlier. The Wild Whisperers of the past had never had to deal with genetically altered animals and especially not animals that had been fused with A.I technology. These beasts were being powered by something different, and Lance worried that even the Wild Whisperer would have trouble influencing their minds.

Meanwhile, the High Commissioner was left feeling confused. He was sure that someone had interfered with his precious predators during the last Predator Pit competition, but the footage showed no sign of this person who would be easily spotted. The fabled Wild Whisperer is said to have glowing yellow eyes when they are communicating with the animals, and considering the lack of colour in the drab and desolate Sector's this person would have been like a lighthouse beacon.

That night in bed, Sasha sought to comfort her festering husband. "What troubles you my love?"

"It's nothing, just a possible problem that might just jeopardise everything that I have built."

"Well, if I can help in any way. Please, I don't like seeing you like this."

"Have you ever heard of the legend of the Wild Whisperer?"

"No. What is a Wild Whisperer?"

"The legend of the Wild Whisperer says that every one-hundred years, someone from a Tamer family will be granted the power to communicate with the animals. They will be able to take control of them and use them for their own will. When I was young, I grew up in a village where some of its inhabitants possessed these Tamer skills. They were far from the Wild Whisperer, but they made the animals attack me for fun. They would laugh at me when chicken's almost scratched out my eyes, or a goat bucked me so hard I couldn't sit down for weeks, they were so cruel," Hector said, beginning to get emotional, "One day I promised to get my revenge. Now I control the animals and they listen to what I say. I control these people who possess this power, ME!"

"Oh, my love, come here. No one can take away what you have built. The animals are under your control, no one can take that away either," Sasha said, brushing back his long golden hair.

"I think that this person may be lurking in the Sector's. I felt their presence in the mind of the beast as it tried to kill that woman."

"Are you sure?"

"I'm not entirely sure, I was so overwhelmed with rage. This woman, the first ever woman. She couldn't survive, she just couldn't."

"It's ok, my love. Calm yourself. There, there. How would you even know if the Wild Whisperer exists?"

"There will be signs. I have checked the footage from the Sector during the Predator Pit and I couldn't see anything, but I'm sure that their presence is near."

"There was a young girl who came over and stroked the Blue-Eye-Tiger when we were out on a visit to one of the Sectors. I just dismissed it at the time. I'm sorry my love. Could this be anything?" Sasha said with fear in her voice.

" A young girl. The legend always talks of a man who would become this creature communicator, but who knows what form it may take. In what Sector did this occur?"

"I'm sorry, my love, but I can't remember. Please forgive me for not divulging this information sooner?"

"It's ok, you didn't know, but I believe that we need to keep a closer eye on things now."

"Let me flush this person out. Even if it's not this girl, you can make an example of them. Show them what will happen if they do exist. Get your revenge on these Tamers for all that you have suffered!" Sasha said with urgency.

The way things stood, the High Commissioner had nothing to fear. Luna, the Wild Whisperer, was stuck in the mines. Her time was running out and if she didn't find a way out soon, she would perish and take with her the hopes, dreams and lives of thousands of people who will be left to die.

Anna was beside herself when Luna never returned home after her shift. She ran around asking and searching for her child, but no one had seen her. Fearing for her child's life she made her way to the mines.

"You, move away. You have no business here," said a guard, pointing a gun in Anna's direction.

"Please, my daughter never came home after her shift. I think that she is stuck in the mines. She has only been working in them for a short time, she doesn't know the risks. Please let me go in to try and find her."

"Have you heard this crazy woman's ramblings? Go away before you end up in a lot of trouble."

"Please, just let me inside, I will find her. She is all I have left. Don't you have any compassion?" Anna screamed.

A shot was fired at Anna's feet. "The next one won't miss. Now piss off."

Anna stood her ground even with the threat of death, but she knew that without Luna everyone would die. She didn't care about her own life, but her daughter must survive. She is the only one that can free the people of the Sectors. The people won't fight, the rebellion would be over if Luna was to die. She held the hope and strength of so many, she just had to survive, she had to!

As the guard took aim at Anna's head, he was thankfully stopped before pulling the trigger by a slightly more sympathetic guard. "Can you go and check the monitors? The High Commissioner wants to know how much was mined on the last shift."

"Ok, but you can deal with this annoying piece of shit," the guard said, spitting in Anna's direction.

"Please, my daughter," she pleaded again.

"Look lady. If you carry on, you are going to get yourself killed. Leave now, you will not gain entry. Look, the next shift has started and I'm sure that your daughter will be found by someone. However, if she does make it out and you are not alive, would that not be just as painful?"

"Just shoot her already. We haven't got time for this charade," shouted another guard.

"Please go! This is your last warning. I won't be able to stop them from killing you."

Reluctantly, Anna took her leave. The guard was right, if Luna did make it out and she wasn't there, she might just be too distraught to continue with the rebellion anyway. Anna knew that her daughter was strong and extremely resilient, but she knew how dangerous the mines could be, and the survival rate if lost in them was even less than the Tourneys.

Deep inside the mines Luna had all but given up. She had wandered for hours trying to find a way out of the pitch-black labyrinth. "What's the point in having all of this power if it has no use," she screamed.

What sort of animals would she come across this far down anyway. Luna wasn't known as a quitter, however, when your senses are taken away from you, panic can set in very quickly. She couldn't see, she couldn't hear, and now she was struggling to breathe. This would have been a complete travesty before knowing what her passing would do to her mother, but now there were thousands of people relying on her. Thousands who would be sentenced to death at the hands of the Commission if she didn't survive.

"Come on Luna, think, think! What would dad have done?"

She thought back to her father's teaching. She was still so young, but she liked to listen in when he was telling her older brother. *'Check for any type of breeze. Try to find a light source. Use your sense of smell to locate the scent of explosives, or foul smelling odours, that might lead you to a stockpile point. Listen to the ground, the vibrations made by any movement above may give you a sense of direction.'*

Luna tried to use all of the hints that she could remember, but it was just so dark that every other sense was stricken with fear. In a last ditch attempt, she tried to use her Wild Whisperer powers, maybe there was something down here that could help. Fear again clouded her mind, she couldn't concentrate, she heard everything, but nothing, all at the same time which started to give her palpitations. "Calm down Luna, you need to calm down," she said, hoping the audible sound of her voice might help because her mind wasn't coping with the silence very well.

Anger saw her lash out at the surrounding walls. She clawed at the loose rock trying to tunnel her way out. After a while she was tired, her hands were bleeding and she had almost run out of oxygen. After slumping up against a wall, she closed her eyes. Even though it was already completely dark, the act itself brought her some comfort. Maybe she would just drift off to sleep, a quiet and painless death?

Once her eyes were closed, she was treated with happy memories from a time before they were rounded up like slaves. They lived off the land and found peace with all its creations. They all ultimately knew that the world around them was doomed, but if they could have spent the rest of their days all together, happy and free, encompassed by a loving embrace, they could have all left this mortal realm with a sense of peaceful freedom.

It was during one of these dreams that Luna remembered a certain moment when they sat upon the top of a mountain. The sound of rushing water from a nearby waterfall seemed to play a relaxing tune. The sun was almost setting, and her whole family snuggled beneath a huge blanket watching the last of the sun go down, after which they slept under the stars all snuggled together, happy and content. The sun, however, never seemed to set, it stayed blazing towards her. Then it began to get brighter and brighter, this wasn't how she remembered it. All of a sudden all she could see was light, was she still dreaming?

The bright light continued to shine until she found the strength to open her eyes. All around her was a luminous glow, it was so bright that it made her head begin to ache. This painful feeling told her that she was indeed awake and this was no longer a dream. As her eyes began to regain focus, she could see that it was some kind of insect that was producing this light. Shuffling forward, she placed her hand over the insect which greatly reduced its glow. The encased glow now illuminated her surroundings with a non-blinding light. Able to see again, her senses started to function properly. She could see, she could smell, she could hear the little feet of the insect as it moved around. After gently cupping the insect into her hands, she made a small opening which allowed her to use her hands like a torch. This little creature had given her a chance. Now she could see, hopefully she would be able to find her way out.

With all of her senses now working together, she managed to navigate towards an opening. She could once again see daylight. Her lungs expanded three times their size when she breathed in the fresh air. There was only one problem, she was still about one-hundred feet below ground. She had found an old venting shaft. This huge opening was too big to climb, the sleek, sheer sides had nowhere to get a foothold. She now had light and air, but she was still stuck underground. These ventilation shafts were never checked and they were situated so close to the shore that rising tides could flood the whole area, causing the shaft to collapse in on itself. Luna may have found a view of the outside, but she was far from being safe.

She watched as the little insect that had shown her the way, fluttered up and out of the shaft. *'If only she had wings'* she thought to herself.

It was the flapping of wings that she started to hear. Looking up through the shaft, she could see hundreds of birds all flying overhead. The cacophony of sound produced got louder as it travelled down the shaft. All of a sudden the noise stopped, like the birds had just fallen out of the sky, the light from the shaft was being closed off by something. Was it collapsing? Was she about to die?

Luna felt a rumbling and heard a humming sound which heightened her fear of her impending doom. The darkness was back, the humming noise was deafening. Why bring her this far if she was going to die anyway? A glimpse of light brought back a little hope, but the heightened vibrations brought more dread. She could feel something around her, a wind-like force was getting stronger. The light flickered in and out like a dying bulb, what was happening?

Completely startled when she felt her feet lift off the ground. She tried to reach out and grab hold of something, but there was nothing there. The light started to get brighter, and she was getting higher. Caught in a swirling vortex, she was being lifted to safety. When she got a glimpse of the outside world, her heart skipped a beat. The birds had come to her rescue. They'd created a centripetal force that had carried her out of the mines. After being placed very gently on the solid above ground, the birds flew away and perched on nearby trees. Luna had been saved by the animals, they had come to her aid in her time of need. Now back out in the open, she could feel the animals around her, she could sense their life-force like a beating heart. She knew then that they were with her, they were on her side and they were ready to fight.

She returned home to an extremely relieved mother. "Where have you been child? I have been so worried. What happened? Oh my god, come here, let me hug you."

"It's ok, I am safe now."

Both women were in floods of tears and an embrace that could have broken bones. Anna squeezed so tightly, she never wanted to let go. Luna explained what had occurred which made Anna furious. They had to keep her safe. The whole rebellion was riding on her shoulders, and as much as she wanted to protect her daughter, she knew that without her they would all die anyway. They had to find a way to get Luna out of the mines. She was too precious and far too valuable to be at risk, however, that was a worry for another day.

After her long ordeal, Luna was over the moon when her mother showed her what she had sneaked out from the slaughterhouse. She hadn't eaten in days and the thought of some real food was tantalising. That night they both ate like queens. Luna was safe and the planned rebellion was saved from disaster, but with so many other hurdles to jump over, it was far from becoming a reality.

The next day the alarm sounded, calling everyone to the big screens. The High Commissioner's face appeared. "Today the Sector's will have a visit from my wife, who will be accompanied by the Blue-Eyed-Tiger. One among you got close enough to pet this fierce creature. This person needs to announce themselves. They are not in any trouble, but I would like to invite them to the Inner Sanctum to help in my Zoo. My precious predators can be difficult to handle, and the Zoo hands could learn how to take better care of them with your help. Your talent is rare and I wish to award any Sector from which this person comes from. For your cooperation in this matter, the Sector who reveals this person, or gives us the information about who it is, will be exempt from competing in this year's Tourneys, if they so wish. We must work together if we are to realise our dream of life on another planet. Remember, if we persist and persevere, we will all prosper."

Armed with the Blue-Eyed-Beast by her side, Sasha took to patrolling the Sectors. This creature looked like a little teddy bear, all fluffy and white, but along with its piercing blue eyes it had an extendable jaw much like a snake which could swallow a person whole. Every female was lined up side by side while Sasha and the creature inspected them. Held on a leash the creature was released to within inches of their faces to see how it reacted.

"What's the meaning of this," shouted a disgruntled father.

"Move away now!" said a guard, pointing his weapon at the man.

"Eeny, meeny, miny, moe, which one of these ladies will get caught by their toe. Oh, It's ok little one, don't be scared," Sasha said to a girl who had urinated out of fear when the huge creature's breath engulfed her head and its teeth got within touching distance.

Three Sectors down and no sign of this girl who could seemingly tame the beast. Some had come forward with information, but as of yet, all who had been inspected weren't who they were looking for. Sadly, some had fallen foul of the creature's jaws. No one was killed, but a few had lost limbs, which was as good as a death sentence. The fierce creature lashed out trying to get to the meaty treats that were on offer. If it wasn't for the four guards who were holding this beast back, it would have eaten them all.

Sector four was next: how could Luna hide her abilities? If she was found out the rebellion would be over. Thankfully, word has gotten out to the other Sectors about what was occurring so they had a chance to prepare.

"What are we going to do? I can already feel the creature's pain. When it comes to me it will feel safe. They will know it's me, I don't know what to do!" Luna said, panicking.

"You must try to cause the animal pain. Make it want to attack you, it's the only way. It must see you as a threat."

"I can't let every other woman in the Sectors be forced into facing this terrifying ordeal. I must come forward. People are losing limbs and you know as well as I do, they are as good as dead now," Luna said, completely beside herself now.

How could she let others suffer for her mistakes? Worst, however, would be to come if she didn't. What was she going to do?

Amid all of the chaos, time was up. The alarm sounded and every single female in Sector four would now be scared to within an inch of their lives. Anna feared what her daughter would do. Luna never wanted others to suffer, especially not for her own actions. She was so overjoyed when she realised that she had the power to help save them all. She had such a good heart even in this death sentence of an existence.

It was too late, the sound of an unmistakable roar sent shivers down everyone's spine, letting them all know that the beast had entered their Sector. Thankfully, Luna was placed at the far end of this very long line of the damned. However, this felt like more of a curse than a blessing. She would have to hear the cries of all who had come before her, all the while knowing that she could stop their pain. With more time to think, her head might just explode before the beast finally reached her. This was such a huge decision and everything was riding on it. What was she going to do?

CHAPTER TWENTY-TWO

Loving Sacrifice

AS THE BLUE-EYED-BEAST got closer to her position, Luna could no longer endure the horrifying screams of the women who had already been subjected to this terrifying ordeal. Her body shaking with fear, guilt and the overriding need to protect. That was it, she could no longer let others suffer for her. After taking in a deep breath she got ready to step forward to receive whatever fate would be coming her way. As she lifted her foot to make the move, however, she felt a hand grasp hold of her own, stopping her forward advancement.

Luna was so overwhelmed with indecision that she never noticed who was standing beside her. A friend of hers who was just a little bit older than her. They had grown up together in this new cruel world and had both given the other help and strength when they felt like giving up. Each one had made a promise to always protect the other and share anything that they could to help keep them on the side of the living. Their families lived together alongside many others when the world descended into chaos and they all lived off the land. Bella was also from a Tamer family, and both girls would practise building their skills on pet rabbits. Both had a strong Tamer instinct and a love of all animals.

"Let me be the one. You have to survive. I have overheard my parents' conversations. I know who you are."

"No Bella, I cannot let you sacrifice yourself for me."

"We both made a promise to protect the other, and now it is my chance to thank you for always being there for me."

"NO! YOU CANNOT," Luna said slightly louder, which got the unwanted glare from some guards.

"Luna, I'm dying. I have an illness. My parents have been trying to treat it with the help of your mother, but I will not survive. You were always the stronger one of us, and I know that it is you who has the strength to save our people. You must carry on. You can save us all. Free our people from this life of terror and become the Wild Whisperer," Bella said, coughing up some blood.

"NO! I will not let you suffer any more. Let me help you. I'm sure we can find a cure, Please, you're my best friend," Luna said, as tears rolled down her cheeks.

"Luna, it has to be you. Please, my life is already over, but you can save so many more. Let me do the one thing I can to help. I'm too ill to fight and I really want to stick two fingers up to the Commission. Please, it's the only way I will have peace before I go to my grave. We will meet again my friend, but now it is you who must go on."

"Silence, you will be quiet for the inspection," said a guard witnessing the chatter.

Sasha and the Blue-Eyed-Beast were getting closer. Unable to say any more, Bella looked at Luna and her eyes said it all. Both were now crying as they squeezed each other's hands tightly.

"Ahh, how sweet, holding hands," Sasha said, before their hands were broken apart by one of the guard guns.

The Blue-Eyed-Beast was now standing in front of Luna. It already seemed a bit more placid, which had Sasha's eyes widening. Luna tapped into the beast mind and caused it pain, her face also showed the torment as she closed her eyes. The creature went crazy, snapping at her with its huge jaws that sounded like a shotgun every time they slammed shut. A commotion behind got everyone's attention. Some people from the crowd started shouting and banging, making as much noise as possible to distract Sasha from seeing Luna's eyes when they started to change colour.

After order had been restored, Sasha was happy that Luna wasn't who they were looking for, but it still wasn't over. Could she send her friend to the certainty of unimaginable suffering and most likely death? However, she was already dying and she wanted to have her own chance to attack the Commission.

Bella was a strong Tamer, but she was nowhere near powerful enough to affect a beast of this nature. Luna would have to use her powers to help calm the beast. Turning away to try and shield her face, luckily, Sasha and the guards just believed that this was because she couldn't bear to watch her friend face this ordeal. The beast started to calm down and soon stopped growling and snarling. It went as playful as a puppy and nuzzled it head into Bella's body.

"We've found the one we are looking for. Guards take this child away," Sasha said, extremely elated that her plan had revealed the culprit.

As the crowds dispersed Luna dropped to her knees, with her head in her hands she sobbed. She had just offered up her best friend as a sacrifice.

Anna rushed to her daughter's side and prized her from the ground, "Luna, please we must get inside. We can't be seen."

Anna helped a broken Luna back to their home where she collapsed again, sobbing so hard her head throbbed with pain. *'What had she done? How could she live with herself now?'*

One person had been sacrificed, but this action may have saved so many more, who now still had a chance to survive. With what the Commission thought was the Wild Whisperer now in their grasp, the Sectors could breathe a sigh of relief. The real Wild Whisperer, however, was in bits. Her best friend had sacrificed her life to save hers and so many others, but the thought still struck her like a knife to the heart every time she pictured her friend being taken away by the guards.

An elated Sasha returned to the Inner Sanctum with her head held high. "I've done it my love. I've found the girl," she announced to her awaiting husband.

"So this is the fabled Wild Whisperer. Only I will control all of the animals, filthy Tamer scum!" the High Commissioner screamed at Bella. "Planning to take control of my prized beasts were you? Not on my watch, little girl," he said, striking her across the face with the back of his hand.

"Well done my love," he said, kissing Sasha. "Take this filthy traitor away. I will deal with her later."

To Bella's surprise, she wasn't killed on sight. It looks like the High Commissioner wanted to study this person who could control the animals without the need for technology. If he could somehow harness this power, he would be unstoppable.

To control his animals the High Commissioner used microchips implanted into their brains. However, he could only use pain to control these creatures and in the past during the first stages of testing, some of the animals managed to override this painful affliction and attack. The High Commissioner's robotic right arm was the result of one of these attacks.

Technology can also malfunction and possibly be tampered with. He wanted to control them without the need for this kind of technological interface. Wanting to have the same connection to the animals as the legendary Wild Whisperer. If he could just work out how this person did it, he could dissect their mind and mould it into his own D.N.A. They had the technology, they just needed the raw material.

With everything that had been happening of late, everyone had almost forgotten about the upcoming Rabbit Run Competition. Most were completely knackered from the extra mining that was required to replace the lost Thorium. A loud ringing in their ears and trembling bodies reminded them of what time it was when the alarm sounded, signalling their presence at the big screens.

"Hello to you all and before we start, let's hear from the person who has shown that anyone can earn their place in the Inner Sanctum. The first woman ever to triumph over both Tourneys, it's Mavee."

After being pulled from her seat, Mavee's face appeared on the screen. "Now Mavee, why don't you tell everyone how good it is to live on this side of the wall," the High Commissioner said, glaring at her.

Mavee looked terrible, even worse than some of those living in the Sectors. It turns out that just because you have made it to this side of the divide, your life is still one of constant work. There was no one here to help carry the load and any respect that she might have had was long gone. Yes they did eat better than those in the Sectors and the winters were no longer a lottery of life, but they felt no love, no belonging on this side of the wall.

At least in the Sectors there was a sense of love and togetherness. Everyone helped each other when the going got tough. Inside the Inner Sanctum, if you didn't fit in you were shown no respect. Many who had made it to the other side now wished to be back where they had come from. They also wanted to warn everyone in the Sectors that the life they had all been promised, the life that they have been fighting for, was just a lie.

After Mavee had been forced to tell everyone how great her life was now, the High Commissioner continued with his speech. "As you are all aware, we have been searching for a certain person. This special person is now helping the Commission in their research. With her help the transfer of my Zoo full of animals to our new home will be a much easier task......... Although this person didn't come forward of their own accord, I understand that she may have had some reservations. However, I'm nothing else, but a man of my word. Sector four will not need to compete in the remaining Rabbit Run competitions. You can still compete if you so wish, but this will be your own decision. As a little extra bonus for the family of this wonderful person, they will all be welcomed into the Inner Sanctum to help support their daughter, while she helps us with our important work. We must all continue to make sacrifices for the greater good. If we don't work together as one, we will be stuck on this dying planet forever. Remember, if we persist and continue to preserve, we can all prosper!"

Cheers reigned out from Sector four, but not everyone was happy about this. Although they were far from ready to enact their rebellious plan against the Commission, their plan required participation in the Tourneys. Luna had to get to the Predator Pit, only then would she have the opportunity to take control of the animals.

Sadly for Bella, her parents would now be used as leverage. They would be tortured in front of her if she didn't do what the Commission commands. In the split second decision to sacrifice herself for the sake of her friend and the chance for the Sectors to rebel against the oppressive organisation. Bella had no idea that her parents would be dragged into this situation. She believed as did many that her life would be taken as soon as she was transported to the Inner Sanctum. This person was the biggest threat to the High Commissioner and he surely wouldn't let her live.

Even with all of the power he already commands, the High Commissioner wanted more. He also had no idea what kind of animals were on Kepler-186F, if any at all. However, the native species might be even stronger than his corpse-crushing-creations? In time, he knew that he could capture these creatures and use technology to gain control over them, but if he could harness the

Wild Whisperers power, it would give him a better chance of being able to control any creatures they may come across.

He had no idea if this fabled creature communicator could influence animals on another planet, but he would still prefer to obtain this power for himself. Having no clue what he might face when he reached this new destination, he wanted to have enough power, money and influence to make his quest to take over the whole planet as simple as it could be. Any established colony would be difficult to infiltrate and he wanted to hit the ground running. He didn't want to give them any time to mount a defensive effort. If he could catch them unawares, his take-over would be much easier.

The High Commissioner didn't want a war, war would only bring destruction to his new planet and he wanted to make sure that this new destination was kept intact. He'd witnessed the fate of planet Earth and if he wanted to rule for as long as possible, he would need to preserve what they had. Of course, some would live luxury lives, but the majority would live like the people in the Sectors. Resources would last so much longer if it was just the few who were pillaging them. He'd worked wonders with the few resources that were left on Earth, imagine what he could do with a brand new, fulling untapped planet?

Who knows, maybe after he's enslaved Kepler186-F, he could set his sights on other planets in the solar system. The universe could become his oyster. He could build the largest force there has ever been. Commanding so much power that nothing could ever dethrone him. Furthermore, he would rule it all and nothing could stop him. With his sadistic wife by his side, they would be unstoppable.

Sasha had always loved the sight of blood and guts, which is why she decided to become a surgeon. It wasn't for the life-saving operations she might perform, but for the gory scene during them. Nicknamed the Night Nurse before the planet fell into chaos, she was already being investigated for an artery of deaths that had occurred on the operating table. Operations that were usually routine and had little risk attached to them. People, however, continued to die under her knife.

With the body count rising, she was suspended from her position until an investigation could be launched. Shortly after the world erupted in chaos, millions lost their lives and every medical personnel was drafted in to help treat the sick and injured from the fallout. Her qualifications saw her become head of the Commission's hospital, which is where she met Hector. She saw something different in this man's eyes, he was as inhumane as she was, and his love for bloody violence saw an even darker side come out in her.

They both liked to see the suffering of others and it was like a match made in Heaven when the two met. Hector quickly found someone who relished torment and torture as much as he did. He was still very wary at first, but Sasha was keen to prove herself. She wanted to be at the top of the pile alongside this man. She too, had a thirst for power.

Before, her victims were always sleeping and unable to fight back, but he showed her how much more exciting it was to see the anguish upon peoples faces when they were still very much alive and kicking. The expressions of fear and the harrowing sounds produced by the dying victims was like cat-nip to the pair of sadistic souls, the gorier, the better.

Sasha was partly due to why the animals were being altered in such brutish ways. They both wanted to see more fear, more suffering, more blood and guts, and the soundtrack produced by the dying was like music to their ears. Metal teeth made a much nicer sound when sliced through flesh and bone. Cauterising jaws made the victims last longer, even after all four limbs had been removed from their torso they were still alive, but they were definitely not *kicking!!!*

Sasha brought a surgical precision to the spine-splitting-savages that already had more than enough deadly capability, and the experimentation would continue. With artificial enhancements readily available, these creatures of the kill could become unstoppable.

They both knew that to be able to take over a whole planet, they would need these altered animals that would strike fear into any who might oppose them. Striking fear into your enemy is usually the best way to win a battle. Once they are scared of what might happen to them, they lose their own fighting edge, they become worried, they can no longer think straight, which all helps to destroy your adversary. Fighting ability, strength and any skills that an individual might have, can be easily overcome when that person is in a fearful state. The body reacts differently when it's feeling apprehensive. Once fear has entered your mind, any hope of winning that you may have had is slowly chipped away leaving a empty shell of a person.

The High Commissioner knew this only too well, but while fear has its place in defeating your enemy, compassion and carrot dangling also has its place in influencing people to do your bidding. Both can be highly effective when used correctly, and now the two of them are working as one, could they ever be stopped?

Hector's original thoughts of believing that the world was his oyster had now been widened to the universe. They had the technology, they had an army of people. Along with a Zoo full of A.I altered animals that were all ready and waiting to do their bidding. With such an almighty arsenal, could any other force survive their advances, let alone hope to defeat them?

CHAPTER TWENTY-THREE

The Predictor

THANKS TO THE BRAVE actions of Bella, the rebellion was still on. Although the one person that everyone was relying on to be strong, was at this present time a complete mess. Luna still couldn't come to terms with the loss of her best friend. However, considering that she plays the most pivotal role in this fight against the Commission, without her there would be no rebellion at all.

Bella was, at present, hooked up to an array of machines, all scanning every inch of her body to try and find out the reason why she had this exceptional ability. Tubes, wires and all sorts of probing devices were attached to the poor young girl. Little did the Commission know that they would find no such evidence from this false patsy.

The real Wild Whisperer was trying to stay strong. She'd lost her best friend, but as many scared faces stared back at her during a meeting about the upcoming rebellion, she realised that there were still so many poor souls that needed her help. It wasn't their fault that everyone was in this position, or that her best friend had been taken. It was all down to the cruel Commission. This oppressive organisation had caused so much pain and suffering, it was time that it was stopped for good.

"We must move up the planned attack. The girl was nearly found out. All will be lost without her," said a member of the crowd.

"We must remain patient. If we strike too early, we will be easily defeated. We must stick to the plan. The crisis is over for now," replied the Sector Elder.

"What shall we do about competing in the Rabbit Run? We have been given a pass. Surely we should take this offer to save our people's lives?"

"We must continue to compete, if we don't and then we ask to compete further down the line, suspicions will be raised."

"So you expect more of us to die for a plan that has more holes than a colander."

"Is the child even strong enough to take over the High Commissioner's A.I altered animals?" shouted another angry person.

"She doesn't look strong enough to complete the Rabbit Run at this present moment."

The crowd was starting to get rowdy. "Please everyone, we need to remain quiet. I grant you that our plan has a few issues, but it is the only way that we can hope to survive........... Do you not understand? We will be left to die on this planet, just discarded waste, another cast off from the Inner Sanctum! Just like their rubbish......... We must fight, or we will all perish!"

Anna stood up. "Please, my daughter needs to feel your strength is behind her. She may be a pivotal cog in this undertaking, but we must all play our part. I wish so much that my only remaining child wasn't the fabled Wild Whisperer, but she is, and she is willing to sacrifice herself to help save our people," she said with pride. "If you can't understand the sacrifice that we are all about to make, you have no place here."

The meeting was interrupted when one of the lookouts came forward dragging someone who was sneaking a peek at proceedings. "He was caught in the trees snooping on our meeting," said the lookout, throwing the man at the Elder's feet.

The only safe place to gather groups of people was in the forest by the sea. Cameras had been mounted there in the past, but the close proximity to the warmer seas kept shorting out the whole surveillance system. Dummy cameras had been put in their place, but everyone knew that this was the case. There were still many in Sector four that were unaware of the rebellion and even fewer that knew of the Wild Whisperers presence, let alone their identity. Maybe this was just a curious person who wanted to know where the majority of people went in the dead of night, or maybe they were spying for the Commission?

One way to find out this person's intentions was to have him connect with the Predictor. The Predictor was a man who had the ability to read people's minds. Technological advancements allowed him to become a human lie-detector machine. He could sense the person's heartbeat, their blood pressure and even the opening of their sweat glands. Like the lie detectors of old, they weren't fool-proof, but this was as close to finding out the truth as you could get.

Thankfully, the Predictor was on the rebellion's side. His whole family had been killed by the Commission during the rounding up procedure. Many lost their lives during that awful process. All because they wouldn't be treated like cattle and rounded into huge pens like animals while the Commission decided what was to become of them.

During the round up, fights broke out, and people tried to escape. No one wanted to be confined to a certain area. Even if the surrounding land was dying, they still had their freedom, but the might of the better equipped Commission was just too powerful to fight against. Sadly, during the round up process, many hundreds of people lost their lives, just for wanting to be free. Even then, they had no idea just how bad things would become for those who lived in the Sectors, but they wanted to keep what little freedom they did have. If they were to die, it would be by their own actions, not forced by another's hand. This barbaric process cemented a very deep hatred for the Commission in many people's minds, however, there are still those who will listen to the lies, believing what they are told is for their own good. These people could be easily manipulated by the Commission and they wouldn't think twice about blowing the lid on this whole rebellion.

Even after they had been captured, it still wasn't the end of their suffering. Those who tried escaping from their respected areas would be forced to fight for their lives against their own people. The evil Commission guards would throw them into a make-shift ring made from hale bales and make them fight each other, all the while laughing and betting on the outcome. Sadly, after they'd their fun any survivors would be shot. This set the tone early on for this take-over by the Commission. If you didn't fall in line, you would be killed. However, some would still betray their own people if they believed that they might get rewarded for their efforts.

The peeping tom who was caught was in fact a man called Tom, or Thomas to be exact. He was old and his broken body would be of little use in the fight that was to come, but his eyes and ears worked perfectly. Until they could find out what this person's intentions were they had to keep him under lock and key. Thankfully, there were so many people all moving around at the same time that one or two bodies wouldn't be missed in the huge crowds.

The predictor had his work cut out at the moment. Anyone who wished to join the rebellion would be checked to see if their intentions were of an honest nature. Although this wise man resided in Sector four, he was having to test those from other Sectors also. It had taken eight years, but all of the Sectors were now linked by a secret underground tunnel system. Each sector had a tunnel into the next. It was still difficult to navigate across the Sectors themselves, but you can literally hide in plain sight when you are being treated like herded cattle. The guards never took a head count and as long as the size of each group looked to be roughly the same size they paid little attention. The workload stayed the same no matter how many people were there, so as long as they still produced what was expected of them, no one ever worried.

This rebellion was their one and only chance to take down the cruel Commission and save thousands of lives from a most horrific death. After the meeting had disbanded, the people of the rebellion returned to their Sectors. All were now tasked with gathering more people to the cause. Discretion was important and they also had to look out for any who might just be trying to find out information for a more sinister purpose. There are always one or two snakes in the grass, just waiting with a venomous bite.

Unfortunately, there was only one Predictor. Only one person could say with a ninety-nine percent chance that they were telling the truth. Being in Sector four was obviously advantageous for those living in that Sector, but it was much harder to smuggle people across from other Sectors to be tested by this human lie detector. However, all it took was for one Commission sympathiser who believed that revealing this information might help provide them with a better life and once again the rebellion would be in danger.

Firstly, they had to find out the motive of the peeping tom who had been captured. Inside an old broken down wooden hut in the forest the man was brought forward. The Predictor sat upon a seat made from weaved branches. A very intricate object, but also very comfy. Just because you don't have much to work with doesn't mean that the end result has to be rough and ugly. Some of the most beautiful creations have been made from the rawest of materials.

"Bring him forward," said the Predictor, his voice crackly and strained.

The Predictor was blind, so it took others to bring them close to this man who could ironically see everything. After placing his hands on either side of the man's head, his eyes rolled backwards revealing a jet-black covering. "Tell me your secrets. Tell me all you know. Reveal your intentions to me."

The interrogated man's eyes also now turn black as the Predictor delved into his mind.

"Release your burdens onto me. Show me your truth," the Predictor said, as the room began to get colder.

Everyone looked on as electricity sparked between the Predictors hands. Everyone present had been through the same experience, but during this process you had no idea what was happening. You were in a trance-like state as the predictor plucked your darkest thoughts and deepest desires from your mind.

All of a sudden, the Predictor let go of the man's head. "He lies. He lies. His thoughts portray malice. He wants to reveal our secrets."

"No, I want to join. Down with the Commission and their cruel ways," Tom shouted.

"Take him away."

"No, please, I have a wife and child. Please, I want to help. I'm telling the truth. I'm telling the TRUTH!" he continued to scream as he was taken away.

Sadly, this man would now have to be silenced. No one wanted to slay one of their own people, but taking a few lives to save thousands more, was a price that they were willing to pay. The rebellion was the most important thing now. This man's dishonest actions had put everyone's guard up. However, they still needed to unite the Sectors. Without the strength provided by the people, they stood no chance against the Commission.

Even if Luna managed to take control of the High Commissioner's blood-boiling-brutes, it still wouldn't be enough to fight back against the army of highly trained soldiers who all had access to high-tech weaponry. They were a force to be reckoned with, and although the A.I altered animals were extremely deadly, they could still be killed by these weapons. The rebellion needed the numbers as well as the rest. Only together as one could they hope to take down the oppressive organisation.

The head of this organisation who believed that he had the Wild Whisperer in his grasp, couldn't be happier. All he needed now was to replace the lost Thorium and blast off from this planet, leaving thousands of people to their deaths. The High Commissioner had decided to stay for one more Predator Pit competition. It would be the last time his bone-crushing-beasts would get to kill, before they were loaded on the spacecraft to make the journey to Kepler-186F.

Another little leaving present he had planned for the people living in the Sectors, might just play into the hands of the rebellion. The High Commissioner planned to invite one-hundred people from the Sectors into the Inner Sanctum to witness the final Predator Pit competition. They would be graciously treated and have the chance to mingle with the higher ups in society. They would get to see what all of their hard work and sacrifice had been for. The life that they could expect when they reached Kepler186-F.

However, after they had been treated to a more luxurious lifestyle, they would be locked inside the Pit and set upon by the High Commissioner's Zoo full of cruel creatures. Not happy with the punishment that these people had suffered for years, he wanted one last massacre to say goodbye to people who had been treated like slaves for so long. His own gruesome desires for more death and dismemberment, however, could be the opening the rebellion were hoping for.

His plan was to have a mass slaughter. He wanted his precious predators so drunk on flesh and blood, that they were already hungry for the kill when they arrived at the new planet. He didn't want to give the people already living there the time to get a defensive strategy in place. He would roll through like a hurricane and after one almighty battle he planned to be standing at the top of the pile. His new heart had given him the strength of ten men and a lifespan of at least another one-hundred years. More than enough time to become the all-powerful leader of a whole planet, and with technological advancements continuing to improve, he hoped that he would actually be able to live forever!

Unfortunately, those living in the Sectors have already suffered so much. Their lives of pain and percussion would end in a most horrible death. Their bodies would blister and burn, one last blistering-hot knife to their hearts. A final farewell from the cruel Commission.

CHAPTER TWENTY-FOUR

Titanium Teeth

IT WAS THE TIME IN the High Commissioner's Zoo that everyone who worked there hated. It was the monthly teeth sharpening session. Sadly for these enhanced creatures, he wasn't happy with the already sharp, flesh-tearing, bone-crunching teeth that they had been born with. No, he wanted teeth so sharp, so surgical that they could almost perform an operation on their victims.

After the introduction of the shield suits which gave the victims at least half a chance in the two deadly competitions, it never quite felt the same. Less limbs were removed and the bites caused less damage. Of course, after many bites and swipes the result would still be the same, but it had lost the gruesome-gore that the High Commissioner relished. Blood never splattered and ran down the walls like it did before, most would bleed out slowly now, just trickling from their wounds rather than squirting out all over the place.

He wanted to bring back the dismemberment and have torn off body parts flying across the Predator Pit. There was nothing more satisfying than watching a severed head smash into the sleek glass side, while still showing the horrifying expression upon their faces, long after it had been detached from their bodies. If you had enough money you could buy souvenirs from the Tourneys and display them in your house like taxidermy animals. Mounted upon a plaque to forever encapsulate the moment when life drained from the victims eyes. Yes there was more of a competition now, but now the violence had been slightly muted. A less gory tone had been set which didn't please the hardcore viewers, or indeed the High Commissioner himself.

He tried to push for the removal of the shield suits, but the high rollers wouldn't go for it. The only other way to bring back the bloody violence that he loved was to enhance the creature's teeth. All of which were now made from Titanium. Upper and lower jaws formed in one piece like a person's dentures. However, these new metal-mashing-munchers were fixed with something a bit stronger than Fixodent. Huge bolts attached to the creature's bodies made sure they never came loose. Even though flesh and bone was no match for these Titanium teeth, they did become slightly dull over time. To keep them in tip-top, flesh-tearing, skin-stripping shape, they were sharpened once a month. Machines would do the majority of the sharpening, but to get that super fine slicing edge there was nothing better than the skill of a sword sharpener.

Swords, knives, spears, and bows and arrows had become the tools of choice for those who survived the rising tides. They needed to hunt to survive, so a sharp weapon was needed, not only to kill, but to kill with one strike. No one wanted to cause the animals more pain than was necessary. Blades also had to have a very fine-slicing-edge to be able to carve up the animal when it had been captured. Anna used to work as one of these specialist teeth-taperers, but after her accident during pregnancy, she could no longer produce the power required to grind the teeth to paper-slicing-perfection. Thankfully, her skills with a knife could be utilised elsewhere.

Like many who don't like to visit the dentist, the animals would have to be sedated to perform this extremely dangerous task. Many had lost hands and even whole arms after the sedation had worn off and the beast realised what was occurring. This, however, made his prized animals drowsy and they lost a little bit of their aggressive nature after having been put under on multiple occasions. The High Commissioner's use of pain to control the animals during this task was no good. They were already receiving enough torment from the process, sparks flew in all directions and the heat generated would scold the skin, meaning that even more pain just enraged the animal further, making the task impossible. However, now he had the Wild Whisperer, she could tame the beast during the procedure, saving his animals from having to be sedated. This would save time and ensure that his bloodthirsty beasts stayed as deadly as they did before.

The believed Wild Whisperer was at present attached to so many machines that she wouldn't be able to help on this occasion, which was a relief for the real Wild Whisperer because if this false patsy was found out, the hunt would be back on to find the real creature communicator.

The real Wild Whisperer was still trying to get over her friend's sacrifice. Worse still, now her parents had been taken. Luna knew of only one reason why they would transport Bella's parents into the Inner Sanctum, and that was to use them as leverage to get Bella to do what they required of her. This did give Luna some comfort, knowing that her best friend must still be alive, but it still stung her heart like a thousand bee-stings every time she pictured her sad face being carried away by the guards. However, this was no time to be weak. Luna knew what would become of so many more poor souls if they allowed the Commission to continue their cruel ways. They had to stand united and strong if they were to have any chance of taking down this oppressive organisation and save her people from certain death. She wouldn't let her friend's sacrifice be in vain. Those responsible would pay with their lives.

Word had now reached the rebellion that they had until the Predator Pit competition to get their act together. After that the Commission would take their leave from this planet and leave thousands of people in the Sectors to die under the blistering-hot sun's rays. That's if they weren't swept away by the rising sea level first which everyone in the Sectors could see was slowly encroaching on their land. Once the land had been swallowed up by the sea, there would be nothing left. The seas no longer provided any sustenance and without land for animals to graze upon, the people would eventually die of starvation, that's if they survived long enough for that to happen. Either way a slow, painful, and agonising death awaited thousands of people once the Commission left. A few small boats had been made and hidden from the Commission spying eyes, but they would only be able to carry a few people, and this would only serve to prolong the agony. There was nowhere else to run; this was the last of the planet's dry land.

This sped up timeline had many worried that they wouldn't be able to get everything in place in time. Only one segment of this operation had to fail to see the whole rebellion fall apart at the seams. The decision had been taken to hold a meeting. It was time that everyone living in the Sectors knew about the Commission's plan to leave them all to suffer a terrible fate. They needed extra people to help make weapons for the attack, but in doing so they risked an uprising from the disgruntled Sectors that would see all their planning and effort be wasted.

These people had to hold onto their anger until the time was right, but when most found out that all of their sacrifice, all of their hard work, and all of the pain and suffering they had endured for many years now would all be for nothing. The Commission had used them and they would be discarded like rubbish. Just a used commodity that no longer has a purpose. To say that their blood would be boiling would be a massive understatement, many would whistle like boiling kettles through gritted teeth when they found out about this evil act.

No one liked having to bow down to the Commission and being treated like slaves. Many had lost their whole families to the High Commissioner's totally terrifying and utterly traumatic Tourneys. However, they all believed they were all working towards a better future, one where they would once again be treated as human beings. A new life on a distant planet where they could rebuild their shattered lives and start again. Gain back the respect that had been stripped from them and once again walk around with their heads held high.

To find out that all of this pain, suffering, torment and torture was for nothing, would be more agonising than losing your life in one of the Tourneys. At least they had a chance, even though the odds were disgustingly stacked in the Commission's favour, but this act would see them discarded like vermin, left to die a most excruciating death where no matter how hard they tried the outcome would still be the same. How could they do this to so many people? Especially when it has been their hard work that has made it all possible. To say these people would be angry would be a huge understatement, but a fiery and flared response would only see them lose their lives quicker. The Commission still held all of the power, and if they so wished they could treat the people living in the Sectors to a prequel to how their lives would end.

If the High Commissioner believed that there was any threat towards his plan to leave this planet, he would stamp it out before it became a real possibility. As enraged as the people living in the Sectors would become and rightly so, they had to keep a cool head. They had to play along with this sick charade, all the while knowing what would become of them if they never took a stand.

One person who was pivotal to this whole rebellious plan was far from ready to fight. She had just lost her best friend and the pain of this still weighed heavy on her mind.

"Luna, you must eat something. You need to keep up your strength. You will have to face the Rabbit Run at some point, and the sooner the better. We need to have your place firmly fixed for the Predator Pit. There is no way that the High Commissioner will leave this planet, knowing that another woman has made it to the main event. The sooner you triumph over the Rabbit Run, will ensure that he stays to see it through. They have everything they need to leave this planet now and we cannot risk them leaving any earlier. He will not be in the least bit happy that this has occurred again. His own hatred will ensure that he remains until the end."

Luna rolled over and faced the wall. Anna hated the pressure that had been placed upon her daughter's shoulders. She hoped more than anything that she wouldn't be the fabled hero that everyone had been waiting for, but if they were going to save themselves along with thousands of others, it was only Luna who could join up all of the dots. The One Beast's Eye wouldn't have chosen her if she wasn't strong enough, but this gave Anna little comfort, still knowing what lengths her daughter would have to go to.

For now, she would give her the time she needed to come to terms with the loss of her friend, but with the timeline set there was so much that had to be done. The non-stop regime that was forced upon them, meant that every single second counted. Time was now as much an enemy to the rebellion as the Commission itself. Only united could they hope to pull off this uprising and save the lives of thousands of people. However, would cool, calm and collective be the mood when the full truth had been revealed?

While Luna tried to find the strength she required to bring thousands of people together as one. Word of the rebellion was slowly spreading throughout the Sectors. Thankfully, not everyone had to go in front of the Predictor. These people had lived, worked and watched loved ones die side by side, so most had a pretty good understanding of that person's disposition. The majority of those living in the Sectors wanted nothing more than a chance to fight back against the Commission. Some weren't even worried about the outcome, just to strike a few fatal blows at their oppressors would see these people smiling from ear to ear as they went to their graves.

There were others, however, who wanted the same, but they had been so dragged down, so destroyed mentally and physically by the Commission that they didn't have any fight left in them. They obviously backed the rebellion, but they would just be supporting bystanders, cheering from the side lines as they watched their favourite team go into battle.

Still there were a few who, even after all the torment and torture that the Commission had put them through, would still believe in their lies. They wouldn't join the fight, but worse was that they could inform the Commission of any planned rebellion against them, in the hope of gaining reward, or a better life for themselves. Sadly, the only reward that they would receive would be a slow and agonising death. Turned to charred remains by the blistering-hot sun's rays.

CHAPTER TWENTY-FIVE

Severed Head Show

REPRESENTATIVES FROM every Sector came together to hear the rebellion's plan. "Thank you all for joining us. I know the trouble that you have endured to even be here. However, listen when I say that the pain we have all suffered, the sacrifices we have made, are all for nothing. The Commission plans to leave us to die on this planet. They will blast-off to pastures new, while we are left to a fiery fate. Once the satellite shield has been removed there will be no hiding from the scorching sun. We will be burnt to a crisp, the temperature outside has now reached a scorching seventy degrees. We will suffer blistering skin, extreme heat stroke and dehydration. Our bodies will suffer like never before and the Commission will look down upon us as they always have, laughing as we die. We are the ones who have made this journey possible. It is our hard work that has mined the Thorium fuel required to make this space expedition possible, but our seats have not been booked on this life-saving flight......... If we are going to save ourselves from a terrible fate, we must join together and fight. The Commission plans on leaving after the Predator Pit competition. A cruel contest that has claimed so many lives. A cruel contest that we have all endured for far too long. We must fight if we are going to take down this oppressive organisation, so we can finally free ourselves and our families from certain death," said the Elder from Sector four.

"Why would they do that to us now? The Commission has never been more generous," asked a sceptical person from the crowd.

"They told us that we are all in this together. Why would they leave us? Who would work for them if not us?"

"How do we know what you say is true? Have you got any evidence?"

"Do you not understand? You want evidence? Here's your evidence. They treat us like slaves, they control everything we do, and they will discard us as easily as taking out the trash. We have lived in fear for so long. Done everything that has been asked of us, and still they plan to leave us all to die. The only way that we can save our people, is if we are united. We have a plan, but it relies on everyone working together. Take this message back to your Sectors and convince them that there is no other way."

"What sort of plan? How can we take down such a powerful organisation? They have high-tech weaponry and what do we have sticks and stones? Not to mention the High Commissioner's Zoo full of blood-thirsty-beasts."

"We have a way to take back some control. Please, I can't say any more. There are still those who spy for the Commission. Only tell those who you know you can trust. We have people on the inside who are willing to help us, but unless we unite as one, we can never hope to succeed......... I do not say that this plan is foolproof and I don't say that there are issues that still have to be resolved. However, this will be our only chance to save ourselves. We must unite, we must fight, we must stay strong, it's the only way that we will survive. Please keep tempers in check. This news is sure to make many extremely irate, but if we show our hand too early, it will all have been for nothing. The Commission wants us dead, it's that plain and simple. They have already taken so much from us, let's not allow them to put the final nails in our coffins."

Cheers came from those who were on board, but many still believed that following the rules was the only way that they would be saved. The rebellion knew that they needed proof of the Commission's treachery. The word of a few wouldn't be enough to convince everyone living in the Sectors, and unless they were all fighting as one, the job just wouldn't get done. In the coming days, every Sector tried to recruit as many people as possible to join the rebellion. Some, however, wouldn't listen to a word of it. Unless they had hard evidence of the Commission's actions, they wouldn't come on-board.

The revelation about the Wild Whisperer was being kept under wraps. Until they could trust everyone with this information, it would stay concealed. Especially the information about who this fabled saviour's identity was. The Wild Whisperer was an integral part in this planned rebellion and they had to keep their identity hidden for as long as possible. Without this person, they wouldn't have the animal help they so desperately needed for this plan to succeed. With Luna still in a world of suffering, it would be up to Anna to obtain concrete evidence of the Commission's plan. She had to speak with Lance as soon as possible.

In all of the excitement everyone had almost forgotten about the up-coming Rabbit Run. This did, however, allow Anna her chance to communicate with Lance. The slaughterhouse always stepped up production the closer it got to the Tourneys, especially the Predator Pit which saw mountains of food being prepared for the event. Once again the mincing machine helped Anna to conceal her conversation with Lance.

"Many in the Sectors are willing to join our fight, but some do not believe what the Commission has planned is true. We need evidence."

"How can I get the evidence needed? I don't have that kind of access."

"You need to speak to Charlie, he is the only one who may be able to get such information."

"Come on lady, how long does it take to mince some meat?" shouted a guard, getting suspicious of the time being taken.

It was now up to Lance to contact Charlie, so they could hopefully get the proof they required. Charlie was at present trying to make sure that his other activities weren't found out. He had doctored the camera footage from the last predator Pit to hide Luna's actions, and he was also responsible for the explosion that destroyed precious Thorium. His actions were to give the rebellion more time. He knew that heads would roll for this mistake, but he never imagined they would literally roll. Sadly, two people lost their heads along with their lives. This was never what Charlie expected to happen, he knew they would be punished in some way, however, he never believed that the High Commissioner would go as far as he did. Especially towards those living inside the Inner Sanctum! Although Charlie had the blood of two people on his hands, the Commission has killed hundreds of people and would kill thousands more if they weren't stopped.

It was while Charlie was trying to access the information the sceptical people of the Sector needed to see, that the High Commissioner approached. "Charlie, I hope to find that you are working hard. Did you notice anything wrong with the Sector footage that I asked for?"

"No sir, why was there a problem with it?" Charlie replied as his temperature began rising.

"Not that I'm sure of. Did you have time to view the footage?"

"No sir, you said you needed it ASAP, so I never had time to look through it," Charlie said as beads of sweat began forming on his forehead.

"Well, I want you to go through it with a fine tooth comb. Look for anything out of the ordinary. I'm still not totally convinced."

"Yes sir, right away sir."

"Oh, by the way, did you ask to gain access to the Zoo the other day?"

"UMM, yes sir," Charlie paused, trying to think of a suitable excuse for his actions. "I was looking to see if any of the animals came back differently from that visit to the Sectors. I wanted to see if I could gain any more information about what had occurred sir."

"What a good idea, I don't know why I never thought of it. To save time, use the computer in my office so that none of the footage gets accidentally deleted. The password is Hunter Killer. I'm sure that I'm missing something. I just don't know what. I can trust you, can't I Charlie?"

"Yes sir, of course sir," Charlie said as a drop of sweat fell from his face.

"Sadly, I believe that there are some who cannot be trusted. I'm sure something is going on, I'm just not sure what is yet... Very well, carry on."

"Yes sir," Charlie's voice sang with relief.

Charlie was trying to figure out how he could sneak in and obtain access to the High Commissioner computer and now he had just given him permission. Charlie's initial elation to this piece of good fortune, quickly turned to suspicion. Was the High Commissioner trying to set him up and catch him out? Did he know what was happening? Was he baiting the trap to see who bites?

Regardless of what might occur, Charlie knew that he had to get this information. The Sectors had to be united. Only when they realised that the Commission's plan to leave them all to die was in fact true, would they join in the rebellion. Time was ticking and with only nine months to get everything organised, one missed step in the plan could see it all fall to pieces. Deciding to strike while the iron was hot. Even if this was some kind of trap. If he could get the information he needed to prove the Commission's plan to the Sectors, he would be happy to lose his life shortly after.

No one was usually allowed in the High Commissioner office, which did fill Charlie with dread as he pushed open the door. As with everything that the High Commissioner has, his office was a huge space. Totally oversized for its purpose. This greedy man had a desk that was five times the size of the beds on which the people in the Sectors slept. This lavish room was adorned with paintings and other arty-type sculptures. Charlie decided that because this may be his one and only time that he would be allowed in this office, he was going to make the most of it. Sadly, alcohol of any kind was forbidden in the Sectors. Obviously some managed to make a kind of homebrew, but this never had the velvety smoothness of a one-hundred-year old whisky as it travelled down your throat, and the High Commissioner obviously had the best of the best.

A very fancy drinks cabinet that was stocked with all manner of alcoholic beverages, was illuminated as soon as he touched the golden handles. Whiskey, Vodka, Gin, and all manner of other fancy drinks, many of which Charlie had never heard of before. Charlie wasn't the biggest of drinkers before the world fell into chaos, but when something is forbidden you tend to crave it that much more.

"Just a little tipple, no one will notice," he said, as he unscrewed the top.

Even the sound of the liquid glugging as it was poured into the glass was like music to his ears. It sounded like releasing freedom. The glass was so finely cut that his fingers sunk into the elaborate pattern that was carved upon it. After raising the glass to his nose to smell the wonderful aroma, he nearly got drunk off the fumes alone. The spicy, wooden flavour was like smelling salts, snapping his eyes wide open. After a quick check behind him, he raised the glass to his mouth and took a sip. As the smooth liquid ran down his throat, his eyes were taken to the top of the fancy drinks station. The shock of what he saw next caused him to drop the glass.

At the top of this cocktail cabinet were rows of glass boxes all highly illuminated with different coloured glows. It wasn't the bright, vibrant colours that shocked him, but what was inside. In each glass box was a head, a HUMAN HEAD! And they were all displaying a look of shock and horror. Each head had been shaved and shined up like a bowling ball. Some were men and some were women, but it was hard to decipher the sex of some. All of them had names and dates beneath them and Charlie quickly figured out that many were past Predator Pit winners. If that wasn't cruel enough, a big illuminated button had emerged from the base of the cabinet which said play. Charlie hesitated to press the button, but he was curious to know what it did.

"Press it. No, don't press it. Come on Charlie."

Deciding to press the button, he had no idea what would happen, but he secretly believed that it wasn't going to be good. After pressing the button, he watched as the heads became animated. Some of their eyes popped out on poles and rotated around. Some mouths opened so wide that the head was almost split in two. Others were pulled apart in sections displaying the many different parts that make up the human head. Totally disgusted at what he was seeing, Charlie pressed the button again which stopped the horrific severed-head-show. The display he'd just witnessed certainly wasn't worth the tiny sip of whiskey he had. Quickly cleaning up the mess, he was thankful that the glass never shattered into millions of little pieces. Why did he have to be so curious?

After putting everything back in order, he went to the computer to try and find information about the journey to Kepler-186F. He needed to show what the Commission had planned for those living in the Sectors. Looking through the manifests he could clearly see that there was more than enough space to take everyone who was still left on this planet, but as he found lists of the different areas and the people's names who would be in them, he saw that none of the Sectors were listed.

Deciding to see who and how many would get to travel in the High Commissioner's exclusive section of this huge craft, he was shocked when he read his own name. His space booked on this life-saving journey. There it was in black and white, *Charlie Watts.* He was on the High Commissioner's list of very few who would be travelling with him. This area alone could have carried fifty times the amount of people it was going to and still very comfortably, however, the High Commissioner would travel in style. He literally had almost half of this huge craft to himself and very few others.

This revelation gave Charlie a bit of a dilemma. He assumed that he would be cast aside just like everyone else from the Sectors, but he had a place at the high table, so to speak. Should he be selfish and take this opportunity to better his own life? He no longer had any family left in the Sectors and knowing that he was so highly thought of gave him a more positive outlook. It's always better to be inside the Lion's den, affiliated with the Lions, rather than being thrown to them as food. However, thousands of people would die, if he failed to pass on this information, but in a world where survival was the only outcome that everyone was striving for, could Charlie jeopardise his own safety and prospects going forward?

He'd tasted the finer side of life. Ok, he wasn't living as lavish a lifestyle as many in the Inner Sanctum, but he never felt the pain of being hungry. He never felt the extreme heat in summer, or the biting cold in winter. His hands no longer bled from constant hard labour. Now and then he got a bit of cramp in his fingers from all of the typing. He was also respected by many, and he had earned his place in the High Commissioner's exclusive club. Would he be foolish to throw all of that away? Charlie had the information that the rebellion required, but would he still pass that on after realising what he would be sacrificing?

CHAPTER TWENTY-SIX

A nimal Importance

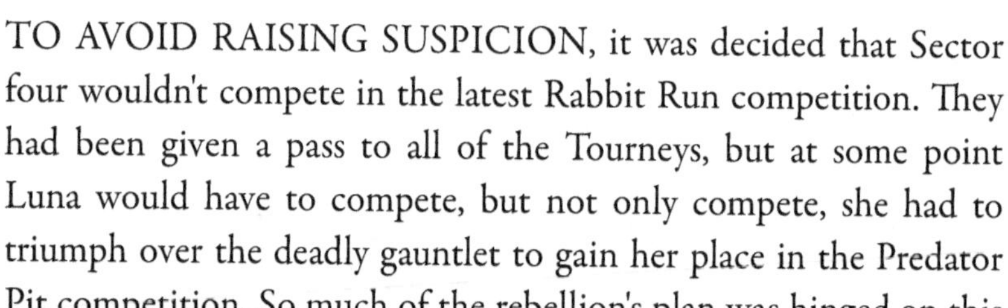

TO AVOID RAISING SUSPICION, it was decided that Sector four wouldn't compete in the latest Rabbit Run competition. They had been given a pass to all of the Tourneys, but at some point Luna would have to compete, but not only compete, she had to triumph over the deadly gauntlet to gain her place in the Predator Pit competition. So much of the rebellion's plan was hinged on this eventuality.

The High Commissioner was a clever man and no one would be foolish enough to compete in a contest where the outcome was more often than not death, if they didn't have to. This action would certainly raise suspicions. They had to wait until it looked as if they needed the supplies that would be given to the Sector if their contestant managed to survive. With everyone working overtime to replace the lost Thorium, any supplies would dwindle a lot faster than usual. The ground was still frozen which meant that the growing of food wouldn't be possible for at least another month or so. All of these factors might just work together to hide Sector four's real reason for entering the Rabbit Run Competition.

Now that there was no longer a choosing ceremony, the people in the Sectors had a little more time to rest until they were called to view what would more than likely be the slaughter of their friends and family members. Seven hopefuls stood on the starting line, all shaking with fear. The extra chill in the air always made the winter

Tourneys much more difficult. The frozen ground and more slippery apparatus made an almost impossible task even harder. The icy structures were a lot deadlier, and cold hands made getting a firm grip much more difficult.

Regardless of the conditions, there was no more time to transverse this obstacle course before the Hunter Killer was released. Luna would also not be allowed to interfere in this contest. For now, she would have to hone her powers with the farm animals. Goats, pigs, Chickens and cows would become her training partners, but would that be enough practice to allow her to command the minds of the High Commissioner's prized predators?

Now that Luna possessed this amazing gift, she wanted nothing more than to help all who had to put their lives on the line to compete in the Tourneys. She believed that she could get into the Hunter Killer's mind and stop the beast from harming the contestants, but that would just shed more unwanted attention upon them. They had to be smart, but while more of their people were dying, it was an extremely hard pill to swallow.

The seven hopefuls raced off the starting line, all hoping to be saved from the jaws of death. Within seconds the first person lost their lives. After slipping from the A-frame, they fell and broke their necks. The resounding crunch that was heard almost toppled two more of the slippery apparatus. As the six remaining people made their way to the next obstacle, they were pleasantly surprised when the usually very unstable surface was made a lot sturdier by the ice that had formed around the connecting points. Thankfully, the ice had melted from the lattice rope structure and they all flew across with ease.

The rope swing was next, and the ice that had built up around the connections to the ropes limited the swinging motion. They had to hold on longer and forcefully swing their bodies further to break the icy obstruction that was stopping a free swinging motion. Any time that had been gained from the last obstacle was now gone as they all struggled to get the frozen ropes to move. The extra gripping time needed was just too much for some and two more found themselves plummeting to their deaths. That left only four contestants. Could any of them make it all the way, or would the Rabbit Run claim all of their lives?

The unmistakable roar of the Hunter Killer let the remaining hopefuls know that they were now being hunted. Screams echoed out from the tunnels soon after when two more were unlucky enough to find the exits blocked. As they made their way to the monkey bars, the contestant from Sector six couldn't help but look behind. He wanted to see where the Hunter Killer was and he was left totally shocked when it burst through the end of a tunnel still carrying someone's arms in its mouth. A loud roar reverberated outwards, stopping the other contestant in his tracks. The Hunter Killer spat out the arm he'd been chewing on and locked eyes on the last two victims.

Tired arms and ice-cold bars made the monkey bar transverse extremely difficult. After only two rungs another victim fell, sadly a fate worse than breaking your neck awaited them, a pool full of hungry crocodiles below were waiting to tear them limb from limb. Somehow, the unlucky person had a little bit of luck. He landed at the start of the obstacle right next to the pool's ledge, and all of the snapping-jawed-crocs were at the other end chasing after the other contestant as he swung precariously above. His tired body left him weak, but he clawed at the side of the muddy bank trying to pull his body from the water.

Once the other contestant had finished the monkey bars safe and sound, all of the crocs honed in the man's wailing and splashing legs. The contestant gouged at the muddy surface, each time pulling himself closer to freedom, however, a cloud of hot steamy breath engulfed his head. Slowly raising his gaze he caught sight of two piercing blood-red eyes looking back at him. Before he could blink his mouth was inside the Hunter Killer's huge jaws.

By this time the crocodiles had reached the other end; they just managed to get their teeth into the poor souls' legs before they were devoured by the Hunter Killer.. Both flesh-tearing-fiends now tousled over the man's body, pulling and tearing his body to get their piece of the meaty treat. The screams were harrowing, not to mention the sound of bones breaking and flesh tearing as they slowly tore this person apart. A loud popping noise saw the man's body split in two halves, the Hunter Killer claimed the man's head and torso and the crocs had its feet and legs.

The last hopeful looked back with sadness, he stood there mourning for a second before he realised that his own life was still on the line. His shaky legs stepped onto the balance beam, grasping hold of his knees, he tried to gain some stability. "Clam down, stop shaking. Please!" he pleaded with his body.

Heavy breathing produced huge plumes of steam as his lungs released each almighty breath. A slow and steady walk was needed on this apparatus, but with a hungry beast on your tail this wasn't an option. The obstacle shifted violently when the Hunter Killer pounced onto it. The extra weight saw it undulate like a ship on stormy seas. The beast slowly approached, moving the beam from side to side like he was playing with his food, just moving the peas around the plate, making sure there was enough space for the meaty treat he was about to receive.

As the creature closed in, the last hopeful knew that he wasn't going to make it. Looking at the huge salivating jaws that would soon be feasting upon his body, he took the decision to jump to his death rather than being torn apart by this bone-chilling-beast. Leaping from the beam his body was impaled upon a cluster of shiny poles all protruding from the ground in different directions. His body now looked like a pin cushion, and was full of more holes than a strainer.

As blood poured from his body, its lubricating effect on the poles saw his body slip further down the sleek, shiny surface, taking it clear from the hell-cats' jaws. This was in no way a painless death, but it was probably a lot less painful than if the Hunter Killer got hold of him. Seeing as he would be the last victim, the Hunter Killer would have more time to torment and torture this poor soul.

The Hunter Killer was declined a meal, but the Rabbit Run had claimed all seven contestants. Many, however, noticed an extra skip in the Hunter Killer's step. It seemed faster and more agile than before. It looks like even the KING OF THE HUNT could be enhanced and that's exactly what the High Commissioner did. This already deadly beast which contained the attributes of three apex predators was seemingly not enough for one man and he sought to make it even deadlier. It now possessed extra long retractable claws. These extended like a set of kitchen knives from its paws, now affording it the pleasure of slicing its victims clean in half with one swipe if it so pleased. It also had a set of shiny metal horns protruding from its head. They looked like bull's horns, but longer. These protruding poles could now impale any fleeing victim. They were not really made to kill, although many wouldn't live long after being impaled upon the prominent head adornments. However, the purpose was to disable his future meals, giving it more time to enjoy his food. These new additions to the Hunter Killer had everyone worried, none more so than Anna. This was a whole new beast and she worried about her daughter's chances when she faced the already gruelling gauntlet.

Luna was being kept away from viewing the deaths of others who had to compete in the Tourneys. Her fragile state wasn't equipped to see any more slaying of her Sector family. Luna was key to the rebellion's plan, she couldn't be overshadowed with any more unnecessary pain, anger or fear. Her mind had to be clear, she had to be fully focused on the task in hand. Her training also had to be performed discreetly. If the guards saw the farm animals all marching around in a straight line, or performing tricks, she was sure to be found out. In the dead of night she did manage to communicate with the birds. She envied them so much for their ability to just fly away from all of the suffering, however, they were also stuck on this dying planet. There were still some mountains that were above sea level, but there was no sanctuary to be found on these desolate positions. Some used to contain life, but without the satellite shield, no animal or human would be able to survive there. With no sanctuary to be found at sea either there was only one way off this planet and that was via the spacecraft.

Luna knew she had to find her inner strength. She had to find a passionate will to survive. She was needed, not just for the thousands of people, but also the animals. Ever since the One Beast's Eye touched her skin, she could feel their pain. They also wanted to live and she believed that without them they wouldn't be able to survive when they reached the new planet. No one knew what kind of ecosystem was on Kepler-186F. They knew that it could support human life, because there was fresh water there, but without insects and animals the humans didn't possess everything they needed to survive. She hoped that the first travellers to this new planet would have had the foresight to realise this fact, but with many just wanting to escape what they knew was an imminent death sentence, certain important commodities may have been forgotten. In the blind panic to flee did they remember the most important assets of all? THE ANIMALS!

For all anyone knew the first people to set foot upon this Earth-like planet could already be dead. Human beings have a tendency to jump first and ask questions later, however, without animals they would all die of starvation. This revelation had opened Luna's eyes. Everyone was so worried about saving their own arses that many wouldn't have given the animals a second thought. Even she hadn't really thought about this eventuality. She was just a child and although everyone knows this fact in the back of their minds. A selfish nature to survive could see them leap from one dying planet to another.

The animals were so important to build a strong and sustainable ecosystem. Without them, they just as well stay where they are. There would be no new life without these incredible creatures. They were every bit, if not more important than human beings. Let's be fair, without the greedy human-race, planet Earth would still be a habitable planet. It was the humans who destroyed this planet, not the animals. Maybe it was best that the human-greed-disease didn't make it to this new untouched planet. They were sure to repeat the failing of the past. Does anyone really learn from their mistakes, or are we all pre-programmed to be this way?

Left alone the animals could make a thriving ecosystem, the planet would be more fruitful than ever. Maybe even Earth could have survived if the humans were removed from the equation sooner? Luna was now questioning whether it was worth saving the human race? It would only take one greedy person to start the ball of death and destruction rolling again. She knew that her people had proved that they could live and survive beside the animals. Both living off the land and helping one another to flourish and endure. Both species were needed to make any new planet a viable, habitable home.

One thing that Luna knew for sure was that the High Commissioner and the vast majority of those living in the Inner Sanctum didn't deserve to get another chance. Their selfish nature would just repeat the failings of the past. Greed would see them pillage and plunder this new planet as they did with Earth, and once again they would slowly kill off this new sanctuary.

Her goal was to save the people, but now she realised that she had to save the animals as well. Only together could they hope to make a new life on a distant planet. The stakes have been raised again, this was about so much more than just the human race. Luna was the only one who could bring animals and humans together. She held the power of a new life for so many in her hands, but would this extra pressure help stoke the fire inside, or would it be too much to comprehend?

CHAPTER TWENTY-SEVEN

Hard Decisions

AS THE DAYS, WEEKS, and months continued, more suppressed souls lost their lives to the cruel Commission. The Lost Thorium had been replaced, but greed saw the strict regime continue. Due to the extra long, hard work forced upon them, no one had managed to triumph over the Rabbit Run. It was halfway through the year and soon Luna would have to face the contest. Her training of a different kind had been improving, but there was still no telling if she could take control of the High Commissioner's altered animals. Thankfully, everyone in her Sector decided to pick up her share of the workload so she could train for the Rabbit Run.

Luna's previous confidence in triumphing over this competition had been significantly reduced. Originally she only had her mother and herself to worry about, but now she held the fate of thousands of people along with hundreds of animals, all relying on her to save them from certain death.

The Sectors had been experiencing a lot more freedom of late. There were fewer guards and less announcements from the Commission. It had been ten years since they felt this kind of free rein to wander without the feeling of judgemental eyes, or the barrel of a gun pointed in their direction. The reason for this lack of supervision was because the Commission was getting the spacecraft prepped and ready for departure. Many supplies had to be loaded and the finishing testing and preparation were being carried out.

Once the last Predator Pit competition was over and he had the pleasure of watching his blood-boiling-brutes tearing apart one-hundred unlucky Sectorites, they would be setting off on the journey to their new home. The High Commissioner, his precious predators and the inhabitants of the Inner Sanctum would all be aboard this life-saving vessel. Sadly, they would be leaving thousands of people living in the Sectors to die an extremely painful death. Once the satellite shield had been removed, their skin would blister and burn under the sun's incandescent heat. There would be no escaping the blistering-hot, radioactive rays coming from the scolding sun. There would be no hiding, no way to escape. All would die an awful, agonising death.

If by some amazing stroke of luck they managed to shield themselves from the death-star in the sky. It would only give them the shortest of reprieves before the sea level rose and swallowed up the last of the dry land. This kind of realisation would be too much for a seasoned adult to comprehend, let alone a young girl of only sixteen-years old. Anna could see the pressure building upon her daughter's shoulders. She was literally weighed down with the huge task that had been placed upon her. She was also having to deal with the pain and suffering of countless animals on top of everything else.

"Luna, are you ok my sweet child? I can see the strain that this has put upon you. You can still refuse to compete. We will make the rest of our time on this planet as enjoyable as possible. Before your father died he made a raft. We were all going to sail away and let the sea decide our fate, at least then it would be on our own terms! Unfortunately, after he won the Rabbit Run we believed that he really did have a chance at surviving the Predator Pit. Sadly, that was not to be.............. Come away with me, we will sleep under the stars. I have been saving some food for us to take and we will once again have our freedom. Away from the Commission's rule. Far away from all of this suffering. Who knows, we might even find another piece of land."

Luna gave her mother that don't be silly look. "Mum, I love you so much and the thought of sailing away with you sounds, well .... Just about perfect. I can't........ I just can't leave these people to die without trying. I have been given these powers for a reason. We must save our people, or at least die trying. I will not give up on everyone while we still have a chance."

"But, what if you fail? We have already lost so much. I just couldn't bear to see you lose your life. Please, Luna, let's just leave this all behind us," Anna said, sobbing.

"Oh mum, come here," Luna said, embracing her mother, "We have to fight! We have to take back control of our lives. We have to do it for everyone who has died at the Commission's hands. We have to do it for dad and Baron. I will not let them take any more innocent lives. If we don't try we are going to die anyway...... I would rather die knowing that I did everything I could to survive. Let's make them pay for all the hurt they have caused. They cannot get away with treating us like slaves any more. We must show them that we are more than just rubbish to be tossed aside. We will make them suffer, like we have suffered for so long. It's our time to rise up. It's our time to take the fight to them. We can do this, we can. I just know we can. You have to believe. I need you by my side. I need to know that you are with me all of the way. I need your strength, I can't do this alone. Please mum, please!"

Both women were now sobbing and unable to speak. Anna grabbed Luna's face in her hands. After looking into her big beautiful blue eyes she pulled her close and kissed her on the forehead. "I am with you always, always Luna! I love you, I love you so much."

"I love you too mum."

After this passionate exchange, the two women went for a walk on the beach. Luna could just about remember when they would go to the seaside, build sand-castles and look for shells to make into necklaces, having so much fun. It's where her dad taught her how to swim and how to catch fish and other sea creatures for them to eat. Sadly, the sea's no longer provided this kind of bounty, if they did the vast majority of the people living in the Sectors would have fled long ago. Unfortunately, the rise in temperature and all of the contaminants that were washed into the once blue water had stripped any life-giving qualities that it used to have.

There was nowhere else that these people could go and the Commission knew that. Some had tried, but many returned to the Last-Isle, the only remaining piece of habitable dry land left on the planet. Sadly, when you are totally reliant on something to keep you alive, you can be forced into doing just about anything, even risking your life for the entertainment of others. Unfortunately, this realisation and the promise of better days to come allowed the Commission to treat these people worse than rodents, just pawns in their sick and twisted games. Then to top it all off they would be left to die while their oppressors sailed away to pastures new. This had to stop! If not for her own people, but for all of those who had already made the trip to Kepler-186F. The Commission would infect the planet like a plague, and soon have a whole planet full of people to torment and torture.

With the backing and feeling of strength coming from her mother, Luna was ready to take the fight to the Commission. They had to be punished for their actions. They could no longer treat good people this way. Furthermore, they wouldn't make it off this planet if she had anything to say about it. These cruel people would be the ones who would be left to a coffin-less-cremation, even if they had to suffer the same fate, which would still not be enough suffering for all they had inflicted upon others, but at least their reign of terror would be no more. They could go to their graves knowing that no one else would have to suffer by their hands.

With the main ingredient in the rebellion's recipe for revolution, now fully focused on the task in hand, the word that this person did actually exist was also getting around the other Sectors. Most knew that without this fabled hero they stood no chance against the Commission, but now they knew this person was real they were willing to fight. This gave many the extra kick they needed to get on board. Unfortunately, many still wanted to see proof of the Commission's plan to leave them all to die. Some still couldn't believe that this would be the case. Even after all the Commission has put them through, they still held onto a little thread of hope that even the Commission wouldn't be that cruel.

This vital information had been relatively easy to obtain, especially considering when it had to come from. However, now in the hands of one of the rebellion's own people, this material had yet to make it to the Sectors where it was desperately needed to convince the last few to join in the fight. Charlie Watts was the person who had this important information in his possession. Up until gaining this intelligence, he was strictly on the side of the rebellion. He'd survived the High Commissioner's cruel Tourneys and earned his place inside the Inner Sanctum.

His affiliation into this other world was much easier and better than anyone else's. He was extremely bright and after he was tested he found himself working for the Commission's technology department. Years of having to survive living in the Sectors gave him a greater ingenuity and resilience that many of the Inner Sanctum lacked. Only recently had he been promoted to the head of this department and life for him was pretty good. Still, he hated what the Commission had done and was still doing to the poor people living in the Sectors. He'd suffered at their hands and watched as many loved ones died as a result of this cruelty. Status and belonging, however, were what everyone in the Sectors had been striving for ever since the Commission took over.

Now Charlie had a respected position, a good life. Many who used to look down upon him, now had to rely on him. He was needed, he was accepted and he'd just found out that his seat on the life-saving-shuttle that was leaving this doomed planet was booked. Not only booked, but he was to take this journey with the High Commissioner himself. Only a select few had their seats booked in the same section as this man and he was among them. This made him feel extremely important and highly respected. This was unheard of, someone from the Sectors earning their place alongside this powerful organisation's big-wigs. What more could he expect? How much further could he progress?

Sadly, after being physically defeated and mentally destroyed on a daily basis, any small glimmer of hope for a better life was like a star shining in the night sky to anyone who had suffered this cruel treatment. What Charlie had, however, was like a bright-shining-beacon. So bright you'd go blind if you looked directly at it. A blazing beacon of hope and a better life awaited him if he wanted it, but the fate of thousands of others would be certain death. What was he going to do?

He now held the fate of the rebellion's plan in the palm of his hand. He knew that the High Commissioner wouldn't stop when he reached Kepler186-F. In fact, he expected things to get a lot worse for the people he'd imprison on that planet. The Tourneys would go from a competition with a chance of survival to a straight-up slaughter to any who didn't toe the line. The Commission's cruelty would increase ten-fold, if that was even possible.

Charlie, however, would be on the other side this time. He wouldn't have to live in fear, hoping and praying that he wouldn't be the next one to be chosen to face the torturess Tourneys. He would never feel the pain of bloody hands and a broken body from relentless hard labour. His stomach would never sing that awful, painstakingly-hollow tune again from malnutrition. Who knows, he may even be able to have a family of his own?

This decision was weighing so heavily on his mind that the High Commissioner had seen the change in his behaviour. *"Charlie to the High Commissioner's office,"* came a voice over the tannoy system.

As soon as he heard this announcement, he began sweating profusely, his face went as red as a plump juicy tomato, producing a heat that would melt plastic. What was happening? Had the High Commissioner found out about what he had done? Would he now be made an example of and be thrown to the wolves, quite literally inside the Predator Pit to have his body torn apart?

The walk to the office felt like his final judgement. His actions had ruined everything that he had worked for. Now the thought of losing the life he had was like a knife to the heart. When he entered through the office door, he was actually holding his chest with his hand because the pain he was experiencing felt like this extremely fast pumping organ was about to burst through his ribcage.

"Take a seat Charlie," the High Commissioner said in his mono-tone.

"Umm, yes sir. How can I help?"

'*Calm down Charlie,*' he said to himself, realising that he was acting extremely guilty. '*It might be nothing. No he knows, we are dead meat. We are going to die.*'

"Is everything ok?" Hector asked, seeing Charlie erratic actions.

"No, I mean yes, everything is ok. Umm, you wanted to see me."

"Yes I did. Now that footage I ask you to get, is there anyway that it could have been doctored in some way. After reviewing it again, I noticed a break in the feed. Here, let me show you."

His heart was pounding so hard and fast now that he had to look down to check that it wasn't visible beneath his shirt. '*That's it, he has been found out,*' Charlie thought to himself.

Charlie knew what he would be seeing because he was the one who altered the video to cover up any chance that Luna would be seen.

"Right there. Did you see that," Hector shouted while pointing at the screen?

"Umm, I'm not sure. Can you play it again?"

Charlie could clearly see the time when the video feed changed. Even though he had done a very good job when doctoring the video, he was in a rush and couldn't do it as well as he might have if he had more time.

"You see. Look! Right there."

"Oh yea. Now I can see," Charlie said sheepishly, thinking that at any moment he was going to feel a hand clasped around his neck.

"Someone is responsible for this and I want you to find out who. I want a name by the end of the week. Whoever did this will suffer for their actions. They are obviously trying to cover something up and I want to know what. That will be all. The end of the week Charlie!"

He couldn't get out of the office quickly enough and almost tripped over his own feet. He had just dodged a sharp-tooth-shaped-bullet, but now he would have to throw another person under the bus to save his own skin. It was at that moment that he knew this had to stop. This man created so much fear and foreboding, he commanded so much power, they had to break this cycle of intimidation and violence. He would never stop his tyrannical ways, and many more would suffer as his rise to be the master of it all continued.

Deciding to give the rebellion the information that they required. He, however, now had a huge decision to make. Would he sacrifice another person for his actions, or would he own up and take the punishment that would definitely be coming his way?

CHAPTER TWENTY-EIGHT

Important Steps

NOW WITH THE VITAL information about the Commission's plan to leave all those living in the Sectors behind to die while the people of the Inner Sanctum jetted off to pastures new. The majority of those living in the Sectors were now onboard with the rebellion's plan. There were still some who believed that if they continued to follow the rules and do everything the Commission asks of them, they would still be saved. Thankfully, there were very few of these deluded people, but just any single one of them could jeopardise everything they had worked for. The identity of the Wild Whisperer was still being kept under wraps for now. This information would only be revealed when the time was right. The less people who knew, the better. One loose-lipped conversation could see it all fall down around their ears.

With the majority of resources being pulled to get the spacecraft packed and ready for the trip to Kepler-186F, the sparsely guarded Sectors now had the freedom they required to make weapons, coordinate strategies and get themselves ready for the planned attack. As long as they kept the number of people moving around to the many different jobs roughly the same size, some could be off carrying out the vital steps required for this rebellion. Some would now have to work much harder to pick up the slack of these missing people, but when you know that you are working for a higher purpose, one where you might finally get back the freedom that had been taken away from you, you can usually find the extra motivation required.

Thankfully, the people in Sector four were eating more than usual. They had to deplete their resources to hide any suspicion of them wanting to compete in the Rabbit Run. If you have been given a pass to the Tourneys, it would seem highly incredulous that anyone would want to put their lives on the line if they didn't have to. The only way they could hide this action was to make it seem like they needed the extra supplies received for winning this cruel competition. Hopefully the increased workload would also help to provide a reason for the quickly depleting rations that would usually last a lot longer.

Many still lost their lives in the Rabbit Run due to the Hunter Killer enhanced attributes. It was faster, stronger, more agile and even deadlier than before. This resulted in no one winning this competition so far this year, and this also had the rebellion worried. Luna had to win, it was a pivotal part of the whole plan. Without her, they just as well take their own lives now, because what was to come would be experiencing more pain and suffering than ever before. All hope would be lost. Their days always felt like they were numbered, what with the two deadly competitions and the precarious jobs they had to carry out, but this would be it for sure. They would all die a most horrible death if they didn't make a stand and take back their chance of living.

With fewer guards keeping a close eye on the Sectors, it allowed Luna more chances to hone her animal communication skills. She would have to be so focused and at one with her skills if she was to have any hope of tapping into the minds of the High Commissioner's cruel creations. Pigs, Goats, Chickens and Cows were one thing, but Lions, Tigers, Wolves and Bears were another, especially considering that these already deadly predators had been altered in some way. All had metal teeth and they'd all been changed in colour to make them look even more menacing. He'd also managed to combine different creatures together to make the already deadly beast's even more lethal. The Hunter Killer was a mixture of three meat-eating-monsters, a Lion, a Tiger and to give it that extra speed a Cheetah. This creation was as deadly as it came and no one would have survived five minutes inside the Predator Pit if this was their deadly foe. Five seconds would be an achievement. Fortunately, the Hunter Killer was the serial suppressor who was in pursuit of the unlucky Rabbit Run contestants.

Although the victims would be spared a fight for survival against the Hunter Killer inside the Predator Pit, they could also be unlucky enough to be facing the huge Liger, or a Crocmodo, two savage combinations that fused the blood-thirsty nature of each creature to make an even more murderous monster.

Luna had to triumph over the Rabbit Run if the rebellion was to have any chance of taking down the Commission. Even though Luna was the fabled Wild Whisperer, she would have to face this competition without the help from her creature communicating powers, having to rely upon her own physical abilities. If the High Commissioner had even the slightest notion that his spine-splitting-specimen had been influenced in some way, he would kill all those who were in that competition. Not only that, he would probably open up the satellite shield and cook all those living in the Sectors for good measure. He wouldn't take any chances. Although he believed that he had the Wild Whisperer chained up and subdued, he was still on high alert. This young girl had yet to show him that she was this fabled hero, but while testing continued, the spotlight wasn't shining so brightly upon the Sectors.

It was imperative that Luna survived the Rabbit Run and earned her place to compete in the Predator Pit. Only then would she be able to have access to the High Commissioner's altered animals and turn them against their master. There was so much riding on this plan that if one step was to be compromised in some way, the whole rebellion would be over and death would follow shortly after.

Meanwhile, Charlie was trying to work out who he would name to take the fall for his actions. He didn't want to send another to be torn apart inside the Predator Pit, but he had too. He was still a very vital part of the rebellion's plan and if he owned up to his duplicate behaviour the rebellion would be over. It should have been easy for him to choose someone to die because almost every single person in the had been mean to him, or looked down their noses at him when he first arrived in the Inner Sanctum. However, after sending two men to early graves, his guilty conscience wouldn't let him forget what he had done. Especially as Blake Markson was still so young. With time ticking he would have to make a decision, or risk the fate of thousands more.

It was a beautiful morning when the alarm sounded waking everyone from their slumber. This was the day when Luna would present herself as a contestant in the Rabbit Run competition. The huge elaborate display played out as usual. Everyone was still on tenter-hooks even though they knew who would be facing the deadly gauntlet. As each Sector presented their contestant there were sadness and tears. Many were leaving loved ones behind, but for some it was a slightly easier pill to swallow, because they knew that their sacrifice would help to free their people from the Commission. They would no longer suffer under the tyrannical rule of this company, and hopefully their families would finally be free.

Three Sectors had given the names of who would be running the Rabbit Run and even though Sector four had an exception from competing the High Commissioner always asked the question. "Sector four, Sector four, Sector four. Any takers?" he asked.

"Yes, I would like to compete in this Rabbit Run competition," said a meek voice.

"Well, isn't this a turn up for the books? What is your name child?"

"It's Luna sir."

"Luna, and Luna, why do you want to compete? Your Sector has been given a bye, and I believe that you still have plentiful resources left," the High Commissioner probing tone was worrying.

"I want to save my mother. She is in so much pain, and she has sacrificed so much for me. I can't watch her suffer any more. We both deserve a better life inside the Inner Sanctum and I plan on making that happen."

"Well, that's what we like to hear. Someone who wants to strive for a better life. I love your confidence young one, and we will all look forward to seeing you compete. Let's all give Luna a round of applause."

Thankfully, the High Commissioner knew of Anna's problems and happily brought the story that Luna was selling. To be fair, he didn't believe that this young girl stood any chance in the competition, but she would help to make up the numbers. Not one single person had survived the Rabbit Run so far this year and the High Commissioner was hoping for a very special Predator Pit seeing as it was to be the last one of this planet.

He could just force eight people to compete in this deadly competition as he has done in the past, but the people never really had that fiery-feisty-fight in them. Those who had triumphed over the Rabbit Run were a lot more competitive. They held more hope in their hearts and a greater thirst to win. Unfortunately, his hyped up Hunter Killer had left no one alive. He couldn't change the Hunter Killer now and he didn't want to. This beast would be key to taking over the Planet Kepler186-F. This was his most loyal creation and he was even certain that the Wild Whisperer wouldn't be able to break that bond.

To hopefully gain some thirsty for the challenge competitors to face the Predator Pit, he decided to have double the contestants for the rest of the competitions. That way hopefully there would be more chance of them winning, in turn providing a better contestant for his final Tourney on this planet. He wanted this last contest to be so spectacular, so spine-tingling that it would be remembered forever. Sadly, any who did manage to survive the Predator Pit wouldn't get the life that they were hoping for. The spacecraft was full and all who triumphed would be left to die with thousands of others.

With sixteen contestants now facing each Rabbit Run, it would be much easier for Luna to survive. There were some who had promised to give their lives for hers to make sure she had the best chance of winning. Almost everyone now realised that they were already dead unless this child completed the first part of the rebellion's plan. Mother's, father's, son's and daughter's were all willing to sacrifice themselves to provide their loved ones with a chance at a better life. The die had been cast, and now everything was resting on this competition. Luna was a key part in the rebellion's plan and now all eyes were firmly fixed in her direction!

CHAPTER TWENTY-NINE

M ore Sacrifices

SIXTEEN SCARED INDIVIDUALS now stood facing down the Rabbit Run's deadly gauntlet. Some couldn't help but look behind themselves. The grunting, snarling Hunter Killer was pacing around its cage just itching to be set free. Most people who faced this Tourney wouldn't dare look back. Being so close to this meat-eating-machine was enough to turn the most fearless of competitors into a frightful mess. Some had gotten so terrified in the past that when the buzzer sounded to start their fight for survival, their bodies wouldn't move. Stuck in place like their feet were trapped in concrete, they never even made it off the starting line. This beast was so terrifying that many also couldn't keep hold of their bodily functions, thankfully it was usually just the liquid-kind that leaked out from the bottom of their trousers, but the more solid substance has been known to make an appearance in the past.

Luna stood facing forward, her eyes like the crosshairs of a gun-sight locked onto its target. Her body was primed and ready to attack this Tourney with everything she had. Everything and everyone was relying on her to survive this competition. Without this vital step in the rebellion's plan being achieved, it would all be over.

The buzzer sounded initiating the start of the contest, everyone shot off like a rabbit from a trap, but there was a clear leader and that was Luna. Her light-weight frame allowed her to create great speed off the starting line. She was first to reach the huge forty-foot tall A-frame climb. The massive tree-trunk beams made it difficult to get a good grip. Thankfully it was in the summer months and the beams weren't slippery like they were in winter.

Again, Luna's lighter frame allowed her to ascend rather quickly, leaping off the beam below like she had springs attached to her feet. Her descent was also swift and she was first to finish this obstacle. Sadly two had fallen from the apparatus, one was killed out-right, but the other only broke their leg, however, this kind of injury signalled the end of their life soon after. Leaving just fourteen to move forward in the deadly gauntlet.

The cargo-net was next and Luna flew across its rope lattice structure as if it was a solid surface. This young girl was also causing a stir inside the High Commissioner's mansion.

"Who is this young girl? She's amazing," said one person who was about to put a bet on her.

The highest in society would bet on the Tourneys. You could bet on almost any aspect of the competition.

Who would be the first to die?

Who would be the first to complete an obstacle?

Who would be the first to fall?

Who would be the first to fall foul of the Hunter Killer's jaws?

Very rarely, they would bet on a person to survive. However, no one usually took this very unlikely bet.

One young girl's performance so far actually had the High Commissioner rubbing his hands together because no one put a bet on this skinny waif of a girl to even complete the first obstacle. Her performance had surprised many and now she was starting to get the attention of the crowds.

Luna struggled with the increasing gaps between the rope swing apparatus and this slowed her progress. Three others had now caught up with her. Unfortunately, two more fell on the cargo-net and their stuck bodies were soon to be snuffed out. The dreaded buzzer sounded alerting the contestants to the release of the Hunter Killer. This enhanced beast was better than ever and its time taken to traverse the Rabbit Run had been significantly reduced. The only saving grace for those competing was the fact that double the contestants were now competing which would hopefully slow its progress. However, the beast never took any notice of the first two fallen victims, not even a sniff in their direction as he passed by hunting down the rest.

Now safely inside the tunnels, Luna scrambled for her life, sadly four others had lost their lives on the rope-swing. The tunnels were still a lottery of getting an open-ended hole to freedom. This was unfortunately an eventuality that no one could predict. Four had entered, but none had yet to exit the enclosed scramble. When the first person to exit the tunnels was revealed, many were totally surprised that it wasn't Luna. Her small stature should have been great for this obstacle. Two more appeared, but Luna was nowhere to be seen. What had happened to her? The Hunter Killer had now reached the tunnels and with Luna still inside would this be the end of her life and the rebellion's hope of salvation?

Horrifying screams echoed out from the metal tubes as the Hunter Killer claimed more victims. Luna had reached the end of the tunnels to find it blocked. Her smaller frame allowed for agility and speed, but her strength was limited. She kicked, punched and tried everything she could to break through this blockage, but it stuck solid. The sound of the Hunter Killer's claws striking the metal tubing reverberated throughout like mini jack-hammers as it made its way towards her. Glowing red eyes now shone in her direction. This was it, everything that they had worked for would be over. Even if she could influence the Hunter Killer into not taking her life, if it exited the tunnels leaving Luna alive, the High Commissioner would have definitely known that there was foul play.

"Luna, this isn't over yet," came a voice from outside.

A loud clanging noise shook the tunnel system sending vibration throughout. To keep the beast from her position, another competitor was bashing the sides of these tubular tunnels to create as much noise as they could to hopefully disorientate the Hunter Killer. This stroke of genius was working and the Hunter Killer fled in search of the mind-numbing noise that was sending him crazy.

"Push Luna — As hard as you can."

"I'm trying. Just leave me, save yourself."

"I have sacrificed a lot for you to be our saviour. I have two children that need to live. Only you can help them to survive. You are the only one that can save our people from the cruel Commission and a certain fate. You must continue, so many lives depend upon it. Now push! Tell my children that I love them," pleaded the contestant from Sector six.

"It looks like this could be the end for the young girl from Sector four who had surprised us all," said the commentator. "Wait, what is this? Yes, I believe that two competitors are now trying to help the young girl."

Meanwhile, the Hunter Killer had found the noise-making-menace and quickly brought an end to the commotion. Now fully focused again, it headed for Luna's position. With the help of others Luna had now managed to break-free from the tunnels. However, as she fled to the start of the next obstacle, her two saviours stayed where they were.

"Come on. What are you doing! The beast is coming," she screamed, realising what was happening.

"Please go. Go now! You must survive. Do it for us all," said the contestant from Sector Eight, just before his head was ripped from his body and threw across the ground.

Luna ran as fast as she could after seeing the dismemberment. Her other saviour faced down the beast, trying to give her as much time as possible. She reached the monkey-bars, but instead of swinging across the horizontal ladder using her arms, she pulled herself up and ran across the top of it, like she was a stone being skipped across a lake. The snapping crocs below didn't even phase her as she raced across the top of this obstacle. The screams of others dying caused her to take a quick look behind her before she mounted the last obstacle in this deadly gauntlet.

"It looks like this young girl might just make it to the end. Is it just me, or has the Hunter Killer gotten even more savage than before?" said the commentator, completely overcome with excitement.

Anna couldn't watch as her child took on this deadly gauntlet. She didn't care what else was riding on this, she just wanted her daughter back safe and sound. One thing she knew for certain was, if her daughter never returned, she would follow her into the land of the dead very shortly after. Her painful suffering could only be eased by the sparkle in her daughter's eyes. If it wasn't for Luna, she would have killed herself long ago, so she could reunite with her husband and son in the afterlife.

"What's happening? NO! Don't tell me, I don't want to know," she said all in a panic.

"Please come back to me, child. My dearest Luna, why did I allow you to do this?" she mumbled.

In the mansion, the High Commissioner's initial pleasure in witnessing this young girl defy the odds had turned to anger. He was making a lot of money until the people realised that this young girl might just have a chance. Another woman, however, but not just any woman, this was a girl of only sixteen. He was slightly suspicious of the help this young girl had received during the contest, but after Mavee had won the hearts of many, how could they stand by and let a little girl be killed. Still, his suspicions had been heightened by these actions.

Thankfully, the High Commissioner had no control over the course, other than the hundreds of cameras that captured every gory detail in high-definition. He loved to watch the Tourneys over and over again to make sure he didn't miss a single second of the slaughter. Usually these competitions happen so fast that small details can be missed and he wanted to see all of the gruesome moments. Along with his wife they would have movie nights watching the two deadliest shows on Earth, not some soppy love-story while sharing popcorn.

Luna was making her way across the balance beam when she felt the presence of the Hunter Killer. The huge beast's heavy body created a wave like motion which travelled throughout the beam almost toppling her off the side and onto an array of shiny-spiked-poles. She had the foresight, however, to jump when the beam shifted haphazardly, something the remaining two contestants who were in front of her didn't. Both were toppled off the unstable surface and impaled upon the spikes.

Trying not to look as she made her way past these two impaled people. However, a hand grasped at her ankle stopping her from moving forward. "Make our sacrifices count. Only you can set our people free, you must complete the course. Tell my family that I.........." said the dying person, before his life was snuffed out.

After feeling the grip go limp she watched as this person's eyes closed for the last time. During this little interaction the creature hesitated for a moment like it could sense some kind of force. Could this cruel creature actually feel the love emanating from the impassioned exchange?

After this momentary pause, the Hunter Killer was soon hurtling across the beam at great pace. Luna jumped from the beam into the safety of a cage. She'd done it. She'd survived the Rabbit Run. The High Commissioner wasn't at all happy with another female of the species triumphing over his deadly gauntlet. However, he knew that this young girl along with everyone else living in the Sectors would soon meet their ends. There was no salvation waiting at the end of this Predator Pit competition. No better life, just more pain, misery and death.

If by any slim chance that someone did survive the Predator Pit, they would join the one-hundred unlucky people who had been invited to the Inner Sanctum to join in the festivities. The High Commissioner's cruel treatment of these people would see them get a glimpse of what life could be before they were slaughtered for his viewing pleasure. All in an effort to keep his spine-splitting-savages thirsty for the kill. He needed them to be ready to tear apart anyone who stood in his way when they reached Kepler-186F. The strewn body parts would also be collected to provide sustenance for his precious predators during their travels. Little did he know what the Sectors were planning, and now a vital part in their rebellion had been achieved, it looked even more promising.

Luna's victory now gave her the chance to be right where she needed to be. There were still many pieces of this elaborate plan that could go wrong, but with the Wild Whisperer on their side, many could almost taste their freedom. This young girl had just given everyone a huge confidence boost. Some hearts began pumping so fast that many collapsed to the ground. This feeling of hope washed over them like a huge wave, knocking them over like bowling pins. Could this really work? Could they finally take back control of their own lives?

One girl had united thousands of people. Hope in the Sectors was at an all-time high, but were there still some jealous people who couldn't stomach the fact their saviour was in the form of a weak, scrawny, young girl?

CHAPTER THIRTY

Praise to Percussion

LUNA RETURNED TO HER Sector to cheers and adoration. She'd surprised, amazed and totally dumbfounded many living in the Sectors with her heroic actions. Anna was first to charge down her child like she was on a rugby field. Producing a hugging force that almost took Luna off her feet. "Come here, are you hurt? Are you hurt Luna? Please answer me."

"It's ok mum, I'm fine. I think that you're doing more damage."

"Sorry my love. I just, I can't, oh come here," Anna said, kissing her daughter on the cheek.

Before Luna had a chance to breathe after her mothers bear-like grasp, she was hoisted into the air and was being paraded around like a show-pony.

A few, however, were not happy with this young girl's achievement. "Look at the silly little bitch. She's no hero."

"I could have survived the Rabbit Run if they let me compete."

"Yea, me too!"

"I think we are going to have to teach that little girl a lesson."

"Yea, stupid little cow!"

"And this time there will be no animals around to save her."

Devilish laughter came from the group of unimpressed, angry and jealous young men.

Luna was taken to the Elder's hut along with her mother and others who were involved with the rebellion.

"Here she is. Luna my child, you have shown us all the strength you have inside. I never doubted you for a second, but now everyone can see that you truly are a hero," said William who began welling up.

"Can we please just take a moment for our fallen brothers and sisters. They too, showed great strength and courage in their actions. I wouldn't have made it, if it wasn't for their brave sacrifice," Luna added, bowing her head.

All those who faced the Rabbit Run did so with the knowledge of Luna's true identity. They chose to sacrifice themselves to make sure she was triumphant. After the document containing the Commission's plan to leave all of those living in the Sector's behind had been unveiled, many more joined the rebellion. These people knew there was a plan, but only a very few knew about the identity of the Wild Whisperer. Now that Luna had survived the Rabbit Run, she was more valuable than ever.

After a hearty meal prepared by her mother, Luna was absolutely exhausted. Her body ached all over and she had little energy to do anything. The land of nod would be her home for a while now. Thankfully after winning a Tourney that person was allowed one week off from working to recover from their ordeal. You might believe this to be kindness, when in fact it was more of a knowing on the Commission's part that this worn-out person would be of little use in their current state. The sun stayed shining until the late evening, not that Luna, or her mother knew. Both were so exhausted from recent events that they could have slept if the sun was mere inches from their faces. However, would this snoozy siesta leave them vulnerable?

Thankfully for the Sectors, their workload had finally decreased, the lost Thorium had been replaced and they were tasked with gathering supplies for the journey. With only a few months before the Commission planned to jet-off from this dying planet to start their new lives on Kepler-186F, it was all hands on deck. Most of the guards had been pulled away to get everything ready for their trip. This meant that they didn't have enough people to keep the mines going twenty-four-seven. This resulted in the Sectors getting their nights back. Usually this would be used for sleeping, because even though they no longer had to work throughout the night, their workload was still immensely difficult and after the uplift in production from the mines, the majority of people's bodies were about to give up. However, for some this time would be used to make weapons, dig tunnels and do anything that the rebellion required.

There was no way the people living in the Sectors could get past the boundary wall defences to access the Inner Sanctum. Only one person had the access to this deadly barrier. There would also be a decreased guard presence during the Predator Pit competition because as soon as it was over, the spacecraft would be boarded, and ready to take-off the following morning.

Thankfully the soft ground that the Last Isle sat on wasn't only good for mining, but it allowed the Sectors another way to gain access to the Inner Sanctum. Luckily for the Sectors, they had become extremely good at digging tunnels. Each Sector was now linked by a tunnel, allowing movement between the once cut-off sections. Some were as good at burrowing through the ground as moles, and they used their hands like shovels, digging through the dirt like mini J.C.B'S. The people dug day and night to have the tunnel ready for when the last ever Predator Pit would be taking place. Knowing that during this Tourney, the majority of the guards would be pulled away from the Sectors to help tighten security around the mansion. This would leave very few guards patrolling the boundary walls. Those who were left would be taken out using bows and arrows.

Animal intestines were used to make the bow strings of these very powerful and accurate weapons. Sticks tipped with bone sharpened into points would have no trouble penetrating through flesh. For extra added effectiveness these arrows would also be dipped into a poison secreted from a cane toad just to make sure they had no chance of surviving.

It was in the dead of night when Luna felt something shape pierce the skin on her neck. "What's going on? Who are you?" she said, completely shocked.

"Shhh, keep your voice down, or we will cut your throat," said a masked man.

"Why are you doing this," Luna pleaded.

"Keep your mouth shut, or we will slit your mother's neck as well."

"Not so clever now, are we?"

Luna looked over at her mother who was only visible in the moon-light. "Please, do what you want with me, but don't hurt my mum, Please!"

Those were the last words she spoke before she was gagged. Fearing for her mother's life she decided not to put up a fight. Shortly after, her hands and feet were bound and her eyes were covered, leaving her defenceless against this group of individuals. It was the scent of the sea that told Luna where she was being taken, but why?

The slowing pace and undulating movement told her that she was now being taken across sand. "Why are you doing this to me? Please let me go, I have an important mission to complete," she pleaded again.

"Yea, you've got a mission to complete alright," sniggered one of the men.

"Quickly bring her over here."

Still bound and gagged, Luna felt her body being laid down on a hard surface. Soon after, she felt the tightening embrace of something around her body. The sound of the crashing waves drowned out the conversations between her captures. So she couldn't hear what was happening?

"Theo, hold her down."

"I don't want to be involved. You said that you were just going to scare her."

"You either help us, or you will be taking a ride with her. Now grab her legs," someone ordered.

A searing pain on the side of her head was the last thing that she remembered before she was knocked unconscious. A while later it was a cooling splash of water that brought her out of her unconscious state. Still bound and gagged, she couldn't see anything, but the motion that she was experiencing told her that she was out at sea. A huge wave crashed over her body, pushing her beneath the surface, cutting off her air supply. Fighting hard to pull herself back to the surface, her bound body made this extremely difficult. Although this almost drowning dip beneath the expanse of water caused many problems, the cooler water did help to ease her burning skin which felt like it was on fire.

Luna had been strapped down upon a raft and pushed out to sea. Her capturers were a group of young men who weren't happy that this scrawny, little girl had survived the Rabbit Run competition. Luna's big mouth and confident nature had rubbed many up the wrong way in the past and after she had basically proved everyone wrong, they couldn't stand this realisation and sought to get rid of her. They knew that heads would roll if she was killed outright. Believing that a sea-faring adventure would do what they were hoping, leaving their hands free of any blood. With no body to be found, it would be assumed that Luna had run away because she didn't want to face the Predator Pit.

This fleeing occurrence has happened many times in the past. After surviving the deadly Rabbit Run gauntlet, many just couldn't bear the thought of being inside an enclosed space with one of the High Commissioner's' altered animals, so they tried to run away. Some hoped that they might find land, but for most they would take their own lives by drowning, because their bodies couldn't endure the blister-hot sun's rays. Skin would blister and burn without the satellite shields protection. This meant that Luna was now in a race against time to return to the Last Isle, or she would die at sea, leaving thousands of others to the same gruesome fate.

When Anna woke the next morning she wasn't at all alarmed at first because she knew that Luna liked to get up early to train, or just have some peaceful time to herself before the pain and persecution, which was their daily lives, began. Keen to continue with preparations for the planned rebellion, she needed to speak with Lance to make sure that everything on the Inner Sanctum's end was still proceeding as planned.

Lance hadn't been able to get hold of Charlie since he'd given him the information about the Commission's plans. Charlie's mind was still in turmoil over his decision of whom to throw to the wolves. His devious actions had been found out, but it was he who had been tasked with finding out who was responsible. At first, he had no trouble throwing any of those who lived in the Inner Sanctum under the bus. He saw them all as guilty as the Commission itself. However, after working beside some of these people, he realised that many of them were just as afraid as those living in the Sectors. Ok, they didn't have to risk their lives every day to mine for Thorium. They didn't have to face the Tourneys and they weren't starved to within an inch of their lives, but they were still being oppressed. Many still lived in fear of the Commission, it just so happens that they ended up on this side of the divide.

There were still many who had been absolutely horrible towards him, and one of them would be named as the culprit for his actions. However, after realising that the majority of the Inner Sanctum residents were as scared and persecuted as those living in the Sectors, he just couldn't stand by and watch them all die. He had to get the word out to the rebellion that not all who live on this side of the wall were evil. He also wanted to make sure that there would be enough room upon the spacecraft for some of the Inner Sanctum residents. Just because they ended up on the other side of the divide, it didn't mean that they should all be left to die along with the rest of the Commission. That would make the people living in the Sectors no better than the Commission themselves.

This kind of persecution and control had to stop. They all had to be on the same side when they took the trip to Kepler-186F. The High Commissioner and the top brass of the organisation were the real enemy and any who wished to fight by his side when the battle began would also be judged accordingly, but those who surrendered should be allowed a seat on the flight to freedom. Finally, out from under the oppressive rule of the Commission these people could be rehabilitated, and many would actively help the rebellion if they believed that they had the slightest chance of defeating this cruel company.

CHAPTER THIRTY-ONE

Lost at Sea

IT WAS NOW LATE IN the day and Anna was starting to get really worried. After her shift in the slaughterhouse she searched high and low for her daughter, but could find no signs of her.

'*Maybe the pressure was too much for her to handle?*' Anna thought to herself. '*No, Luna wouldn't leave without saying goodbye. She would never turn her back on her people. She had made the decision to fight and that's what she would do!*'

At this present moment, Luna was at the mercy of the sea. Still bound and strapped to the raft, she had no control over anything. The sun's rays burned like a roaring fire, at times it felt as if the flames were dancing on top of her body. Dehydrated and almost burnt to a crisp, Luna knew that if she didn't do something soon, she wasn't going to last much longer.

The sea no longer held any sort of lifeforms. The rising temperature and toxins that were washed into it when the ice-caps melted, left it an extremely inhospitable space. Not only would the blazing sun become a problem, but the sea itself could be extremely harmful if your body was exposed to it for too long. Unfortunately, getting into the sea was the only way that Luna could hope to stop herself from being turned into a pile of ash.

Whilst Luna fought for her life, Charlie was trying to decide who would lose theirs. "You have to do it Charlie. Just make a decision," he mumbled to himself.

The High Commissioner had noticed Charlie's distracted nature of late, but believed that it was the pressure of finding out who was responsible for tampering with the footage. And he was right, but not in the way that he thought. Charlie had already moved the goal-posts on his decision to buy himself more time. Thankfully, with all of the extra activity taking place at the moment with everyone getting ready to blast-off to a new planet, the High Commissioner had his plate full, allowing Charlie some unexpected leniency. However, he knew that his time was running out. He wanted a name before the next Rabbit Run competition. With only three left before the last ever Predator Pit, he wanted to make sure that the blood of those that will be spilled inside the Pit will be cleaned up in plenty of time before the final contest. He wanted the glass structure so clean that you would get the feeling that you were inside the pit next to the unfortunate victims.

There wouldn't be time for delays. The satellite shield was continuing to degrade and soon there would be no hiding from the scolding sun's rays. This operation had now been given a time limit. The head controllers warned the High Commissioner that time wasn't on their side and the continued degrading of the satellite shield would make things extremely dangerous. They were gambling with their own lives now, but the High Commissioner would have his last savage-slaughtering-show before he left the planet for good.

Charlie's decision was made even harder by the fact that the High Commissioner was directly in his eye-line, and that man could stare-down a charging bull and stop it in its tracks. His eyes were like the sights on a gun and it felt like their glare could literally burn into your skull. It was a man named Pierce who brought the decision-making to an abrupt end, and he had just signed his own death certificate. This man was as stuck-up as they come. He definitely didn't think that his shit stunk and he paraded around like he was a king. This man was in control of the Sector guards and he had personally been responsible for many unjust beatings, whippings and killings. Some of which Charlie had witnessed first hand when he was just a young boy living in the Sectors.

After Pierce had walked past and kicked Charlie like he always did on his way to the High Commissioner's office. It rang out like a struck bell in his head. This man had access to the camera footage and had forced Charlie to erase certain transgressions in the past. This man was about as cruel as they came, but even some of his antics wouldn't be tolerated by the High Commissioner. Yes, Hector was cruel and evil, but he did always like to give people a chance to own up to their mistakes, or have the chance to fight for their lives in one of his deadly Tourneys. Pierce, however, was completely ruthless, drunk on power he treated the people living in the Sectors like they were dogs, sub-humans who didn't deserve to live. In fact, this man was feared more than the High Commissioner himself. At least he had some kind of compassion, ok it wasn't a lot, but when Pierce entered your Sector, you could be sure to hear blood-curdling-screams soon after.

He liked to torture people just for the fun of it, even if they had done nothing wrong. With control over the Sector guards his actions were never reported and he was in complete control of the narrative. He'd even banished some of his own guards back to the Sectors if they questioned his activities. It wasn't just inflicting pain that this man thrived on, but also certain acts of a more depraved nature. Being so high-up in the organisation, however, would the High Commissioner believe Charlie?

Thankfully, some of Pierce's past discretions that he thought had been erased were still kept safe and sound. Charlie hated this man with a passion and always knew that he might need some kind of insurance against him in the future, so he kept hold of this supposed erased footage. He almost floated off his seat when the weight of this decision was lifted from his shoulders. He felt stupid for being so slow to finger this man for the transgression. This man deserved everything that was coming to him and Charlie didn't feel at all guilty about naming him as the perpetrator.

After Pierce had left the High Commissioner office, Charlie got up from his seat to go and make the confession, but as he did Pierce walked past and shoved him backwards whilst grabbing him around the throat. "Hello Charlie. Mind your step, you wouldn't want to have an accident now would you?" he said, glaring into Charlie's eyes.

If this man had walked on by and said hello, or even walked on by without kicking him in the leg like he always did, Charlie might have had a slight second thought about what he was about to do, but this just confirmed to him that this horrible man deserved to die.

With one person's life soon to be in a very precarious situation, another had already been thrown from the frying pan and into the fire. Luna was literally being burned alive, and her only saving grace was when the cool seawater splashed up over her body. Still strapped down to the raft and bound by her hands and feet, she needed to get free before it was too late. Dehydration had left her mind hazy and she wasn't thinking straight. Pictures of her mother's smiling face flashed before her eyes. Her father and brother also came into her visions, picturing a time before the Commission rounded everyone up like cattle. She was in the forest, the sound from the babbling brooke trickled through her ears. The sound of laughter and happiness was intertwined with the chirping of birds, a delightful melody that transported her back to a wonderful time.

Shortly after the laughter faded, the smiling faces were gone and all she could hear was birds chirping. The sound got louder and louder until it felt like she was inside an aviary, *Chirp, chirp, chirp, chirp, chirp, chirp, chirp,* it became so loud her ears started to sting, it felt like they were red-hot and bleeding. Suddenly the chirping went quiet, and she could once again hear the sounds of the sea. Soon after, everything went dark, she felt like she was falling through the air. What was happening?

Luna had been saved by the birds again, they came in their hundreds and pecked away at her binds until she was free. But after being tossed off the raft and into the ocean, she was now drowning. She had to swim, but she was so disoriented and dehydrated that her body wouldn't respond. After opening her eyes and realising her predicament, she managed to claw her way upwards. Her first gasp of air when she reached the surface felt like she had inhaled the clouds from above, filling her lungs so full it actually helped her to stay afloat. Scrambling onto the raft again, she knew she would need it to get home. Back on the raft and unbound, Luna had been given a little bit of hope, but she had no idea where she was and how far out to sea she had drifted. For now, she was safe, but without food and water she wouldn't last much longer. Thankfully she could dip in and out of the sea to cool her burnt skin, but if she didn't find land soon her survival and the survival of thousands of others was at risk.

Anna was now beside herself with worry. It was clear that something had happened to her daughter, but what? Her first thought was that the Commission had taken her. Maybe they were worried that she might actually win the Predator Pit?

Had she been killed by the guards?

Had the Commission found out her true identity?

Was it a Commission sympathiser among them who had hurt her daughter in some way?

Unfortunately, Luna's life had been put at risk by a group of jealous young men. They were jealous of her ability to conquer the Rabbit Run. They were jealous of her inner strength and smart wits, but they were mostly angry at the fact that she wouldn't have sex with them. This precious prize of a woman was what many desired. Her milky-white skin was in stark contrast to everyone else and her beauty was positively glowing. However, Luna's heart belonged to another, and she hoped to be reunited with him again. Lance was her one and only, and Luna would never take another man. Love for Luna was pure, a precious feeling that was worth holding onto. Sadly, love had become obsolete in this new world where the sexual act was a more savage undertaking with unsavoury intentions, rather than being about a heightened connection to one another.

Women used and abused their bodies almost as much as the men did. They'd been forced to become baby-making-mules. There was no love involved in making a child any more, especially when that child was either snatched away by the Commission, or they would have to watch it suffer and die. Sadly, the Sectors were full of many young souls that didn't make it. This completely desensitised many and the love that they were looking for just wasn't there any more. Luna, however, held onto this love. She wouldn't become like the rest. If she was to bear a child it would be with the one that she loved.

At present, love was the only thing that was keeping her going. She was losing hope fast. Lost at sea with no food, no water and no direction. She didn't want to risk paddling in the wrong direction which could see her move further away from where she needed to be. She needed a sign, something to give her a heading, but with the blazing sun scolding her body, her milky-white skin was no more and she was quickly losing any hope of survival.

After talking with the rebellion about Luna's whereabouts, more people were now on the case to find this special young girl. Anna had talked to Lance and he in turn to Charlie, and it was quite clear that Luna wasn't taken by the Commission. Someone living in this Sector knew of her whereabouts and Anna planned on grilling every single one. She would find her daughter if it killed her, or if she had to kill others to get to the truth. She just wanted her back safe and sound. The rebellion was now far from her mind, the pain she was experiencing knowing her daughter was missing was immeasurable, she just wanted her back!

CHAPTER THIRTY-TWO

Flashing Beacon

"CHARLIE TO THE HIGH Commissioner's office!" came the call over the tannoy.

This was it, he couldn't put it off any longer. The High Commissioner wanted a name, but would the one that Charlie was offering be believed. Had he made the wrong decision? Should he have chosen a more insignificant person in the organisation to finger from his crime? It was too late to change his mind now. He had some evidence to back up his false claim, so hopefully the High Commissioner would buy what he was selling.

"Charlie, times up, I need the name of the person who thinks that they can hide their deceitful actions from me."

"Umm, it's someone who you wouldn't ever believe. All I can go by is past evidence. I haven't got evidence of this particular act, but I have obtained proof that this person has performed similar deceptions before. They have the required access and the knowledge to carry it out. I can't be sure if this person is working alone, but they are definitely the master-mind behind this," Charlie said, drawing in a huge breath after speaking without stopping.

The High Commissioner looked at Charlie with wide eyes. "So who is it?"

"Did I not say? Sorry, umm it's Pierce, the leader of the Sector guards."

"Pierce! What Pierce Collings!?" The High Commissioner's tone showed his shock to this named person.

Charlie went to speak, but the High Commissioner held up his finger stopping him. He then got up from his seat and started slowly wandering around his office.

"Sir," Charlie said, but was again cut off by a finger pointed in his direction.

Charlie was now red-faced and sweating buckets. It looked like he had just come in from the pouring rain. The beads of sweat on his forehead rolled down into his eyes making them sting. *'He doesn't believe me. What am I going to do now? Run, no that's stupid, where would I run to? Oh god, calm down Charlie, you would already be dead if he thought that you were lying.'*

The silence was killing him. He just wanted to know what was happening. At this point the tension was so overwhelming that Charlie wanted to throw himself to the wolves, at least something would be occurring.

"Charlie......... Leave the evidence with me. You can go now."

Charlie now wished to go back to the silence. Did he believe him, or not? This was complete torture, the not knowing was literally killing him inside. If he was no longer needed in the rebellion's plan, he might have taken his own life there and then, but he was still needed if they were to have any chance of pulling off this coup. All of his work up to this point in time, however, might very well be for nothing if the most important person in this rebellion was killed. Luna was still lost at sea, however, as the news of her true identity spread throughout the Sector, someone just couldn't keep quiet any longer.

"Right, we all know what we have done."

"Yea, but we didn't know that she was the Wild Whisperer," said a panicked voice.

"What have we done? She could have saved us all."

"Right, calm down, this is no time to panic. If we all keep quiet about it no one will ever know what we have done," said John, the leader of this group of young men.

"But, what if we say that we are sorry and we help to find her."

"Find her! It's been five days, there is no way that she is still alive. We need to stick together. We are all guilty of this and we will be treated as so."

"What if they find out? What will happen to us? Please, I don't want to die," blubbed Jacob.

"Stop being a bunch of pussies. If you don't keep your mouths shut, you will answer to me," John said with a glaring look and his fist in his hand.

"What about Theo? He was also there."

"That little twerp will be too scared to say anything, but to make sure I will pay him a little visit."

As the group came out from behind a hut they saw Anna on the warpath. She was going to question every single person in the Sector. Someone had to know something, and she would bleed it out of them if necessary. However, it wasn't Anna who this group of lads were now worried about. They'd managed to dodge her advances all day, but it was who was accompanying her to the Elder's hut that had them all shaking in their boots. Theo was now walking alongside Anna. The group were sure that the younger lad would be too scared to say anything, but they couldn't be sure.

"Theo, how are you doing today?"

"Fine thanks."

"Theo, Luna has gone missing and we need to find her. Do you know anything that could help us find her?"

"Umm, if I, umm, but they will hurt me."

"Who will hurt you? Theo, you are completely safe and you will be protected. Luna is the Wild Whisperer and we need to find her. Please Theo!" Anna pleaded.

"They made me do it. I didn't want to, but they said that they would hurt me. Please, I never wanted to hurt anyone, especially Luna, she was always so nice to me," Theo said, now crying uncontrollably.

Anna put her arm around Theo and pulled him tight. "It's ok. We just want to find her before it's too late. Please help me find my daughter."

"She's............ She's in the............. In the ...."

"Where is she Theo?"

"She's in the sea. Sorry, I never wanted to hurt anyone."

"What do you mean in the sea? What, has she drowned?"

"I don't know. They said it was just a prank. They tied her to a raft and pushed her out to sea. She's dead, she's dead. It's been too long. I should have said something sooner. Please forgive me."

Anna shot out from the Elder's hut like a bolt of lightning. Her bad hip and legs wouldn't hinder her from finding her daughter. She knew what she had to do. She just had to hope with all her heart that it wasn't too late!

Many had previously talked about and carried out a sea-fearing escape from the Last Isle. Almost all of them, however, had been lost at sea, most starved to death, or drowned, only a very few lucky ones somehow managed to find their way back. This was probably just dumb luck, but very few returned once they entered the big blue. Luna and Anna had discussed a sea-born escape, but they had seen many failures. They always said that if they did try this daring activity they would leave a mirror in the trees so that its glinting surface in the sunlight would give them a signal, a flashing beacon to lead them back home. Rushing to her hut, Anna grabbed the biggest mirror they had and made her way to the shore. The sea was relatively calm and there were very few waves. Looking out to sea, hoping to see her daughter on the horizon, but there was nothing. Has it been too long? Was her daughter lost to the sea forever?

Anna chose not to believe this, she knew how strong her daughter was, she would endure until the very end. Armed with the mirror, Anna began flashing the sun's rays off its surface out to sea. Like a mini lighthouse, she moved around in a semicircle to reach as much of the ocean as possible. Anna stayed on the beach until the sun went down. It was now coming into winter and the temperature would drop drastically by night, but she refused to leave the beach. She wanted to be there for the very second the sun rose, so she could start the process all over again.

Thankfully, her fellow Sectorites brought her blankets, food and a hot drink. "Please eat something Anna," said a worried friend.

"I'm fine, I couldn't eat anyway, I feel sick. Do you think she is still out there?"

"Luna is a very special girl. Even from a young age, I could sense something magical inside her. She has endured where others have failed. She is the strongest little girl that I have ever seen. She certainly won't give up without a fight."

Luna was still alive, but only just, in and out of consciousness, her body was losing what little strength it had left. After the birds had come to her aid, she tried again and again to call on the animals for help, but she was just too weak and delirious to concentrate. Looking for anything that might guide her home again, but her eyes hurt just to open them. The sun had burnt them so much that they were now blistered and extremely sore. The contaminated salty seawater was also making a bad situation worse. Her body was covered in sores and every little movement felt excruciating. Thankfully, the usual drop in sea temperature at this time of year would have given her hypothermia by now, but the blistering hot sun's rays kept this prolonged cold exposure from being fatal.

The next morning, Luna opened her eyes to see what she believed was a little island. It had palm trees and a place to shelter from the sun. Filled with hope, she started paddling towards this unexpected place. It took everything she had to get her limbs to move and each movement caused her so much pain. If she wasn't so dehydrated, tears would have steamed from her eyes. *'Come on Luna, you can make it. Just a little further.'*

As this oasis got closer, her body began to respond to the hope in her heart and she managed to keep going. It was so close now, it seemed only finger-tips away. *'One last push, come on, you can get there.'*

Closer and closer she came to her salvation. When she reached this place, she was going to drink the fluid from the coconuts. Make a cooling balm from the leaves and work out where she was. After resting for a while, she would hopefully be able to find her way back home. This was it, she was saved. Reaching out to feel the soft sand on the shore. She even believed that she had a handful of this substance from a moment. "Yes, sand, beautiful sand," she announced.

It wasn't until she brought the handful of sand up to her face to smell its Earthy aroma, but all she smelt was the same old seawater that had invaded her nostrils for the last six days now. "No, No, NO, NO! Please, I can't do this any more," she screamed after releasing it was all just a mirage.

She was so tired, she had given everything she had left to reach this false Eden. As her body slipped off the raft, she barely had the strength to hold on. *'It's no good. I'm done. I'm so sorry mum, please move on without me.'*

Closing her eyes for what she believed would be the last time. She would hold on to the edge of the raft until her body gave up and let go, leaving her at the mercy of the sea. Her mind already had one foot in the afterlife and she now wished to be reunited with her father and brother. A flashing light glinted in her mind. It got brighter until she could see a figure walking towards her. The bright light made it difficult to see who this person was, but as they got closer she could clearly see that it was her dad.

"Luna, my darling little girl. It's not your time yet, you still have so much to do. We will be waiting for you when the time is right, but that time is not now. Follow the light Luna, follow the light, follow the light, follow the light" her dad said before disappearing into the brightness.

All she wanted to do was let the darkness in. She'd given everything and believed that she had nothing left. The darkness would now be her friend, however, this blinding light continued to glint in her tightly shut eyes. *'Why can't you just let me go?'* she said in her mind.

It was annoyance and anger that made her prise open her eyes to see what this persistent and irritating luminous glow was. Her stinging eyes hurt so much to open, but she needed to know if this was just another mirage, another false hope. If so, she could slip away knowing that all hope was lost. Her blistered eye-lids struggled to open, this would be her last act before she left this world to join her father and brother on the other side. To Luna's surprise she could see this blinking light with her eyes open. Was this real, or was she still seeing things?

Using her fingers she prised open her eyes to get a clearer view. Was it? Yes it was, this was real. This was her guiding light back to her mum and back to salvation. The hope in her heart made it pump faster, soon her mind was fully awake and thinking clearly, and that's when she realised what was possibly producing this flashing beacon. With blood pumping around her body at a much faster pace, she found the strength to move her limbs. It was slow and painful at first, but hope spurred her on, and soon after the blinding light brought her to more familiar surroundings. She could see the mountains in the distance, they still looked to be so far away, but she knew that she was on the right track now, soon she would be reunited with her mother.

It took until the sun had almost set on that day before Anna saw a shape in the distance. Highlighted by the setting sun, a silhouette gave her hope. It had to be Luna, there had been nothing else for days. This realisation saw her run into the sea and swim with all her might to reach her daughter. She swam through the water like a torpedo locked on to its target. Her ailments never caused her as much pain in the buoyant sea water, and she soon reached Luna who was literally hanging onto the edge of the raft with the tips of her fingers and the last piece of her life.

With Anna now acting like a speedboat out-motor, they were soon back to the safety of the beach. Hundreds of people were there waiting. The whole Sector had pulled their resources to make sure that Luna had everything she needed to survive and recover from her ordeal. With all hands on deck, Luna was taken back to her hut where she was treated for the many problems she'd picked up during this unscheduled ocean adventure. It would still be touch and go for a while, but Anna couldn't get a bigger smile across her face if she tried.

CHAPTER THIRTY-THREE

Truth or Lies

WITH THE REAL WILD Whisperer back on solid ground, the suspected individual was at present being given the water treatment. Bella refused to cooperate with the High Commissioner, and all the tests they had performed so far hadn't shown any special gene, or attribute that gave this person the power over all animals. He'd tried everything to figure out how this person did what they did. With tests revealing nothing, the High Commissioner turned to something that he was extremely good at. "Tell me how you do it?" he screamed in her gasping face.

Still, Bella stayed quiet, she knew how much was at stake and she wouldn't ever crack, or would she? The High Commissioner had yet to reveal his trump card and when her parents and younger brother were brought into the room her expression changed to one of dread. "Please, they don't know anything. Let them go, you horrible man."

"Bella, why are you being so difficult? Just tell Hector what he wants to know. It's ok darling, he only wants to help," said her mother.

"You don't need to suffer any more, my child. Hector has given us all a place in the Inner Sanctum. We can all live together without pain and suffering, together as a family. Just do what he wants, please my darling daughter," begged her father.

Who were these people? They looked like her family, but they were acting very strange. They hated the Commission for what they had done to thousands of people.

"Listen to your parents Bella. They are happy and you can be too. Just tell us what we want to know," said Sasha, caressing her wet brow.

"I don't know what you have done to my family, but I will tell you nothing. You have enslaved our people and your actions can no longer continue."

"Stupid girl. Without the Commission everyone would already be dead. We saved the last of humanity. Your obedience and loyalty is a small price to pay for your lives. You people would have nothing, NOTHING! If it wasn't for my gracious husband," Sasha said, pulling Bella's head backwards by her hair.

"It's ok, my love. Unfortunately, this young girl responds well to pain and torture. However, how will she feel when it's her family that gets hurt."

"Leave them alone!" Bella screamed.

The High Commissioner led Bella's mother down some steps and placed her within touching distance. *Don't you dare hurt my family,* she screamed again.

After placing a large knife in her mother's hands, the High Commissioner looked deep into Bella's eyes. "Not to worry, child, it's not me who will be hurting them."

Bella was completely confused. If this man thought that he could get her to hurt her parents, he would be sorely mistaken. She looked up into her mother's eyes, but there was nothing there, it was her, but she seemed to be a million miles away. She wore a blank expression with a slight grin.

"This is your last chance child. Tell me what I want to know, or your family will hurt like never before."

Bella stayed quiet and stared at the High Commissioner with an angry determination.

"Don't say I didn't warn you. Beatrice, please cut into your arm," he instructed.

Bella watched as her mother began cutting into her arm. "No! Stop, what are you doing?" she screamed in horror.

The High Commissioner enjoyed every minute of the terror portrayed on Bella's face that he never once looked at the act itself, he got all of his pleasure from the growing fear in his victims eyes. Beatrice continued to slice through her arm. She did this without making a single sound. The pain must have been excruciating, but she kept the same blank expression upon her face all the way through the horrifying ordeal. A resounding thud was heard when Beatrice's forearm crashed to the floor. Still her mother stood there like a statue, no movement, or emotion. Blood was pouring from her wound and it was only when her complexion turned grey, did she finally collapse to the ground. Bella was now crying profusely, the pain in her heart was excruciating, but she wouldn't give up any information. Her family were a heartbreakingly-sad price to pay, but she knew that the only way to stop this tyrannical reign was to take down this man and the organisation that he controlled.

While Bella was staying strong in the face of an absolutely awful tribulation. The real Wild Whisperer was still in a lot of pain. Herbal creams and medicine had started to ease her blistered skin, which still glowed like a red-hot poker. Even after being cooled with buckets loads of ice, her body still poured with sweat. She looked like a human sauna, steam bellowed from her body when the ice made contact with her scolding-hot skin. Such lengthy exposure to the sun would have killed the average person. However, Luna wasn't out of the woods yet, who knows what this has done to her mind, could she still access her powers? If the condition of her body was anything to go by, then her mind must have been in a relentlessly tormented state.

Everyone railed around the girl who could hopefully still save them from a fate worse than death. Anna, unfortunately, couldn't stay by her daughter's side. She was the best butcher in the business and an unexpected event needed to be catered for. After reviewing all of the evidence the High Commissioner also believed that Pierce Collings was the one responsible for tampering with the footage. Thankfully, his past discretions were enough to convince the High Commissioner of his guilt. Once again, this deceitful person would be made a spectacle of in a most gruesome fashion.

Even though the High Commissioner believed that he was only taking subservient people with him to Kepler186-F. This highlighted another hole in his majesty. He wanted to show the people once again what would come of them if they dared to challenge his rule. He held all of the power. He was the one and only king on this planet and any other that they might find themselves inhabiting. He knew that he needed the numbers for now, but once he had positioned himself at the top of the tree, would even his closest followers be safe from his tyrannical thrust for whole universe domination?

With the Commission's time being taken up with preparations for the trip to their new home, the Sectors had been saved from the mind-numbing alarm that they used almost daily to announce the most trivial of communications. So everyone was taken completely by surprise when it sounded off one morning. Even in Luna's comatose state you could see the pain that this horrifying alarm had on her.

"Hello to you all. Firstly, I would like to thank everyone's efforts to replace the lost Thorium. We now have enough fuel to transport us all to a new life on another planet. Correspondence with the newly formed Kepler Federation has brought good news. They already have some important infrastructure in place and the planet is turning out to be plentiful.

Now, as you may be aware, the extra time and resources taken up by the busy Commission to get everything ready for this trip, has left certain vigilance of some activities that fall below the expected standard."

"That's it, we're in the shit now," said a scared person.

Was this all just a test? Was the slackly guarded Sectors just a trap to see what they would do with more freedom?

"That being said, it has left me with a very difficult decision. The three final Rabbit Run competitions will not take place."

There were many relieved and unexpectedly shocked faces among the Sectors. "There's got to be a catch. There is always a catch," said one susceptible person.

"Now, I know that many of you would have relished the chance to better their lives, not only for the rest of the time on this planet, but also going forward on our new home. This opportunity that has been taken away from you will not be without recompense. Every sector will receive extra resources for the next three months. These will be supplied to every Sector, not just those who may have triumphed over the Tourneys. I want everyone to be fighting fit and ready for our journey. Now, with that being said, the last Predator Pit competition on this planet will have to be a very special one. Each Sector will provide two people to face this last Tourney. Those who have already won the Rabbit Run will also still get their chance to compete. However, the extra competitors will help to make the final Tourney on this planet the best that there has ever been. Let's all go out with a bang!"

There was a mixed response in the Sectors. Some believed it was a good gesture, but those who knew of the Commission's real plans, felt sick knowing that after everything they had done, they still wanted to have fun and entertainment at the poor Sector's expense.

"For added incentive for those who compete in this final Predator Pit contest. Any person who manages to survive will win the chance to upgrade from the cramped and uncomfortable conditions in the animal quarters, and get to travel in an area where all aboard will have beds to sleep on. Along with extra rations and a much more comfortable surroundings. This journey will take us many years to complete, so trust me when I say that you will definitely want to win this prize. Sadly, spaces are limited and resources are now at a premium, so only ten lucky people will be able to claim this prize. This is your chance to fight for a better life. A much more comfortable journey and also the knowledge of knowing that when we reach our new home, an improved existence of life awaits. The Kepler Federation will look to work with the Commission in the transition period, so being on the right side of the divide will open up a lot more opportunities going forward. Let's make our last days on this dying planet a triumphant one.................. The mines are going to be shut, they have given us all that we need now, but other resources will need to be collected. I leave it to you in the Sectors to procure anything that you believe might be necessary for our new lives. Deposit your findings to a guard station and they will make sure that it gets loaded onto the vessel. Take this extra time to train, to give yourselves every chance of surviving the Predator Pit. I want everyone competing to be in their best shape possible. As this will be the last ever competition on this planet. Myself and my lovely wife Sasha would like to, well, I will let her tell you as she is the one who came up with the most generous idea. Remember, if we persist and persevere, we will all prevail."

"Thank you my love. Let's have a round of applause for your High Commissioner....... Now, seeing as this is the last ever Tourney to be carried out on this planet. I have decided to invite one-hundred lucky people from the Sectors to come to the mansion and witness the competition up close and personal. You will be wined and dined and have a glimpse of what a new life may look like for you. These people will be selected at random and all will have a first class experience. This is our way of saying thank you for all of your hard work. Together we have endured, together we have succeeded and together we will conquer any challenge that awaits us. Remember, if we all persist and persevere, we will all prevail."

The Sectors were full of intrigue and gossip. This didn't sound like they planned on leaving the people of the Sectors behind. They were giving them the chance to gain a more comfortable journey. Why would they leave us behind when they obviously need us? This little speech had left some doubting the rebellion's claims. Those who were not so stupid knew why the Commission was spouting this absolute bullshit.

After the screens went blank, everyone believed that was the end of it. However, shortly after the screen was once again illuminated and it showed the Predator Pit in all its sparkling glory. Inside stood one man, a man that everyone was completely shocked to see inside this death den. It was Pierce Collings. Thankfully, the High Commissioner believed Charlie's lies and this man was about to become another lesson to all those who might be thinking that they were safe. This man was highly respected and held a very powerful position in the Commission, but this just showed everyone that no one was safe from the High Commissioner's fury.

There was elation and happiness in the Sectors. This man had killed, kicked, beaten and tortured many of their friends and family members over the years. They were overjoyed to see this man get what was coming to him. The Inner Sanctum residents were as shocked as anyone when this man was revealed. If such a powerful and well integrated man could be sacrificed, were any of them really safe?

As an extra display of dominance the glass tubes that fed the Pit were all filled with deadly beasts. Usually it would only be one of his flesh-filleting-fiend's that would get the pleasure of the kill, or it would be afforded to the Hunter Killer. However, eight altered animals slowly walked down the sleek glass tubes towards the pit. Pierce would be torn limb from limb. There would be no running, no hiding, this would be an obliteration of a person's body. Nothing would be left after they had all had their pound of flesh. Many in the Sectors watched intently on as this cruel man was torn apart, but some still couldn't stomach the slaughter. Yes this man was guilty of some of the most brutal and barbaric behaviour, but to be judged in this way was still an act that didn't sit well with many.

CHAPTER THIRTY-FOUR

Painful Information

AFTER HAVING TRIED everything in his power to find out how the Wild Whisperer controls the animals, the High Commissioner was at a loss. He'd killed Bella's parents and her younger brother, and although this was extremely painful to watch, she stayed strong and kept to her word. Bella knew that this kind of cruelty would only continue if they didn't stand up and fight against the Commission. She'd sacrificed herself so that the true Wild Whisperer, her best friend Luna would have the chance to take down this oppressive organisation. Thankfully, Luna was now on the road to recovery and thanks to the Commission's easing of work details, it gave Anna and others the extra time and resources they needed to nurse Luna back to full health. Only fully recovered and strong would she have the strength and stability required to take control of the High Commissioner's blood-thirsty-brutes.

"Luna, how do you feel? You are looking so much better today. Is there anything that I can do to help you further?"

"Mum, you have saved me from near-death, I think you can take some time for yourself now."

"No Luna, I will never leave your side again. I will find out who did this to you and they will pay with their lives. Dirty low-life SCUM BAGS!" Anna's raised voice showed her anger.

"Please mum, too many lives have already been taken. If it's not the Commission's then we should spill no more blood. I know who is responsible and they will receive their punishment in the form of my strength. They will see my face and know what they have done. The Commission is responsible for this hatred and anger that has bred among our people. Their oppressive rule has shaped many awful decisions over the years, it's time that it stopped. They are the ones that must fall. They are the ones that shall be punished," Luna said, her strained voice cracking as she got more animated.

"Ok, my love. Just save you energy, I will say no more about it."

Anna still wanted the heads of the people responsible mounted on spikes, but she understood her daughter's sympathy towards these people. Luna showed a maturity well beyond her years. She was extremely articulate and wise for someone so young. However, living in the Sectors was a baptism of fire and you either survived, or you died.

A group of people were stalking Luna's hut. Watching the comings and goings of many different people. Unfortunately, her mother was still needed in the slaughterhouse. "Are you sure you will be ok without me?"

"Yes mother, please go, we don't want to invite any more trouble. We must keep everything as normal as possible, or suspicions might be raised."

"Mike will sit with you while I'm gone."

"Please, it's not necessary, I feel so much better now and I would like a little privacy," she said, glaring at her mother.

"Ok, but he will stand right outside the door."

"Fine, just go before you get into any trouble."

As Anna left, she was stalked by many sets of eyes. Were these people avoiding her, or were they up to something more sinister?

Were they working for the Commission and planned on putting an end to this creature communicator?

Had the High Commissioner found out that Bella was just a false patsy, and the real Wild Whisperer was still at large?

Luna was looking at herself in the mirror when she saw a hand appear on the edge of her huts window opening. Keeping her eyes on this reflection she slowly backed up and positioned herself next to the opening. Another hand appeared and a body was being pulled upwards.

Luna swivelled on her heels and grabbed this person around the throat. "What are you doing here?" she asked forcefully.

"Please don't hurt me. We came to say sorry," came the frightened reply.

Luna immediately saw red, she was ready to tear out this person's throat if need be, she wouldn't let herself be caught by surprise again. After the red-mist had cleared, she could see that it was one of the people who was responsible for her a sea-faring, skin-blistering, nearly-drowning, close to death adventure. Still feeling a lot of anger towards this person, but after looking into their eyes she could see that they were extremely frightened and truly sorry.

After releasing her tight grasp and dropping this window watcher, she looked outside to see more sorry-looking faces. "Please forgive us, we never meant for it to go so far. We were childish and stupid and we offer our wholehearted apologies. Please accept these offerings as a gesture of our forgiveness," the group of men said, all presenting these gifts above their heads.

"Keep your gifts. Your apology is enough. I will ask just one more thing of you. Will you fight with me against the Commission? Will you help to set our people free? We need to be united as one if we are to have any chance of winning this battle. Fight with passion, fight with pride, stand strong against the people who are responsible for our persecution. Only together, can we save ourselves from certain demise."

"We will, we will. We will fight beside you. Thank you for your forgiveness."

Luna was grateful that these people still had the sympathy and strength to apologise for their actions. Sometimes the hardest thing of all is to admit when you are wrong and repent for your transgressions. This group of young men's actions could have seen their own lives along with the lives of thousands of others being terminated. However, the strength and resilience of this young girl had given them all another chance. The long road was far from over and many twists and turns lay ahead. Luna had cheated death once, but could she do it again?

Has this sea-faring adventure cost her more than just a bucket-load of pain and suffering?

Could this girl still find the power to take over the High Commissioner's flesh-tearing-tyrants, or had all of her energy been taken up recovering from her horrific ordeal?

Time was getting near and the battle would soon be upon them. The people living in the Sectors had never felt so at ease. They were no longer forced to work until their hands bled. They had enough supplies to get them through the colder months and they weren't struck with crippling fear knowing that one among them would have to face the deadly gauntlet known as the Rabbit Run. Maybe this was what the Commission wanted. Allowing these people to let down their guards so they would be unimaginably shocked when they were left all alone on this dying planet, watching as their ride to salvation flew by.

The news of Bella and her family's demise had now reached Luna. Her mother first thought to keep this information from her daughter, but it wasn't right to keep Luna in the dark. She would find out eventually and she wouldn't thank her mother for keeping such a secret from her. This terrible news had hit Luna hard, however, it was some other undisclosed information that made her heart ache even more. Unaware of Bella's conversation with Luna, Anna revealed that Bella was healthy, she didn't have a terminal illness like she had told Luna. Bella knew that this would be the only way that she could get Luna to allow her to make this sacrifice, if she believed that she was going to die anyway. This revelation shocked Luna like an Earthquake, she couldn't stop her body trembling with agony and anguish over her friend's sacrifice. "Why did she do that? Why did she sacrifice herself? She was my best friend," Luna sobbed.

"She did it because she loved you. She did it because she knew that you were the only one that could save us all. Her sacrifice gave us all another chance at life."

"Did you know?"

"Know what?

"That she was going to tell me that she was sick."

"No! Of course not. I would never."

"I'm sorry, I just miss........ I just miss her so much. Why? Why Bella?" Luna said, breaking down completely.

Anna wrapped her arms around her daughter and held her close. "I'm so sorry for your loss. Bella was a lovely girl," she said, now also sobbing.

This information had devastated Luna, but she wouldn't let it bring her down. She would use this added torture and torment to get revenge upon all of those responsible. This had ignited a fire inside of her and she was now more determined than ever to take down the cruel Commission and take back their lives from these oppressors. They would suffer, they would know what it feels like to live in fear. They would hurt like never before for all of their transgressions and they would be the ones left to die on this doomed planet. The weapons had been made. The tunnels had been dug. Everyone was waiting for their chance to strike a deadly blow upon the people who had made their lives feel like a living hell for the last twenty years. Everything was now in place, everyone was ready and soon they would fight to take back their freedom!

That night, Luna went for a walk along the beach, looking up at the stars gave her comfort. This planet may be dying, but the world above still looks full of promise and wonder. If they were to win this rebellious battle against the Commission she just hoped that where they were headed would really be a new start for her people, one where they were free, one where they lived without fear. One where they could watch their children grow and not suffer the most horrific pain of having to watch as they slowly die. There was a whole new world out there, and Luna just hoped that wherever they ended up they could live in peace with that planet's lifeforms, and that the people of Earth wouldn't make the same mistakes as before. They would nurture the planet and not strip it bare for greed and innovation that only brings suffering to others. This was a huge ask, and she knew it, but the stars provided her with something to reach for, something to hope for and something to strive for. Hopefully her people would live on and make the place they arrived at a home and not just another framework for failure.

CHAPTER THIRTY-FIVE

The Attack Begins

THE GROUND SHOOK LIKE never before, the ringing sound was so loud and relentless that many began to bleed from their ears. This was the last alarm that anyone would ever hear and the High Commissioner sought to start the torment and torture of the people living in the Sectors early.

When everyone arrived at the big screens, there was a steely determination in their eyes. This was it, soon they would be storming the castle to take down this oppressive organisation who were responsible for so much pain, suffering, torment, torture and death. However, they had to wait until the opportune moment. If they were to strike too early it would give the Commission time to close their ranks. Everything was now hinging on Luna. If she couldn't gain control of the High Commissioner's Zoo-full of blood-curdling-creatures, they wouldn't have the extra force they needed.

Charlie still had a part to play in this rebellion along with Luna's one true love, Lance. Lance worked in the Zoo and he would have to make sure that the deadly predators would be perfectly positioned for the attack. The carousel of creatures rotated above the pit itself, so any who were inside could witness their frightening foes in all their gruesome glory. Eight sleek glass tubes fed the pit allowing for multiple animal entries, however, only one has ever been needed. This was more so another fear tactic by the High Commissioner.

The thought of one of these beasts was enough to scare the living daylights out of you, but eight of them, well that was just inconceivable. Lance would make sure that the carousel of deadly predators would be released into the mansion once Luna had gained control. Once this part of the plan had been executed, he would release the rest of the animals in the Zoo upon the Inner Sanctum. The chaos caused by these wild running-free animals would help to disrupt the guards who could then be taken down by the rebellion.

Luna would actually be in grave danger. Surrounded by an impenetrable glass structure, she would be stuck inside facing one of the spine-shaking-savages. If she couldn't gain control of this cruel-creation she was sure to be killed. There was still no telling if she could connect with these altered animals.

Firstly, the High Commissioner's control over the animals had to be severed. He used implanted microchips to coerce these beasts into carrying out his will. These devices had to be interrupted in some way to give Luna every chance of taking control. Charlie would be the one who would make this happen. Using the control system, he hoped to sever this connection long enough for Luna to have an opportunity to gain a connection with whichever deadly foe she would be facing.

Anna still feared greatly for her daughter's safety. What if she couldn't control these A.I altered animals? What if Charlie failed to relinquish the High Commissioner's control? Her daughter would be trapped inside a huge fishbowl with a blood-thirsty-beast. Worse still, if the High Commissioner noticed something fishy going on he could release the other seven primed predators upon her.

All of these questions ran around Anna's mind like a cat chasing a mouse, thankfully Anna was one of the lucky people chosen to watch the last ever Tourney up close and personal. She obviously didn't want to witness her people being slaughtered, but if something went wrong she would be close enough to hopefully help her daughter.

She was like a ninja with a sharp object, and after stealing every single blade from the slaughterhouse she was well and truly armed.

The High Commissioner's sadistic need and depraved greed for wanting to witness the slaughter of one-hundred people from the Sectors would actually help the rebellion. They would now be inside the belly of the beast and well within striking distance of the man himself. It would be his slaughter they would be witnessing if everything went to plan.

There were still so many variables that could cause this rebellious plan to fail, but at least they would go down fighting. For once in control of their own actions. They would fight, or die, however, it would be on their own terms. No longer would they let this organisation play with their lives like they were just pieces of meat. They still had hopes and dreams and regardless of the outcome, they could happily go to their graves knowing that they did everything in their power to save themselves from certain death. Everyone was ready, everything was set, now all they had to do was pray that it all fell into place.

Luna would get the chance to stare this cruel man in the eyes before the competition. The High Commissioner always likes to witness the fear building on these unlucky people's faces before the event takes place.

"Hello, who do we have here?" he said with the rye grin that was always upon his devilish face.

"It's Luna sir."

"Ah yes, the young girl from Sector four. You surprised many people with your performance in the Rabbit Run. Let's see if you can survive this competition?" he said with a sinister grin.

"I will try my best," she said through gritted teeth.

Luna was absolutely fuming beneath the surface, but she had to keep her anger in check. All she wanted to do was jump up and rip this smug man's throat out, but she had to bide her time. If she could have just one element out of this whole rebellion to be enacted, it would be to see this man's head on a stick. Remove the head of the serpent and hopefully all others shall fall.

Everyone in the Sectors were now waiting for the glitzy, glamorous over the top show to begin. It was then they would make their move on the Sector guards. Using the dazzling display as a cover for their actions, they hoped to get within striking distance without being seen. They needed to be ready to storm the Inner Sanctum when Luna entered the Predator Pit.

Sadly, three people would have to lose their lives before it was Luna's turn. They all knew what was at stake and although they would be trying to evade their chosen deadly foe to survive, they were happy to give their lives for the sake of so many more. Willing to make this sacrifice in the hope that their families would have a chance at a better life on Kepler-186F. Considering they were all marked for death anyway, this decision was slightly less painful to comprehend.

With the spectacular show well under way, the first part of the rebellion's plan was being carried out. The guards were all in lofted positions and the only way to take them out was with a bow and arrow. Everyone had been practising their aim, but could these malnourished, weakened bodies still have the strength to propel these arrows with enough force to take down the armoured guards. They had to try and take the guards out in the open. With access to the control hub, if any weren't killed quickly they could sound an alarm with the press of a button located inside.

A person from every Sector now walked up to the guard towers in their area to draw them out into the open. "Oi, you. Yea, you, you ugly looking idiot. Why don't you come down here and take me on? Stop hiding behind that uniform and have a go," shouted a man from a crowd of people.

The guard at first paid him no attention, however, when a rock hit him on the side of the head, he was giving this man his full attention.

"Guard tower. I have a rowdy person over here. Could you come and take over watch while I go and deal with him. Come and watch me stomp this piece of shit into the ground," said the guard, laughing.

When the guards left the control station a volley of arrows was shot in their direction. It was extremely overkill, but they couldn't take any chances. While the guards fell in each Sector, the people left to gather the weapons and get themselves in the tunnels. So far, so good. All of the Sector guards had fallen, and none had managed to raise the alarm. Charlie had put the footage from the Sectors on a loop so it didn't raise any suspicion. The High Commissioner always had one eye on the monitors, just in case. On closer inspection you would be able to tell, but hopefully the High Commissioner would be far too busy showing off his majesty and watching the slaughter to notice that it had been tampered with.

Unfortunately, the three people who had entered the pit before Luna all lost their lives. Their demise came rather quickly, a lot quicker than in the past. It seems that these bone-breaking-beasts had all had an upgrade.

The first competitor faced a Grizlion, a mixture of a Grizzly bear and a Lion. This huge beast took little time in killing the contestant. Its power and speed were just too much to overcome, and the sounds of blood-curdling screams were soon resonating throughout the mansion.

The next person faced the Crocmodo, it was slower than most of the predators, but once the pit began closing in around them its huge elongated jaw soon had a meaty snack between its teeth. Two more poor souls had fallen and it was a hard pill for Luna to swallow. She knew that these people all knew what they were expecting, but it still hurt hearing their painful screams as they were torn apart.

The third flesh-tearing-tyrant to enter the pit was a Liger. Its huge metal teeth shone brightly under the pit's lighting. Just the sheer look of the creature had the contestant shaking uncontrollably. Its bright white fur and blood-red stripes made it look very devilish. Jet-black eyes followed its victim as they tried to create some distance. Luna couldn't watch as the man ran around trying to escape this creature's jaws. His fear was clear to see, and the tormented look upon his face struck her like a knife to the heart.

Like the first two, this person soon fell, but after his head had been torn from its body, the blood-covered-beast walked to where Luna was sitting. Looking at her dead in the eyes it slowly opened its huge jaws to let this poor soul's head drop to the floor. The poor man's eyes were still wide open with terror. This was a message from the High Commissioner to Luna, to show her that there was no surviving this competition, all would perish today.

Luna was next. This was it, the time had come and now everyone was trembling with anticipation and fear. If just one step in this plan failed, it would all be over. They just as well take their own lives there and then, because the alternative was a dreadful experience that no one wanted to end up with.

Anna began to tremble as she watched her daughter walk into the Predator Pit. Luna showed no fear as she took her place inside the glass structure. Her eyes locked onto the High Commissioner and they were so striking that he had to turn away. Even the rotating carousel of creatures above her head never fazed her and she remained as focused as ever.

This young girl had a strength that worried him slightly. However, after seeing which one of his prized creations she would be facing, a grin appeared on his face. Luna would be facing the Black-Wolf. With the size and strength of a Black Bear fused with the speed, cunning and down-right savagery of a Wolf. This deadly creation had the blackest of bodies, it was like looking into a deep, dark abyss, so dark and dreadful, its body gave off a chilling concern. Two piercing red eyes and long shiny fangs were all that broke up this black beast. The only thing deadlier on this planet was the Hunter Killer.

This creation had rarely been seen. Even the High Commissioner himself stayed clear of its unpredictability. This was one creature that he never walked around with, when he displayed them like pets. He had control over the beast, but it was so vicious that even he was wary. It was so cunning that its behaviour was also extremely erratic. Luna stood no chance against this beast and the High Commissioner even turned away for a moment to speak with patrons. This cunning creation liked to play with its victims. Tearing limbs off first to cause as much pain as possible before finally tearing them apart with its claws, gouging organs out like they were dirt from a pit, sending them flying in all directions. Little was left when this beast got his victim in its sights.

The Black-Wolf took its time, slinking down the opaque tube towards its victim, slowly stalking their movements. Most who faced this blood-thirsty-beast never moved a muscle. Once you looked into its piercing eyes you were frozen to the spot with a crippling fear. Luna stood strong, all the while wondering if she would have the strength to gain control of this terrifying animal. Now finally inside the Pit the wolf circled. This creature never grunted, snapped its jaws, or used any other intimidating tactics to put the fear of god into his victims. Its presence alone was all it took to scare the living daylight out of you.

As the wolf got closer, Luna closed her eyes. "Concentrate Luna, you can do this."

Her eyes remained closed up until the huge snapping jaws of this beast were mere millimetres away from her face. This was it, shit or bust! Opening her eyes suddenly they revealed a yellow glow that shone brightly. The High Commissioner spat out his drink in complete shock, this young girl was the fabled creature communicator, how could this be? He tried to regain control over the wolf, but thankfully Charlie had managed to interrupt the signal used to manipulate the A.I altered animals. Slowly reaching out her hand and placing it on the wolf's head. Her eyes glowed even brighter when the two connected, sending a wave of yellow out from the pit, binding onlookers and bathing them in a luminous glow.

When everyone's eyes adjusted after the snap blindness, there was complete shock as their gaze was focused into the Predator Pit. Luna had mounted the Black-Wolf and her gaze was firmly fixed in the High Commissioner's direction. The hundred Sectorites who had been brought to the mansion revealed hidden weapons and started to gain control of the room. Noise from outside saw guards rushing into the mansion when Lance released the animals upon the Inner Sanctum streets.

"Sir, sir, High Commissioner, what do you want us to do?" screamed a guard to a completely dumbfounded man.

The High Commissioner couldn't believe what he was seeing. Witnessing her husband's shock, Sasha gave the order to kill. Soon bullets and arrows were flying in all directions. "My love, we must flee, hurry, we need to get to the spacecraft," Sasha shouted.

Still, the High Commissioner stood there with an extremely shocked look upon his face. '*How could this be? This young girl is the Wild Whisperer? It's not possible.*'

His dismay at the whole situation suddenly got a lot worse when the carousel of creatures rose from beneath the mansion's ballroom floor and opened to reveal seven more of his precious predators, all snapping their huge metal jaws in his direction. The sound was trembling and he was filled with overriding trepidation. What was happening to all he had built?

Soon after, there was a clear path through the huge ballroom littered with dead Inner Sanctum guards. Realising he no longer had control over his cruel creations, he fled for his life with Sasha and a group of guards. If they could make it to the spacecraft in time, they may still be able to leave this doomed planet with their lives intact before it was too late. Even though Luna had gained control over his precious predators, did he still have an ace up his sleeve, something that might just help him to stay alive long enough for him to flee to safety, all the while getting revenge upon the Sectors by leaving them to die?

CHAPTER THIRTY-SIX

Fleeing For Their Lives

WHEN THE HIGH COMMISSIONER reached the outside of his mansion he was shocked at the chaos unfolding. Animals were running amuck, his guards were fighting against the people from the Sectors, it was complete pandemonium.

"Quickly, sir, into the vehicle."

As the High Commissioner, his wife and a group of guards were bundled into a huge armoured vehicle, they looked behind to see the Black-Wolf and seven other predators all running towards their location.

"Go NOW!" the High Commissioner screamed.

The armoured truck set off at break-neck speed, but soon the beasts were on its tail. An already infuriated man was left spitting when he witnessed Luna riding on the back of one of his creations. "Take them down," he shouted.

This vehicle had an array of weapons mounted upon it and soon every gun was manned trying to take down these rampaging beasts. Sonic cannons producing a force like being hit by a train, began to pick off the chasing pack. The creatures weren't killed, but they would be out of action for a period of time. No matter how hard they tried Luna and the Black-Wolf continued to evade their attacks. After being lured in too close, the High Commissioner used the huge truck to ram the bounding-beast, knocking it over and sending Luna flying through the air. "Take that you silly little girl," he said feeling triumphant.

When the dust settled, they were free from the chasing creatures. Luna was battered and bruised, but she wouldn't give up until she had this man's head on a stick. Meanwhile, back at the mansion the rebellion had overcome the guards and now had control over the Inner Sanctum. The majority of the freed zoo animals fled into the surrounding forest leaving a much less chaotic scene.

After rounding up the guards and placing them inside the Predator Pit, the rest of the Inner Sanctum residents had been confined to the mansion. These people were crying like babies. They loved watching pain and persecution being inflicted upon others for their amusement, but when the tables were turned they acted like children, crying, begging and pleading for their lives to be spared. Many from the Sectors wanted nothing more than to cause these people the same pain and suffering that they had seen inflicted upon their family and friends for years now, but Luna wanted them to be spared. Yes, they were responsible for some atrocious acts, but many were only scared of what would happen to them if they didn't follow the High Commissioner's sick rules. These people would still be judged, but it would be at the hands, or should I say claws of the predators they have cheered on in the past, happily watching as they tore people limb from limb.

Luna was still on the hunt for the High Commissioner and she knew exactly where to find him. This man who commanded such power and dominance over others had been made to flee like a scared little rabbit. This irony wasn't lost on Luna and she hoped that this horrid man was feeling every bit as terrified as the poor people who have faced the Rabbit Run in the past. Remounting the Black-Wolf she headed for the hanger.

After having reached the hanger, the High Commissioner believed that he was home and dry, however, Charlie had managed to put the hanger on lock down and the doors wouldn't open. The guards opened fire on the doors, but these doors had been constructed to withstand a huge blast, *"Give me that,"* the High Commissioner said, snatching one of the guns.

It was no use, these doors weren't going to be opened in this way. A low growl that travelled through the ground and up into the High Commissioner body stopped him in his tracks. He turned around to see Luna standing there with eight of his precious predators, all snarling in his direction. The guards immediately fled for their lives. They'd seen what these flesh-feasting-fiends were capable of and wanted no part of it.

The High Commissioner opened fire on the creatures, but these beasts had been made to withstand this kind of attack. Realising that his own creations were too strong to stop with gunfire, he turned to the last card he had to play. It was the eight vicious animals that now backed away nervously as the Hunter Killer stepped out from the shadows. Its roar alone was so terrifying that even the other vicious beasts were scared. This creature was like the grim reaper. It was so strong, so fast, so agile that before Luna had a chance to think, it had already killed two of the other predators. Luna desperately tried to connect with this beast, but the High Commissioner's control was so overpowering. This creature was more android than animal now, and that stopped Luna from taking over control. She could feel the creature's pain, but couldn't break through the technological control that this man possessed. With this beast being more cyborg than creature, she just couldn't get through to it. Had the High Commissioner just saved himself from certain death?

The Hunter Killer went on the attack and even though it was six against one, he was having the upper hand in the battle of the beasts. There was only one way to stop this rampaging creature and that was to stop the person controlling it. More guards who were defending the hangar rallied to the High Commissioner's aid after witnessing the unfolding events. They'd also managed to find another way into the hangar. While altered animals fought, hundreds of the people from the Sectors had come to help Luna. There was only one, however, who could stop this war, only one who had to finish this before any more lives were lost.

The majority of the Inner Sanctum residents were now being held inside the mansion. Some fled for the sea, but they would soon find out that there was no sanctuary to be found. After the guards had been killed, most ended up a blubbering mess that was absolutely pathetic.

"Stop snivelling, you baby. You people know nothing of pain and suffering," said a Sectorite totally bemused at the way in which these people were acting, they haven't even been harmed, YET!

With Luna in control of the predators, the Commission's army had fallen, only the few guards that were with the High Commissioner remained. They had almost won this war, but the person who they really wanted to suffer, could still sleek away like the snake he is, and take their ride to freedom with him.

Luna, accompanied by a handful of Sectorites, sneaked their way into the hangar. The Hunter Killer was still winning the battle against the other predators even with the help of hundreds of Sectories who also joined in the attack. Could this one spine-splitting-savage turn the tide on this war, or at least allow the man responsible to escape?

While the guards battled with Luna's little rebellious group, the High Commissioner and his wife had sneaked onto the spacecraft. Believing that they were home-free, they sought to get this huge lump of metal in the sky. However, Luna wasn't going to let this man leave this planet. She followed the pair and kept out of sight. This huge craft would only take a short while before it was ready to depart so she knew she had to make her move soon. Seeing her opportunity she pounced. After launching herself from the shadows, she tussled with the High Commissioner. He was much stronger than her, but her lightning agility allowed her to escape his attacks and soon she had her arm around his neck.

"Please, don't kill me, please I want to live. I'm sorry, come with me to our new home. You can all still have this flight to freedom, please," he blubbed.

Suddenly, Luna was struck from behind by Sasha. In her blind anger to take down this cruel man, she had completely forgotten about his wife. "You stupid little bitch. How dare you attack my husband?" she screamed in Luna's face.

"Kill her now, my love. Rip her tiny little head off," Sasha said, totally enraged.

The High Commissioner grabbed Luna by her hair and lifted her off the floor. "All of that power and still my Hunter Killer reigns supreme. Only I can control that bone-crushing-beast. You stupid little girl, did you really think that you could defeat me?" the High Commissioner said with a smile across his face.

Luna looked deep into the High Commissioner's eyes and waited for the moment when he realised she had him right where she wanted him. It was that fearful look that he had put on so many other faces, and Luna took delight in knowing that he now knew what it felt like to be totally petrified. One swipe with a hidden knife, and the High Commissioner's neck was sliced open. After dropping Luna, he grasped at his throat trying to stop the bleeding. Sasha ran to her husband's aid, but it was too late.

She cradled her dying husband. "Hector no, no! Don't die. You evil little cow, you will pay for that," she screamed up at Luna.

Luna looked at the pathetic woman and gave her a swift kick to the side of her face which quickly silenced her. Outside and now free from the High Commissioner control, the Hunter Killer had stopped its murderous onslaught. Luna was now able to reach the beast, however, without the High Commissioner's painful control it fled the scene, finally feeling free for the first time in its life.

This was it, they had won the war. The High Commissioner was dead, and his altered animals were now under Luna's control. Luna came out from the hanger to ear-splitting cheers. This young girl had fought back against years of oppression and helped her people gain back their freedom! It would be her persecuted people who would get to flee this awful existence and start a new life far far away.

CHAPTER THIRTY-SEVEN

Are They Finally Free

THERE WAS ELATION AND frustration among the people of the Sectors. They were happy that they had taken down the cruel organisation known as the Commission, but they all wanted to see the High Commissioner fight for his life inside the Predator Pit. This man had taken great pleasure in watching hundreds of people die over the years, and many wanted nothing more than to return the favour. They wanted to see his eyes grow in size with fear. They wanted to see his body shaking uncontrollable with sheer terror. They wanted to see his body ripped into tiny little pieces by his own devilish creations. However, this man was already dead and his oppressive company had been taken down. Many lost their lives during the battle, but those who remained have never felt elation like this before. Not only had they stopped pure evil, they had also saved themselves from certain death.

"Luna, you have saved us all, you are so special, thank you," said a relieved person.

"Thank you child, thank you," said another grateful person.

Luna was thanked so many times on her way through the crowds of people who were all so grateful for what she had done. This young girl had helped them to overcome all of the odds and free themselves from Tierney. There was, however, no time to waste, the spacecraft must be boarded. No one knew exactly how much time they had left before the rest of the Last Isle was swallowed up by the sea, but they knew it wouldn't be long.

She took to the woods with the remaining predators. These bone-crushing-beasts had no place in society, or even in a zoo. They were too powerful and unpredictable. Yes she now had control over them, but there was no place for these altered animals. With sadness, she sent them off into the forest. She knew it wasn't their fault that they had ended up this way, but regardless of that fact, they still had to go. All of the animals that could be useful were collected and put on board the spacecraft. This rounding up process would have been extremely difficult if they didn't have the Wild Whisperer. Luna, however, was able to connect with them and they all boarded one by one, just like on Noah's Ark. With the animals on board and the deadly predators set free, it was just the people who had to get onto the life-saving-vessel.

Before they could leave, some wanted to have one last look at the place that had kept them prisoners for so long. There was a peace to be found wandering around a place that definitely wasn't a home, but now knowing that they would never have to return, many feel at ease. It's not like there weren't any good memories from this place, there were very few and far between, but some of the best experiences can come when you only have each other to rely on. Strong bonds had been made in the Sectors and it felt like one big family. They had all done their best to keep everyone alive and support each other throughout the hardest of times, which were an almost everyday occurrence. However, hope can be a very powerful emotion. It filled their stomachs when they felt hollow. It lifted their spirits when they were down. It provided them with the strength to keep going, and it helped them to continue to love even when it felt like their hearts would beat no more.

One person whose heart was absolutely racing was Lance, he just stood looking at the one he loves with tears in his eyes. He always knew that Luna was the one for him, but after the Commission took over he never really believed that he would see her again. He knew she was special, however, this was on another level. This girl had tamed the beasts, taken down the leader and his oppressive organisation and freed thousands of people. To say Lance was proud would be an understatement. His chest felt like it was full of butterflies, his body was tingling all over, he felt so alive, so in love, he couldn't wait any longer.

After rushing towards Luna he picked her up in his arms and gave her the biggest kiss upon her lips. "Luna, you are a very special girl. I love you more than you will ever know," he said crying.

"Oh, Lance, I love you so much," she said looking into his eyes. "We did it, we actually did it. No longer will our people have to suffer. We can start a new life together."

The pair embraced for what seemed like an eternity and although they hoped they would live a long happy life together when they reached Kepler-186F, their time on this planet was running out. The tide was rising and the satellite shield was continuing to break down leaving hot spots that created small patches of fire upon the ground where blistering sun's rays were starting to break through. The High Commissioner had left it until the very last moment before he was going to flee. All because he wanted to watch the people of the Sectors burn, just to make sure that they were all dead. Not satisfied with leaving them to die, he actually wanted to witness the slow, painful and agonising death of these poor people.

The majority of people had now boarded the spacecraft. Most of them wanted nothing more than to see the back of this planet and their lives of torment and torture. The captured Inner Sanctum residents who had been judged by the animals and deemed worthy of life would be allowed to take this flight to freedom, however, there was no luxury in their living quarters, they would travel with the animals. A smelly, cramped space with little supplies. These people would get a glimpse of what the people in the Sectors have endured for years, but they would still have the luxury of reaching salvation on the other side of this journey.

Most from the Sectors wanted to kill these people outright. They were seen as just as responsible for their suffering. They stood back living a life of extravagance, all the while knowing the conditions in which the Sectors were living. Furthermore, they were culpable by standing idle and watching the chastisement of these people. Even the animals didn't want these people aboard the same vessel. Why should they be allowed to live?

This decision was given to Luna. She was the one who had set them free and many were also slightly scared of her abilities. Luna decided that there had been enough pain and suffering, enough blood, butchery, and far too much death. These people would have a chance to redeem themselves when they reached Kepler-186F. Maybe after they had experienced what life is like when you don't have everything you need, you're so hungry and uncomfortable that you want to end your life, they would hopefully be humbled?

The people of the Sectors were finally free. No longer will they have to suffer, be scared, feel painstakingly hollow, or feel like life wasn't worth living. The future was bright, a new planet awaits, one where they could start over and build new lives for their families. Family was what was on Luna's mind at the moment, however, she couldn't find her mother anywhere.

"Has anyone seen my mother?" she asked in every area of this huge vessel.

Unfortunately, she always got the same answer. Where was her mother? Luna couldn't leave this planet without her. Now she would no longer have to suffer. Luna would make sure that the rest of her life was one happy day after another. No longer will she endure so much pain. She will be looked after like the queen she is.

Very few people were left on the streets of the Last Isle now. Most couldn't wait to see the back of this torturest place and were ready to take-off. However, Luna still couldn't locate her mother. Where was Anna?

She asked Charlie to put out a message over the tannoy system calling for her mother to join her on the spacecraft. Everyone was eager to go, but Luna wouldn't be going anywhere if she couldn't find her mum, and no one was going to question her authority now. Using the eyes, ears and abilities of the animals she searched for her mother. With control over these much faster creatures she could search farther and wider much quicker, whilst also staying where she said that she would be, but after roaming the Last Isle, Luna was at a loss. Where was her mum?

Now starting to get slightly worried, her panic heightened greatly when she saw her mother's face appear on one of the big screens. Anna had been taken captive by Sasha. After she'd come around from being knocked unconscious by Luna's swift kick, she slinked through the streets trying to find Luna, wanting payback for the death of her husband. She didn't care about anything else. She could have boarded the spacecraft and hidden away, so she could also flee to salvation, but her anger and rage could only be fed with one act. Her quest for Luna, however, turned up another victim.

Anna went back to the mansion to retrieve a necklace, a family heirloom she wanted to give to Luna, which she'd lost during the battle. Feeling safe in the knowledge that any threats were now over, she was caught by surprise when Sasha ambushed her. After tying her up, Sasha beat her, she was so enraged, not only with the loss of her husband, but she also knew that their Kingdom has fallen, their oppressive rule was over and all she could salvage from this terrible situation was to cause the person responsible for all of her loss a final dose of pain and suffering.

It was now that Luna realised the Hunter Killer deserved just one more meal. As the low rumbling growl travelled throughout the mansion, Sasha was terrified. Her blind rage saw her completely forget about this young girl's abilities. As the sound of its footsteps got closer, Sasha took off like a bolt of lightning, she would now run a deadly gauntlet throughout the mansion all the while being chased down by death itself. She'd witnessed this horrible occurrence many times and revelled in the Hunter Killer's ability to tear bodies limb from limb.

Luna arrived at the mansion to collect her mother. She was battered and bruised, but she would be ok. As a little leaving present, they both got to hear Sasha's screams of blind-panic as the creature began its dismemberment of her body. Her torture echoing throughout the empty mansion almost as loud as the alarm that had awoken the people living in the Sectors on so many occasions. No longer would they be woken in such awful, mind-splitting ways. No longer would they have to work until their hand bled and their backs broke. They would be free. Death would only come from old age, and they would never again have to partake, or witness the brutality of the Tourneys ever again.

Luna and her mother were last to board the spacecraft. Walking among her people she was blessed to see smiling faces everywhere. This occurrence hadn't been seen in such a long time that many wondered if their faces would remember the delighted position. As smiles beamed in all directions, Luna gave the signal to depart. This craft was huge and everyone could have had more room than they had ever had before, but they all crammed into one vast area of the vessel. They'd been together for so long it didn't feel right to be separated from each other. They had come together as one to win their freedom and they would arrive at their new home united.

Never again would they have to suffer, or watch as others suffer in such horrific ways. This was a new day, a new adventure awaited and everyone was full of hope and happiness that when they arrived at this new planet, they could build loving homes that would cherish life forevermore. Hopefully, the mistakes of the past will not be rewritten. This planet and its resources would be protected so that it could always sustain life, and it would never again leave the people in such a precarious position.

Luna had saved thousands of people from certain death. Now she would use her gifts to make sure that animals and humans lived side by side in peace and harmony, providing life for one another. All life should be cherished, every single living thing has a place in the world and she swore to use her abilities to help protect them all!

ATTRIBUTIONS

Cover lettering : Textstudio.com.

Final Editing : Sam Newman.

Cover images from Playground A.I and Canva

Cover art created with Canva.

www.ingramcontent.com/pod-product-compliance
Lightning Source LLC
Chambersburg PA
CBHW051501150726
47997CB00001B/74